THE
SWITCH

THE
SWITCH

ROLAND SMITH

SCHOLASTIC PRESS • NEW YORK

Library of Congress Cataloging-in-Publication Data available

ISBN 978-0-545-80350-2

10 9 8 7 6 5 4 3 2 1   22 23 24 25 26
Printed in Italy   183

First printing, November 2022

Book design by Christopher Stengel

For the real Marie

"*Hunger makes a thief of any man.*"

—Pearl S. Buck, *The Good Earth*

PART ONE

THE SWITCH

October 6

Okay, I made a deal with Mom. Two pages a day. I'm glad that these are small pages. She said I could write whatever I wanted, so I'll write about the Aunt Farm. Here goes . . .

The Ludds have lived on this forty-acre farm for seventy-two years. There are three houses on the farm: the house I live in with Mom and Dad; another house up on Wonderland Road (six hundred feet up from my house), where Aunt Madeline, Uncle Stan, and their kids live; and a third house (the original Ludd farmhouse) occupied by Uncle Chester, Aunt Ruth, and several more kids. The other Ludds (and there are a lot of them) live within easy driving distance to what most of the family have come to know as the Aunt Farm.

My grandparents, long dead now, had ten children. Five boys and five girls who ran as wild as coyotes when they were young and (with the exception of Mom and Uncle Edgar) were as prolific as my grandparents. At our last potluck there were over 150 people wolfing down the home-cooked food. Most of them had Ludd blood running through their veins, and those who didn't, like my dad, Tom Carter, had married into the Ludd family.

CHAPTER ONE

Henry Carter's father, Tom, came into his bedroom just before ten in the morning and cleared his throat, waking Henry from a dream he was having about his neighbor, Caroline Olof, of all people, which was strange because he had never had a dream about her before. In the dream she was bossing him around like usual.

"Didn't mean to wake you," Tom said, which wasn't true.

"That's okay," Henry said, which wasn't true either.

"I'm going to the zoo and thought you might want to come with me."

Henry had been to the zoo a thousand times. This wasn't a *hey, you want to go visit the zoo* kind of invitation. His dad was the zoo director. He went to the zoo almost every day and sometimes brought the zoo home with him. Right now, there were two bobcat cubs upstairs in the living room. Their mother had stepped into a steel leg-hold trap up on Mount Hood and had died. They named the cubs Robert and Catherine, Bob and Cat for short. Two weeks earlier, there was a baby chimp living with them because its mom had refused to nurse it. Henry's mom, Marie, rejected the chimp too, saying she was sick of it tearing the house apart. "The chimp's as bad as Henry was when he was a baby!" she complained, which was a little insulting, but probably true. Henry's dad had moved the chimp back to the zoo.

"I have a birthday present for you up at the zoo," his father continued. "It arrived yesterday after I left work."

Henry had turned thirteen the day before. He had gotten a lot of presents, but his favorite thing was sitting on his bedside table. A sleek, beautiful smartphone that had kept him up half the night.

"You and Mom gave me the phone."

"We did . . . well, mostly I did. Your mom wasn't thrilled with the idea, as you know."

Henry knew. She had made that crystal clear. Henry's mother, Marie Carter, formerly Marie Ludd, had a bad case of screen phobia. The only computer they had was his father's laptop, which Henry was not allowed to use, and his father's cell phone, which Henry had never touched. He had a tablet for school, but it was blocked from doing anything that was fun. The weird thing about his mom's phobia was that before Henry was born, she was the CEO of a billion-dollar international software company.

In addition to the smartphone, they had given him a leather pocket journal and fountain pen. "Quid pro quo," his mother told him. "I want you to write two pages a day in the journal or I'm taking the phone away." His dad would never check the journal, but his mom would . . . every day.

The journal was sitting next to the smartphone. His father picked it up and leafed through the pages.

Henry guessed he was wrong about him checking it.

"I'll write more in it today," Henry said. He had only managed to scribble a paragraph the night before. "I just woke up. In fact, I think I'll skip the zoo so I can do the rest of my pages."

4

Tom laughed. "You better do it before you go upstairs. If your mom checks, your phone is history."

Henry swung out of bed and grabbed his pants. "It's Saturday. Aside from my present, what else is going on up at the zoo?"

"The rumor is there's going to be an animal rights protest. Don't know if it'll happen, but I need to be there if it goes sideways."

"What are the chances of it going sideways?"

"Slim to none. You don't have to go with me. I'll bring your present home. I think you'll like it."

That's when Henry smelled Tuna Day. He had forgotten all about it because of his birthday. Tuna Day was an annual event on the farm. Once a year a couple of his uncles drove to the coast to buy a pickup-load of tuna from a commercial fishing boat and brought it back to the farm. The tuna was gutted, baked, and canned by his mom and aunts, stinking up their little valley and irritating their neighbors for miles. Tuna Day had been going on for over fifty years, long before they had neighbors close by. This was another reason to tag along to the zoo with his father. But for some reason Henry still didn't want to go.

Henry wanted to be alone.

All his aunts and uncles had shown up to his birthday celebration, along with their kids. After a big dose of Ludds, the only way to decompress was to hide out for several hours. Henry suspected that his dad felt the same way and that's why he went to the zoo so often, and why he was going to the zoo today. He was more comfortable around animals than he was around people.

"I think I'll stick around here if you don't mind," Henry said.

"Up to you, but it'll be difficult not to get nabbed for tuna duty. They're canning up a storm."

"Hard not to notice."

His father said that he'd see Henry later and left him sitting on the edge of the bed.

Henry's bedroom was in the daylight basement of their ranch-style house. There was a slider leading to a patio made of large pavers his mom and dad had put in themselves, with a little help from Henry. There was another bedroom downstairs for guests, a bathroom, a small library, and a large recreation room with a second kitchen reeking of tuna at the moment. The recreation room would have been a media room if they'd had a television. Instead, it had a rowing machine, an elliptical machine, a treadmill, and a ton of free weights, all of which they rarely used. The room also had a pool table that doubled as a ping-pong table. The cue ball had a large divot out of it, making long pool shots very challenging, to say nothing about the felt being ripped in several places. The damage was caused by the gangs of little Ludds who roamed from house to house like a troop of young baboons.

Upstairs were two more bedrooms: his parents' bedroom and another bedroom that doubled as an office for Marie and a nursery for visiting zoo animals when Tom didn't have a keeper to take care of them.

It wasn't a fancy house but was comfortable and lively with exotic animals and Ludds running around.

As Henry sat on his bed, he could hear people stomping

around upstairs, which was pretty typical every Saturday, even without tuna. His mom had an open-door policy. Only strangers knocked. Everyone else just walked in. You never knew who was going to show up and hang around for hours, days, or even weeks.

Henry pulled on a T-shirt and a ratty pair of sneakers. He was hungry, but knew better than to go upstairs for something to eat. He would be nabbed for tuna duty for sure. He stepped out onto the patio and looked around. The coast was clear.

CHAPTER TWO

It was a beautiful October morning, crisp, clear, marred by the stench of baking tuna and the *whomp . . . whomp . . . whomp . . .* of Edgar's monstrosity.

Edgar was Marie's older brother by at least fifteen years. He had lived in the barn next to their house as long as Henry had been alive. His monstrosity was a 328-foot wind turbine he erected at the top of the upper field. He put it up within twenty-four hours, almost before Henry knew it, and certainly before their neighbors caught wind of it. Their neighbors were outraged and tried to get Edgar to take it down. This effort was led by Caroline Olof's father, who was a lawyer. So far, it hadn't worked out for them. Edgar had a permit for the wind turbine signed by the county and by Marie, who hadn't paid attention to what she was signing. She let Edgar do whatever he wanted on the farm, much to everyone's dismay.

Whomp . . . whomp . . . whomp . . .

The wind turbine was loud, but Henry was used to it now. It had been whirling away since July.

Edgar had been in the army for nearly thirty years before moving back to the farm. His stint in the service had soured him on the government and human beings in general except for his immediate family. Well, most of them anyway. He became an inventor. No one knew much about his inventions, or how much money the inventions had made, but it was enough to pay cash for the hated wind turbine, which according to Henry's father had cost close to two hundred thousand dollars.

Henry started walking across the lower field toward Wonderland Creek, which split their property in two, hoping he wouldn't be spotted by a curious cousin who would either follow him or rat him out to an aunt or his mom. He had a hiding place carved out of the brush along the creek.

He wished his blue heeler, Boomer, was with him. He had loved that dog. The year before, Boomer had been kicked in the head by one of Edgar's cows and died instantly, breaking Henry's heart and almost everyone else's heart on the farm. It wasn't the cow's fault. Boomer was always trying to herd the cows, nipping at their hooves, because blue heelers are hardwired to herd. One day, after a million nips, Boomer's head was in the wrong place at the wrong time. Right now, Boomer would be running circles around Henry as he made his way past Edgar's barn and his junkyard of old cars and farm equipment.

Wonderland Creek had gone nearly dry long before Henry was born, but his aunts and uncles claimed that when they were kids, they caught spawning steelhead trout in it.

So far, so good, Henry thought. *No one has spotted me.*

The cows grazed placidly in the lower field. A couple of them glanced at him as he opened the creek gate. He walked across the tractor bridge leading to the upper field and looked up at the top corner, where the wind turbine was whirling away.

Whomp . . . whomp . . . whomp . . .

That's when something strange happened.

It was like a lightning strike without the sound or the bolt, or

9

brightening. Like God was snapping a photo using the flash of his celestial camera.

Along with the flash was a crackling feeling like static electricity, but different.

Confused and startled, Henry looked up at the sky.

Bright blue without a cloud.

The breeze was still blowing.

The wind turbine was still turning.

Whomp . . . whomp . . . whomp . . .

The tuna still reeked.

But something had changed. A shift in the universe. He could feel it in his chest.

Dread, he thought. *I feel dread.*

Henry gazed down the Wonderland valley, trying to wrap his mind around what had happened, and that's when he saw the passenger jet.

CHAPTER THREE

The Ludd farm is a half hour from the airport by car. On some days, depending on the prevailing wind, jets fly over the Wonderland valley as they swing around to land at the Portland airport. The planes fly so high they're hardly noticeable. But not this one. It was low. Very low. And it was headed toward the lower field at what looked like a million miles an hour. But the thing that froze Henry where he stood was the silence. No engine noises. None. The jet was barreling up the valley like a glider.

Too fast.

Henry jumped into the creek bed just as the explosion rocked the ground. A cow flew over his head and hit the metal barn like a cannonball, leaving a jagged, bovine-sized hole in the side, ten feet up from the ground. A wing cartwheeled up the hill and came to a stop in the backyard a few feet from his house. A tire bounced uphill toward the wind turbine like it was being dribbled by an invisible giant. All this happened in seconds. The lower field burned with jet fuel.

Shakily, Henry got to his feet and saw his first crash victim. It was a woman; at least he thought it was a woman. She was still buckled into her seat as if she were taking in the view, except there was no view for her, because her head was on fire. He ran over, wondering how he was going to put her out.

"Back off!"

The shout came from his left. Edgar was striding across the field, wearing bib overalls without a shirt. Blood and guts were splattered all over him. How was he able to walk?

"Get over here!" Edgar yelled. "It's too late for her."

Henry ran over to him. "We better get you to a hospital."

"Huh?" Edgar tore off what looked like a loop of intestine dangling over his shoulder. "These aren't my guts. They're cow guts. The barn shredded her like she passed through a freaking meat grinder. Scared the living crap outta me. What a mess."

That's when Henry heard the shrieks. His mother, his aunt Madeline, and his aunt Ruth were running out the back door of the house wearing aprons and disposable gloves, trailed by several little Ludds.

Edgar ran halfway across the lower field, waving his hands and shouting, "Henry's fine. I'm fine. Get those kids back in the house. Adults only. I mean it. They don't need to see this."

It was too late for Henry. He had already seen it. He was still seeing it.

Ruth figured out what Edgar was saying and quickly herded the protesting kids back into the house. Henry's mother and Madeline joined Henry and Edgar in the field. They were crying. His mother threw her arms around him. "Are you okay, Henry?"

"Fine," Henry said, feeling numb and strangely detached from the burning havoc.

Marie looked at Edgar and gasped.

"Cow guts," Edgar said. "Did anyone call nine one one?"

Madeline and Marie shook their heads as if they were incapable of speech. Henry wasn't certain if he could speak either.

"Doesn't matter," Edgar said. "In about two minutes this place is going to be crawling with cops, feds, and the press." He looked at Henry. "I assume you have that new cell phone with you."

Henry fumbled it out of his pocket with trembling hands, nearly dropping it. He looked at the screen. It was black. He tapped it. Nothing happened. It must have broken when he jumped into the creek bed. He knew the battery was okay because it was full when he left the house. "I think it's—"

Edgar held his hand out. "Let me see that thing."

Henry gave it to him. Edgar tapped the screen several times and pushed the side buttons, then he did an odd thing. He sniffed the phone and looked worried.

"What is it?" Henry's mom asked.

"Doesn't matter. Let's look for survivors."

CHAPTER FOUR

Several more aunts, uncles, and neighbors had joined them on the field, shocked and sickened by the devastation. They searched for over two hours. All they found were bits and pieces of dead people and their baggage, laptops, tablets, car keys, purses, and wallets. Henry stuck close to Edgar, who seemed a lot more interested in electronics than he was in the people. Every time he found a phone or a computer that wasn't completely smashed, he tried to turn it on.

"Why are you doing that?" Henry finally asked.

"Because this plane crash isn't the only problem we have. Not by a long shot . . ." Edgar was going to say more, but he was cut off by Madeline's scream.

They ran over to see what could make her scream after all the horrors they had already seen. She and Marie were staring down at three dead people strapped in their seats. A man and a woman, with a girl sitting between them. They were on their backs, staring up at the blue sky through their sightless eyes. There wasn't a scratch on them. Henry had seen a lot of dead people in the past few hours, most of them horribly mangled, but this was the worst.

He knew these people. It was Mr. and Mrs. Olof. Caroline was sitting between them. Caroline had told Henry that her parents were taking her on a cruise to Mexico. The Olofs weren't going anywhere anymore. They had driven to the airport, boarded a flight, then crashed and died less than a half mile from their home.

Henry felt a hand on his shoulder. It was his mom. Tears poured down her face. "This is terrible, Henry. Are you all right?"

Henry couldn't find the words. He gave her a nod. But Henry wasn't alright. He could barely breathe. He had known Caroline his entire life. She was a couple years older than him, and he had looked up to her his whole life. She and her parents had been a big part of his life. He thought about the dream he'd had about her. He could only remember fragments. She was laughing at him, telling him to do something, but he couldn't remember what it was. He turned away, thinking he might be sick.

"So many dead," Madeline said.

"I liked the Olofs," Edgar said. He squatted down and started to put his hand in Mr. Olof's pocket.

"What are you doing?" Marie shrieked.

Edgar ignored her. He pulled a cell phone out of Mr. Olof's pocket.

"We need to leave everything exactly where it is," Madeline said. "There will be an investigation of the crash site. You can't touch anything."

Edgar sniffed Mr. Olof's cell phone. "There isn't going to be an investigation. We've been here for hours. Where are the cops? Where are the emergency vehicles?" He held up Mr. Olof's cell phone. The screen was dark, just like Henry's cell phone.

"Dead battery?" Marie asked.

Edgar shook his head. "Dead world. At least the world we've come to know. This isn't the only passenger jet that went down today. I'd guess there were about five thousand jets winging their way around the country this morning. If this was nationwide, about a million people died in plane crashes at ten forty-two."

"What are you talking about?" Henry asked.

"I'm talking about an EMP. An electromagnetic pulse. Anything that has a circuit board or a silicon chip in it, which is just about everything these days, has been fried. I could be wrong, but I think the pulse has taken it all down."

"That's impossible," Madeline said. "You're basing this on a couple of dead cell phones?"

"What about the power?" Edgar asked.

"What about it?" Madeline said. "We lose power all the time. The jet probably took out the lines when it crashed."

"Listen," Uncle Edgar said.

They listened.

"I don't hear anything except your monstrosity," Madeline said.

"Exactly. We should be hearing traffic noise from the interstate, trucks and cars driving along Wonderland Road, helicopters, and small airplanes flying overhead. That's all gone now. Electricity, phones, computers, texting, social media, landlines, two-way radios . . . all of it.

"Food is starting to thaw in dead freezers and going bad in refrigerators because there is no power to anything."

"Seems far-fetched to me," Madeline scoffed.

"There's one way to verify it," Uncle Edgar said.

"How?" Marie asked.

Edgar pointed to the wind turbine. "We'll send Henry up top to look around."

CHAPTER FIVE

After a long debate, Marie finally relented and gave Henry permission to climb to the top of the wind turbine.

"If you want to," she added.

Henry wanted to, and knew he was the most likely candidate. His mom and Madeline both had a touch of vertigo, and Edgar was old and not in the best of health. It was a long climb up. Edgar had intended to install an automatic lift to make it easier to get up to the top, but he hadn't gotten the parts yet.

"I suspect the parts aren't coming now," he said. "Nothing will be coming. I'll have to figure a way to jury-rig a lift at some point."

The other Ludds were busy wandering around the field, debating what to do with the dead bodies and debris if no one showed up to haul the carnage away.

Henry had wanted to get inside the turbine since Edgar had put it up, but Edgar kept it locked and off-limits, saying that the equipment inside was sensitive. That piqued Henry's curiosity even more. The reason Edgar wanted Henry to climb to the top of the turbine was the view. He would be able to see for miles in every direction.

As Henry and Edgar walked up the hill, Henry stared at the blades. *Whomp . . . whomp . . . whomp . . .*

"So, it's working?" Henry asked.

"The blades are working because of the wind. The electronics are housed in a Faraday locker at the bottom of the ladder. I'm hoping the locker shielded the electronics from the EMP. I don't have the turbine hooked up to our power grid, but the storage batteries are full. All I have to do is throw some switches to power the houses. When you're up in the nacelle, I'll run a systems check."

"What's a nacelle?"

"It's the housing attached to the blades where the guts of the turbine are stored. When you get into it, you'll find a button that opens a set of hydraulic doors to the outside. Remember to keep clipped in at all times, especially when you're in the open nacelle. It's not that windy down here, but by the look of the blades, it's plenty windy up there. And cold."

Half an hour later Henry was strapped into a safety harness and climbing the steel ladder inside the tower, pausing every twenty feet to catch his breath.

All the electronics inside the Faraday locker were working, including a pair of two-way radios stored there. Edgar had given him a pair of binoculars as well.

The two-way crackled, *"You okay?"* Henry looked down.

Edgar was a tiny dot about two hundred feet below Henry.

Henry made sure he was still clipped onto the ladder, then hooked an arm around a rung and pulled out the radio.

"I'm good." He was actually a little nervous.

"I'm going to shut the blades down so you don't get your head lopped off when you open the nacelle. When you get up there, give me a shout and tell me what you see."

"Roger."

He put the radio back into his pocket and continued to climb. By the time he reached the nacelle, which looked like the inside of a spaceship, his arms felt as heavy as hay bales. He pushed the button and the roof hissed open in two sections, like a butterfly spreading its wings.

The October sky was clear and blue. The air, shockingly cold. One of the blades loomed a hundred feet above the nacelle. The other two blades pointed downward the same distance at forty-five-degree angles. He looked down at the lower field. The people wandering through the debris looked like ants. Several little Ludds were standing on the deck, no doubt wishing they could get a closer look at the devastation. Henry hoped they never did. He wished he hadn't seen the slaughter. Hot tears rolled down his cold face. This was the day he learned that there are some things seen that cannot be unseen.

Butch, their bull, and eight cows were grazing among the dead, as if the tragic plane crash were an everyday occurrence on the farm. Despite the terrible sight, Henry didn't think this EMP thing, if that's what it was, could be as bad as Edgar was making it out to be. When Henry was six, Edgar was convinced that they were going to be nuked by a foreign enemy. To get ready for the blast he built an underground bunker on the property and stockpiled it with food and supplies. With the exception of Henry's parents, all the Ludds joined him in his paranoia. When Edgar asked Henry's dad what he was going to eat when the big one hit, his dad laughed and said, "You wouldn't let me starve, Edgar. I'll eat your food." Which became a running joke in the family.

By now, Henry's father must have figured out that the power

outage extended well beyond the zoo, if in fact the power was out at the zoo. Henry was certain that his father was worried about them. The zoo wasn't far from downtown Portland. If his truck didn't start, as Edgar was predicting, it would take him hours to walk home. Henry just hoped that Edgar was wrong like he had been about the nuclear bombs.

"What do you see?" Edgar asked over the two-way.

"Just a sec." Henry reached for the binoculars hanging around his neck. He looked along Wonderland Road. There was absolutely no traffic, which was odd. It wasn't a busy road, but you could usually spot a car or two making their way up the narrow road. When his mom was a kid, the Wonderland valley was filled with working farms. Now it was scattered with five-acre plots owned by wealthy people like the Olofs. Their neighbors might have a horse or a llama, a couple apple trees, or a vegetable garden in the summer. The Ludds' forty acres was the only working farm left. They grew hay and ran a few cows for meat. They had a small apple orchard and a grove of filbert trees. They sold the filberts and some of the hay, but kept the apples for themselves. His mother and aunts picked all the apples every year, freezing them in three-pound bags. Each bag was enough to make one delicious pie. They were all epic bakers.

Thinking about apple pie made Henry smile through his tears.

He was glad no one could see the smile. There he was, two hundred feet up, looking down on a couple hundred dead people, and he was smiling. He wasn't happy about any of this; in fact he was sick with the horror of it. But thinking about apple pie and seeing his aunts looking like ants brought back the farm's nickname.

"The Aunt Farm!" he shouted into the cold wind, but no one could hear him.

He swung the binoculars over to the interstate. The interstate was a parking lot. All six lanes were jammed with stalled cars. People were standing on the freeway, clutching their cell phones and talking with other stranded drivers. They looked angry and scared.

Beyond the interstate, toward Portland, were a half-dozen ugly, black-smoke plumes. Closer to home, on Stafford Road, several more cars were stalled. Some of them had been pushed to the shoulder. A group of people were walking up Wonderland Road. Henry recognized most of them. Among them was his uncle Stan. He was a structural engineer, married to Aunt Madeline. He looked tired, winded, and worried. Henry wondered where his car had stopped.

He knew what time it had stopped.

CHAPTER SIX

There were about thirty Ludds jammed into the Carters' living room. Henry had finished telling them what he had seen from the tower, and Stan was telling them what he had seen as he walked home. His car had conked out in Lake Oswego, a small town ten miles north.

"It was complete chaos," Stan said. "I saw several fires, a dozen fistfights, the aftermath of two small-airplane crashes, and a downed helicopter. People were ransacking stores."

"So quickly?" Marie said, dismayed. "Lake Oswego is one of the most affluent communities in Oregon."

"Not anymore," Stan said. "The banks are closed because the computers don't work. Credit cards don't work in stores. People don't carry cash anymore. Everyone is taking what they need. More than they need. No police. No fire department. It's complete anarchy."

Henry glanced out the window. The sun was going down. The little Ludds were downstairs in the recreation room playing board games, building things with LEGO bricks, and probably tearing up the pool table. The year before, Henry would have been with them, but now that he was a teenager, he was upstairs with the big Ludds. He wished he was downstairs, certain his cousins were having a lot more fun than he was upstairs. It looked like his mother had been put in charge, maybe because she and his dad owned the property or because she was an ex-CEO. Whatever the reason, Henry thought she was doing a pretty good job. She was very calm considering there were two hundred dead people in back of their house.

After Henry came down from the wind turbine, his mother had assigned everyone a task, telling them to complete it in two hours, then meet back at their house. Henry's task had been to feed the little Ludds and get the games out. It had taken twenty minutes to get them set up and twice as long to explain what was going on, which was difficult because he didn't know what was going on. No one did.

His mother was calling on people in turn in an attempt to keep the meeting under control. The Ludds were notorious for talking over the top of one another. She was down to the last two Ludds.

"Can I ask Edgar a question?" Stan said.

"Let's hear from everyone else first," Marie said. "Then we'll open it up. You're next, Ruth."

Ruth's task had been to walk to the Baptist church, a half mile down Wonderland Road, and talk to Pastor Bob about the bodies and the Olofs, who had been members of his congregation. Pastor Bob had been at the church for close to thirty years. Ruth and her husband, Chester, were both in Pastor Bob's small flock.

"Pastor Bob, of course, is very sorry about the tragedy and shocked that the authorities haven't shown up to take care of things. He agrees that something has to be done about the bodies, but there isn't room in the cemetery because it's almost at capacity. Chester and I have four plots at the cemetery. We'll use three of them to bury the Olofs. Pastor Bob will hold the service for them. His truck and car won't start. The cemetery's new backhoe is out too. He's not sure how long it's going to take the caretaker to dig three graves by hand. He said that if no one shows up in the next day or two to take care of the crash site, we'll have to do it ourselves. The bodies need to be photographed where they lie, *in situ*, he said, and identified before we put them in the ground. When I got home, I tried my digital cameras, but like the cell phones, they don't work. I have a couple of old film cameras and film in the refrigerator that I've been meaning to get rid of. Tomorrow morning I'll start taking photos and identifying the victims, but I could use some help."

Henry's mom looked around the room.

"I'll help you," Madeline volunteered. "But I hope the authorities arrive before we have to do anything with the bodies."

Henry's mom looked at Edgar. "I saved you for last, Edgar, because I know you probably have a lot to say."

Everyone laughed a little, which was good to see under the circumstances. Edgar was scribbling something in a small notebook. He put the notebook away, then stood up without a word. He walked into the kitchen and pulled the blinds, then he returned to the family room and did the same.

"What are you doing?" Marie asked.

"I'll need to make some adjustments over the next few days," he said. "But you'll have to pull the shades at night."

He turned on a lamp.

They all stared at it for a moment like it was some kind of miracle.

"Congratulations," Marie said. "I mean that. But why do we have to pull the blinds?"

"There's no use in advertising that we have electricity," Edgar said. "The word will leak out soon enough, but the later that happens, the better it will be for us."

"And why is that?" Madeline asked.

"Let me put it another way. The good news is that we have electricity. The bad news is that we have electricity."

Everyone in the room looked confused. Henry was confused too. He wondered if the stress had pushed Edgar off the deep end.

Edgar continued, "I realize that people will figure out that we have power regardless of what we do. It won't matter for a week or two, but the longer this continues, the more critical that's going to become."

"Are you saying that people are going to come to the farm and take our wind turbine?" Madeline asked.

Edgar shook his head. "I'm saying they'll try to take our farm and leave the wind turbine in place."

"Surely the power will come back on in a few days," Ruth said.

"Let Edgar finish," Marie said. "It's his turn."

"I hope I'm wrong," Edgar said. "But I don't think I am. After food, the most important commodity will be electricity. We need to wrap our minds around this. The first people to realize that this situation is dire are the people who will survive. While you're thinking about this, I have some other things to go over." He got his notebook out. "My fifty-nine Caddy and old flatbed are still working. There are no electronics in either of them." He looked at Chester. "Our old backhoe is working too. You might want to drive it down to the cemetery tomorrow and scoop out three graves for the Olofs."

Chester nodded.

Uncle Edgar consulted his notebook again. "Pastor Bob's idea about photographing the bodies *in situ* and identifying them is a good one. It will be several days before someone shows up to take care of the bodies, if they show up at all. The victims are our problem and we have to act accordingly. Chester, when you finish at the cemetery, can you dig a ditch down the center of the lower field?"

"Sure," Chester said.

"I know this is unpleasant, but we'll have to bury the crash victims in a mass grave. The sooner, the better. If no one shows up, we'll bury them the day after tomorrow."

"I don't like the idea of a mass grave," Madeline said.

She wasn't alone. Henry could see all his aunts and uncles bursting with comments and questions.

"Let him finish," Marie said.

"I don't like the idea either," Edgar admitted. "But we don't have room for two hundred individual plots. We'll need the field for food production, which brings me to my next item. What are we going to eat over the fall and winter? I haven't had a chance to check our food supply."

"*Your* food supply," Stan said. "You wouldn't let us starve, Edgar."

This got a little laugh from everyone.

"Well, maybe not Tom," Uncle Edgar said with a grin. The old joke.

This got a bigger laugh except from Henry and his mother.

Marie had a look of deep concern. Henry felt the same dread he'd felt that afternoon.

Edgar must have noticed. "I'm certain Tom will be along soon, Marie. The farm is a long walk from the zoo. He may be staying overnight at the zoo, not wanting to head back in the dark."

Henry hoped he was right.

"The food belongs to everyone," Uncle Edgar said, getting back on track. "But we're going to need more. I suspect our numbers are going to swell over the next few weeks and months. We're going to have to figure out how to feed everyone. That's all I have at this point."

"I know you all have a lot of questions," Henry's mom said. "But let's try to ask them one at a time, starting with Stan."

Stan seemed startled to be chosen to go first but recovered quickly. "I have a question for Edgar. You seem pretty certain that this thing is an EMP and it's going to go for a long time. What caused it?"

Edgar shrugged. "Nuke in the upper atmosphere? Celestial event? Who knows? Right now, that's not important. Our priority is to figure out what to do. What are we going to eat? What kind of supplies and equipment do we need? How are we going to protect ourselves if this goes on for an extended period of time? As you told us, people are already panicking, and that's understandable. If your car breaks down, it's inconvenient. When the power goes out, it's irritating. When your cell phone suddenly dies, you're surprised. When all three things happen at the same time to everybody, it's the end of the known world."

Henry's aunts and uncles all started talking at once. They

couldn't help themselves. The avalanche of questions and arguments could not be stopped. His mother didn't even try. She simply listened to them, jotting notes down. This went on for a long time, but eventually everyone ran out of steam. One by one, the Ludds grabbed their kids and headed to their respective homes. Uncle Edgar was the last to leave. Henry and his mom walked him to the back door, the same door Henry was hoping to see his dad walk through all evening.

"That went better than I expected," Edgar said. "We'll know more tomorrow and come up with a better idea about what we need to do. I know you're worried about Tom. I am too. I'm sure he had his hands full today at the zoo. He'll show up. I'm sure of it."

He walked off into the cool night.

Marie closed the door and asked Henry if he was hungry.

"Not really," Henry said, surprised that he wasn't. He hadn't really eaten anything all day.

"I'm going to try to get some sleep," she said. "You should get some sleep too. Tomorrow's going to be a very busy day."

"I didn't really get to ask any questions."

His mom smiled. "It's hard to be heard in that bunch. What was it you wanted to ask?"

"How does Uncle Edgar know so much about this stuff?"

"It's a long story. The abbreviated version is that Colonel Edgar Ludd was in charge of a team that analyzed disaster scenarios for the army. Terrorist assaults, nuclear bomb attacks, pandemic outbreaks, and I guess electromagnetic pulses. When he retired, he had no place to go. He's the only sibling who never married. I invited him to come back to the farm and told him that he could do whatever he liked here. I thought the wind turbine was a little over the top but didn't say anything because he paid for it and I had given him carte blanche." She smiled. "Turns out that the monstrosity might just save us all."

"And someone might take the farm because of the monstrosity," Henry said.

"They can try," she said.

CHAPTER SEVEN

Henry didn't think he'd be able to sleep, but he was out within minutes. What woke him the next morning was the rumble of Edgar's ancient backhoe. He got up and looked out the window. Chester was in the lower field, pulling a trailer behind the backhoe. The memory of the previous day came rushing back, and he had to brace himself to stay on his feet. He knew Chester was going to dig the mass grave. But why the trailer?

"The Olofs," he said aloud.

Chester wasn't digging the mass grave. He was moving the Olofs to the cemetery. A couple of his aunts and uncles were unbuckling the Olofs from their seats. He knew he should go out and help, but he didn't have the heart. He didn't want to see Caroline like that again. He'd seen enough death to last him a lifetime.

He got dressed, went upstairs, and found his mother sitting at the kitchen table typing on a manual typewriter. Her fingers were flying over the keys. On a normal day he would have been amazed at what a good typist she was, but not today. She stopped when she noticed him watching.

"Dad?"

"Not yet," she said quietly. "Did you sleep okay?"

"Yeah. How about you?" But Henry already knew the answer. She looked like she hadn't slept at all.

She shook her head. "I wanted to compile my notes from last night's meeting. Do you still have that notebook with you?"

"In my back pocket."

"I guess our deal is off with the cell phone, but I still think you should keep a diary about all of this. Interesting times."

Henry said he would, but he couldn't imagine writing down a bunch of stuff that he would just as soon forget.

"They're moving the Olofs," Henry said.

"I heard. I should go out and help, but . . ." She laid her head on her arm in front of the typewriter and wept.

Henry's mother didn't cry, not like this. He put his hand on her shoulder in an attempt to comfort her. He didn't know what else to do. Eventually, she put her hand on his, gave it a squeeze, and lifted her head.

"I'm glad that's over," she said with a sad smile. "I knew it was coming." She looked over at the slider leading to the deck. "Let's see what's going on outside."

They walked out onto the deck. It was cold and foggy. They could see their breath. The Olofs were lying in the trailer in the same order they had been seated. Ruth was taking a photo of them. Madeline was writing on a clipboard. Chester laid a blanket over the Olofs, then started up the driveway toward Wonderland Road.

"You can go with Chester if you like," Henry's mom said.

"I think I'll stay here."

Marie nodded. They walked back inside.

"Hungry?"

Henry was very hungry, but it didn't seem right to eat.

"Cereal? There's some milk left. If Edgar is right about this, I guess we're going to have to get a milk cow." She wrote *milk cow* on the legal pad next to the typewriter.

Henry poured the cereal into a bowl, emptying the box. He guessed cereal was going to be hard to get too. Edgar walked through the back door as Henry was eating his last spoonful.

"Vehicles are ready," he said.

"What vehicles?" Henry asked.

"The Caddy and the flatbed," Uncle Edgar said. "We're taking a little tour to see what's happening outside."

"Maybe pick up some supplies," Mom added. "Go to the zoo and check on Dad."

"I want to go," Henry said.

His mother shook her head. "There's a lot to do here, and we're not sure what it's like out there."

"I had enough of the field yesterday," Henry said.

"We all did," his mother said. "You can stay inside and take care of the kids while your aunts and uncles are taking care of things outside."

"I want to look for Dad."

"Dad is probably on his way here right now. The chances are good that you'll see him before I do."

"I'll take my chances."

A dark look crossed his mother's face. Henry knew that look. She was about to say no, and that would be the end of it, but Edgar came to his rescue.

"Henry might come in handy, Marie. He knows the zoo and Tom's routine better than we do. It's up to you, but I'd let him go with us."

Marie thought about it for a minute, then nodded.

Close, Henry thought.

A couple hours later they were heading down Wonderland Road. Edgar was behind the wheel of his red convertible Cadillac. The white top was up. Marie sat next to Edgar. Henry was in the back. Stan followed behind in the flatbed.

Edgar brought the two-way radios from the wind turbine so he could stay in touch with Stan. He keyed the talk button. "There are going to be two kinds of people out here. People in trouble and people causing trouble. Keep the doors locked. A working vehicle is precious. We aren't stopping for anyone. Today's trip is about getting supplies and checking on Tom."

"Roger that," Stan said.

Marie said nothing, but Henry was certain she wasn't happy about this proclamation. The Ludds were known for helping people, even complete strangers.

They passed the cemetery. Chester was digging the Olofs' graves.

CHAPTER EIGHT

The interstate was impassable because of the dead cars. Edgar took side streets, zigging and zagging through the metal tangle. They weren't the only working vehicles on the road. There were a handful of old clunkers, classic cars, even a couple newer cars weaving through the snarl.

"Most of the working vehicles are pre-electronic," Edgar said. "The newer ones were probably parked where the pulse couldn't reach or covered with something that acted like a makeshift Faraday box. Lucky for them."

"We were lucky too," Marie said.

"You got that right," Edgar agreed. "I didn't collect old cars and farm equipment because I thought there was going to be an EMP. I bought them because they were cheap, and I like old mechanical things."

"What about the wind turbine?" Henry asked.

"That was luck too. I've always been interested in wind power. I saw a turbine listed on eBay and put in a ridiculously low bid. I was shocked when I won it. No use having it if you don't put it up. Glad we have it now, but as I explained, it's a two-edged sword."

They didn't start seeing people until they got to the commercial area of Tualatin, ten miles from the farm. Some of the people were pushing shopping carts filled with food and other supplies. People who weren't lucky enough to have gotten a shopping cart were carrying stuff in their arms or lugging it over their shoulders in plastic garbage bags. One man was dragging a pallet filled with stuff behind him like he was a sled dog.

They passed a Home Depot that was on fire. No police. No fire trucks. Just a giant bonfire belching thick black smoke into the blue October sky. A large group of people stood in the parking lot, watching it burn. Some of them were carrying rifles. Others had pistols. A few carried baseball bats. One man was wielding a sword.

It got worse the closer they got to Portland. More looting. More guns. More fights. Storefronts and car windows were shattered, and there was broken glass everywhere. An SUV was turned over onto its side, half in its parking spot and halfway into the road. Some shops had wooden boards covering their entryways. Someone had spray-painted STOP THEEF! onto the plywood. Henry suspected that the people who had done it were also "theefs," or thieves, by now.

They passed a few more cars heading south away from Portland, and just to prove that not everyone had lost it, three different drivers shouted at them to turn around.

"Don't go into the city! Nothing but trouble there."

"You go into Portland, they'll 'jack your rig. Probably kill you. We were lucky to get out."

"Turn around before it's too late!"

They did not turn around, but Edgar did pull over.

"What are you doing?" Marie asked.

"Getting something. Stay put."

He got out of the car and opened the trunk. Henry and Marie's view was blocked for a minute or two. When he slammed it closed, he was holding three pistols and a shotgun. He walked over to Stan and gave him one of the pistols. When he got back to the Cadillac, he handed Henry the shotgun.

"Lay it on the floor." Edgar climbed in, reached over, and put the pistols in the glove box.

"Are those really necessary?" Marie asked. She didn't like guns, but there were several on the farm.

Edgar put the Cadillac into gear and started out again. "I don't know what we're going to run into ahead," he said. "The guns are a deterrent that I hope we don't have to use."

They drove for another two hours, taking long detours because some streets were completely blocked, arriving at the zoo in the early afternoon. The parking lot was filled with abandoned cars.

As Henry climbed out of the back seat, a terrified baboon streaked past him. Right behind the baboon was a black leopard. The baboon clambered up a fir tree as fast as a squirrel and disappeared into the branches. The leopard tried to follow but only made it up the trunk six feet before falling and crashing on its back. The cat gave them a nasty snarl, as if its clumsy fall was their fault, and disappeared among the cars.

They were all speechless.

"Wow," Edgar said. "That's something you don't see every day in a parking lot."

"What just happened?" Marie asked.

"The leopard's name is Bathsheba," Henry answered shakily. "The mandrill baboon is Emmett."

"Are they dangerous?" Stan asked. He didn't like animals. He was standing with one foot in the cab, holding a pistol.

"Emmett is okay, but Bathsheba could be a problem," Henry said, thinking that a bigger problem was that there was another leopard named Chauncey and seven other baboons. If Bathsheba and Emmett were loose, their cage mates were loose too.

"How did they get out?" his mother asked.

Henry had no idea. "The leopard exhibit is on the opposite end of the zoo from where the mandrill baboons are kept, and they have separate keepers. A keeper might make a mistake and leave a door open, but that's rare. To have two keepers make the same mistake on the same day is—"

"Impossible," his mother finished.

"What kind of locks do they have on those cages?" Edgar asked.

"There are a few electronic locks," Henry answered. "But most of the enclosures are padlocked. Only a few people have master keys that open all the locks in the zoo. The baboon and leopard exhibits are both newer. I'm pretty sure they have electronic locks."

"The doors wouldn't have just popped open when the electronic locks were pulsed," Edgar said. "Someone had to turn the knobs."

"Maybe a baboon," Henry said. "But not a leopard."

CHAPTER NINE

"What are we going to do?" Stan asked impatiently, obviously unnerved by the escaped animals. Henry was too, but they couldn't turn back now. His dad might still be in the zoo.

"Can we drive through the zoo?" Marie asked.

"If the gate is open," Henry said.

"It must be," Stan said. "The animals are out."

"A leopard and baboon would have no problem scaling the perimeter fence," Henry said, "but might have some trouble getting past the razor wire on top. If the gate is closed, we can't drive into the zoo. It's operated with a remote. Several keepers and grounds people have remotes in their trucks."

"Only one way to find out," Edgar said.

Henry looked at his mother. "We'll be safe in the car."

"Then let's get to it," she said. "Stan, you can ride with us. No use taking two vehicles on this safari."

The security gates into the zoo were wide open. Both of them. One gate was supposed to close behind a vehicle before the second gate opened, to prevent an escaped animal from slipping out.

"We should close the gate behind us," Henry said.

"Forget it!" Stan said. "We're not here to save the animals. We're here to find Tom."

Henry thought Stan's outburst was caused by the escaped giraffe a hundred feet in front of them pulling leaves off a tree.

"Giraffes are safe," Henry said.

"Stop the car, Edgar," Marie said. "Henry and I will close the gates."

Edgar stopped the Cadillac. Henry and Marie got out. Closing the gates was harder than Henry thought. They wouldn't budge. Edgar got out and joined them.

"We'll have to disengage the chain drive," he said. "Without power the gate is anchored in place. It'll only take a sec."

It took several minutes. He retrieved his toolbox from the trunk, removed the cowling from the motor drive, then started the process of disengaging the chain.

A kangaroo came hopping down the road toward the opening. Henry and his mom stood in its path and shooed it away. As it hopped off into the zoo, his mom turned to him and said, "What do you think, Henry?"

"About the roo?"

She shook her head. "What do you think about the gate being open, animals getting out . . ." She hesitated. "Dad?"

"He could be working at the other end of the zoo."

"What do you mean?"

"He might be securing other animals in their enclosures so they don't get out."

"After this much time?"

Henry looked at the ground. How do you tell your mom that you're worried that your dad is in serious trouble? They had driven through the employee parking lot to get to the gate. His dad's truck was parked in his reserved spot, immaculately clean as always. No one had said a word as they drove past it, but he knew everyone saw it. His father was more than capable of disengaging the chain drive. He was nearly as handy as Edgar. If he was at the zoo, and able to walk, he would have gotten the gates closed. Containment is the number-one priority when an animal escapes. His dad loved them and was a great father, but he would never in a million years walk away from the zoo with animals running loose. He would have stayed at the zoo until every animal was secure and safe, knowing that the farm was completely under control with Henry's mom and aunts and uncles there.

"The gate is a problem," Henry admitted, looking up. "He would have closed it."

"Where should we start?" Mom asked quietly.

"His office in the admin building. I doubt he'll be there, but he keeps two-way radios in his gear closet. It's possible that they didn't get cooked. If they work, he'll be carrying one. There might be a spare in his office."

It took all four of them to slide the heavy gate closed. When they finished, they piled back into the car and continued their grim zoo tour.

They passed a dead zebra with a pride of lions feeding on it, but not the whole pride. One of the females was fifty feet down the road being devoured by two polar bears.

"Are we safe in this car?" Stan asked.

"Yes," Henry said, but he really didn't know. A polar bear or lion could tear through the soft top like it was paper. "They have their food," he added, trying not to think what would happen if he was wrong.

They swung around and drove up a small hill to the administration building that overlooked the zoo. An elephant was tearing tiles off the roof and tossing them into the fountain in front of the entrance door.

"How are we going to get by that?" Stan asked.

"Her name is Indira," Henry said. "She's okay." That wasn't exactly true. He'd been in with her a couple of times when his dad was helping to trim her toenails. Tom was the one who said that she was okay, meaning she probably wouldn't step on them, whack them with her trunk, or do a headstand on them during the pedicure. Henry wasn't sure what she would do when they tried to slip past her into the building. He started to open the car door.

"Where do you think you're going?" his mom asked.

"She's standing right in front of the entrance," Henry said. "We need to get her away from it so we can get inside."

"How much does she weigh?"

"I don't know. Eight thousand pounds? Why?"

"And you weigh one twenty?"

"I weigh one thirty, but this isn't a weight contest. I've seen Dad and the keepers work her a dozen times. It has nothing to do with who's bigger and stronger. It has to do with who's in charge."

"Your dad may not even be in the building," Stan said.

"He probably isn't, but we know he was in there yesterday. There might be something inside that will tell us what happened here."

"It's too big of a risk," Marie said. "I don't want to lose you and your . . ."

Henry jumped out of the car before she could say *dad*. He

didn't want to hear it. At the sound of the door slamming, Indira whipped around and faced him. She had a roof tile in her trunk.

"Put that down," he shouted, trying to sound like his father establishing control and authority. Henry didn't sound like his father. He didn't look like him either. His father was a burly, powerful man.

Henry lowered his voice and tried to sound firmer. "PUT THAT DOWN!"

Indira dropped the tile and charged.

Henry dove behind the car an instant before she smashed into the rear passenger door with a loud metallic crunch. Marie jumped out of the front seat, screaming for Indira to back off. Edgar joined her, swearing at Indira for smashing his beloved car. Stan stayed where he was in the back seat because he couldn't open the crushed door. All of this was too much for Indira. She spread her ears, raised her trunk, trumpeted, then fled downhill toward the hippo paddocks, where the lions were still chowing down on the zebra.

Warily, Stan got out of the opposite passenger door.

"Look at this mess!" Edgar pointed at the crushed metal.

Marie looked Henry over. "Anything broken?"

Henry picked the gravel out of his bloody palms, embarrassed by his elephant handling.

"I'm fine. I guess there's more to controlling an elephant than I thought." He looked at Edgar. "Sorry about the door."

"Not your fault," Edgar said. "Not the elephant's fault either. I'm sure this is confusing for her. Terrifying, just like it is for us."

He pointed down the hill at the feeding lions. "It's going to take a while for us to adapt like them."

"Are we the lions or the zebras?" Stan asked.

"We're both," Edgar said.

"Survival of the fittest?" Henry asked.

Edgar shook his head. "Survival of the smartest."

CHAPTER TEN

The inside of the administration building looked like a group of gorillas had torn it apart. File cabinets were tipped over; paper was strewn all over the floors; chairs, computers, and tables were smashed; several windows were broken.

"What kind of animal would do this?" Marie asked.

Edgar walked over to a broken window, bent down, and stood up with a big rock in his hand. "The human kind," he said.

That's when Henry remembered the animal rights protest.

A door slammed closed from somewhere in the building. Stan yanked the pistol out of his waistband.

"That's not necessary," Marie said.

Stan ignored her.

"I think it came from downstairs," Henry said.

"Let's take a look," Edgar said.

Halfway down the stairs they ran into Gary Dulabaum coming up. He was the zoo's ungulate keeper. He was carrying a bicycle pump.

"I thought I heard voices," Gary said cheerfully, as if everything was perfectly fine. "Good to see you, Marie. Hi, Henry." He looked at Edgar and Stan, saying nothing about the gun in Stan's hand, as if that was perfectly fine too.

"This is my brother Edgar and my brother-in-law Stan," Marie said. "What's going on, Gary?"

Gary held up the pump. "Bicycle tire went flat. Gotta fix it."

Henry had known Gary for years. He had always been a bit strange, but now it looked like he had lost his marbles.

"I meant what happened at the zoo," Marie said.

They waited for him to explain. He didn't.

"All the animals appear to be loose," Edgar prompted.

"Not all of them," Gary said. "Mine are still in their enclosures, except for the zebras and one of the rhinos."

"How did the animals get out?" Marie asked.

"You didn't see it on the news?"

They all shook their heads. Gary hadn't seen it on the news either, because there hadn't been any news broadcasts since the pulse.

"It was those animal rights protesters," he continued. "They call themselves the Wild Bunch. Bunch of idiots, if you ask me. A couple hundred of them showed up yesterday morning. They got violent. TV crews were here. We called the cops. Tom tried to reason with the protesters. You know how Tom is . . . forceful, but calm. Heck, he agrees with a lot of their gripes; we all do. But they weren't having any of it. They started breaking windows. Next thing we know they somehow cut our power and the backup generator. I have no idea how they managed that. The mob rushed the gates. We tried to stop them, but they kicked our butts, stole our keys and keycards, and started letting animals out. Nuts, right? Anyway, it was a complete disaster. After they let the rhino and zebras go, I hit a guy in the head with a shovel. He and his gang backed down and took off. I stayed in the paddocks, guarding the animals. Eventually, Tom came by and told me he and another keeper were heading out after Niki and Nuri. You know, our Siberian tigers. The protesters cut the perimeter fence in several places before they left. The cats slipped out into Washington Park. I offered to go with Tom, but he told me to stay at the paddocks until he got back. That's the last time I saw him or anyone else. It got dark . . ." Gary hesitated. "I guess I better be honest. I didn't want to walk around the zoo at night with the cats and bears on the prowl. I hid out at the paddocks until it got light."

Henry wouldn't have wanted to walk around at night either. It was bad enough during the day.

"It took a long time to search this morning because of all the animals wandering around. I went through every inch of every building. This place is a ghost town. I tried to start my truck, but it was dead as a doornail. I couldn't get any of the other trucks started either, if you can believe that. But I remembered that I had left my bike at the commissary a couple of days ago. Flat tire. That's why I was rummaging through the admin building. I knew I'd seen a pump here. Where's Tom?"

"What?" Marie asked, looking confused.

"Dad isn't with us," Henry said.

Now it was Gary's turn to look confused. "Really? I figured he must have gone home like everyone else and come back with you to check on me."

Marie shook her head.

"Then what are you doing here?" Gary asked.

"We came to find Tom!" Stan said.

"He's not here," Gary said. "Have you called him? I'm sure

he has his cell. He always carries it with him. I would have called him, but landlines don't work for some reason."

"You didn't try your cell phone?" Henry asked.

"Don't have one. Don't believe in them."

At least Gary wasn't going to miss not having one, Henry thought.

Edgar quickly and patiently explained what had happened.

When he finished, Gary said, "That'll be different. At least until they get it fixed."

Henry guessed Gary had missed a few points.

"Where do you live, Gary?" Marie asked gently, like she was talking to a five-year-old.

"I have an apartment three miles from here."

"Do you have a roommate?"

"Nope. I live alone. Don't believe in roommates."

"I'm a little concerned about you," she continued. "Things are dangerous out there. If you want, you can come to the farm with us until . . . until this thing settles down."

"I appreciate the offer, but you live too far away from the zoo. Who's going to take care of the animals that are still here? If someone doesn't feed them, they'll starve."

"Set 'em free," Stan said. "Let them fend for themselves."

"Some of them might be able to do that," Gary admitted. "Did you see the lions at the bottom of the hill?"

"Yeah. It looks like they're fending for themselves."

Gary gave Stan a sad smile. "It's pretty easy for a lion to take down a zebra that has never seen a lion. What happens when there are no more zebras?" He shook his head. "It looks like I've been picked to stick around. I don't mind."

"At least let us drive you to your apartment after we finish here so you can pack some things," Mom offered. "We have a truck. We'll drive you back to the zoo."

Gary shook his head. "I'm good. I'll fix the flat, ride over, get some gear, then ride back. When you find Tom, let him know I'm holding down the fort."

Henry liked how he said *when*, not *if*, but he doubted Gary was going to be able to hold down the fort on his own. From what he'd seen, there was a chance that he wouldn't reach his apartment. "Theefs" might 'jack his bicycle.

"We'll let Tom know," Marie said. "What's your best guess about where Tom is?"

Gary whistled. "All I can tell is that he's not here at the zoo. Washington Park is over four hundred acres, most of it wooded. It's hard to say where the tigers went. They could easily be out of the park by now, in downtown Portland. Heck, if the cats found one of the bridges across the Willamette, they could be on the east side heading up the Columbia Gorge."

Marie let out a long sigh. "I guess we better get to it, then. Take care of yourself, Gary."

"Will do." He stopped at the top of the stairs and turned around. "When you see Tom, tell him I borrowed his pump. I found it in his gear closet. I'll put it back when I'm done."

"We will," Henry said. "*When* we see him."

CHAPTER ELEVEN

Tom Carter's office was in shambles.

Edgar started cursing. Marie's face turned crimson as she glared down at the scattered files, books, and smashed picture frames. There were torn photos of Tom with exotic animals, Tom in Africa, Tom in Asia. She picked up a photo of Tom and Henry on the deck with Niki and Nuri when they were cubs. She shook the broken glass out of the twisted frame.

Edgar looked in Tom's gear closet and found a box of old two-way radios. He picked one out and turned it on. "Dead." He sniffed it. "Doesn't smell cooked. Could be out of juice. We'll take them back to the farm and see if they charge."

Henry looked in the closet. "All the guns are gone." The zoo kept several rifles and shotguns on hand as a last resort if an animal escaped.

"Of course they took the guns," Edgar said. "How much ammo was there?"

"Not much," Henry answered.

"Good," Edgar said. "A few bullets won't last them long out in this mess."

Marie gathered more photos.

Stan stood awkwardly in the door. "I'll check the other offices."

Henry helped his mom with the photos.

"Don't cut yourself," she said.

"That's the least of my problems."

Something whimpered.

"What's that?" Henry asked.

There was another whimper, louder this time, more insistent. Henry went around to the back of his dad's desk and pulled out his chair. Behind it was a small animal carrier. A paw scratched at the wire mesh door. He opened it. A young tricolored blue heeler stepped through the threshold, stretched, and wagged its tail.

"Your birthday present!" his mom said, smiling. It was the first smile he'd seen from her since leaving the farm. "Tom was so disappointed he didn't arrive in time for your birthday party."

Henry scratched the pup's head. "He looks just like Boomer."

"Not surprising, since he has the same parents," Marie explained. "He's six months old. Someone bought him, then took him back to the breeder. Their loss is your gain."

Edgar was smiling too. He had loved Boomer as much as Henry and was devastated when he was killed.

Stan walked back into the office. "What's all the ruckus?"

Henry pointed at the dog.

"A heeler," Stan said without enthusiasm. "The vet's office is trashed like all the others. They tried to break into the safe, but they didn't get it open. What's in it?"

"Drugs and tranquilizer equipment," Henry said.

Stan glowered at the dog. He was not fond of dogs, in particular Boomer, who had not been fond of Stan. Over the years, Boomer had nipped him several times. Henry's dad was not fond of Stan and had told Henry on several occasions that if he were a dog, he would nip Stan too.

"What are you going to name him?" Edgar asked.

Henry thought about it for a few moments, then said, "Gort."

"Gort?" Stan asked.

"Klaatu barada nikto," Edgar said.

Henry knew Edgar would understand. Gort was the robot in the movie *The Day the Earth Stood Still*. The only way to stop Gort from destroying the earth was to say *klaatu barada nikto*.

"That was one of Tom's favorite sci-fi films," Edgar said.

Is, Henry thought. *Is*.

"I bet we watched that film together a half-dozen times."

Tom and Edgar spent a lot of time in the barn watching old movies.

"We need to stop talking about movies and talk about our next *move*," Stan said irritably. "I say we burn rubber and start picking up supplies. We don't want to be out after dark."

Marie looked at the photos of Tom she was holding. "I guess we're done down here," she said quietly. "Where do we need to go?"

"I need to go to my company's warehouse on the east side," Stan said. "There's a whole fleet of heavy equipment stored there that hasn't been used in decades. We should be able to get some trucks fired up and running." He pulled out a ring of keys and jangled them. "And I have a key to the warehouse."

Marie looked at Edgar.

"Fine with me. I need to make a stop downtown to pick something up, but it won't take long."

"Okay," Marie said. "Let's get to it."

"Wait a second," Henry said. "What about Dad?"

"No point in searching the zoo," Stan said. "Gary already looked. Tom's not here."

"We'll drive through Washington Park on our way downtown," Henry's mom said. "Maybe we'll get lucky."

They did not get lucky.

All they found in Washington Park was a chimp making a nest in a tree and a rhino wallowing in the mud at the archery range. No tigers. No Tom. No people. They headed out of the park toward downtown.

"The fact that we didn't find him, or any trace of him, means that he might be okay," Marie said from the front seat.

"He might be at the farm right now worrying about us," Edgar added.

Henry knew the exchange was for his benefit. His mom turned around. "We are not giving up on Dad. But we do need to get back to the farm. If he isn't there, we'll go out and search again, and again until we find him."

Or find out what happened to him, Henry thought grimly, looking down at Gort, who was asleep with his head in Henry's lap. He had given him some water and a handful of kibble he'd found in the commissary that they fed to the wolves. They'd taken a bunch of other stuff too, which meant they were now "theefs" like everyone else.

Henry looked out the rear window. Stan was behind them in

the flatbed, about two feet from the Cadillac's bumper.

"Tailgater!" Edgar complained.

"It will be dark soon," Marie said. "Are you sure you need to make this stop downtown?"

"I do," Edgar answered.

"What are you picking up?"

"It's not a what, it's a who."

"Don't be obtuse."

"A friend of mine. If we're going to survive this thing, we'll need his expertise."

"You're bringing him to the farm?"

"If he'll come."

"Where is he going to stay?"

"He can bunk with me in the barn for the time being. Eventually we'll have to figure out living quarters for others."

"You mean Ludds."

Edgar shook his head. "They won't all be Ludds. We're going to need a doctor. We have several nurses in the family, but we need someone who can do more complicated things like surgery. We'll need a teacher. We'll need an agriculturist. We know how to grow a vegetable garden, but we'll need crops to support us."

"Aren't you getting a little ahead of yourself?"

"I don't think so. If this thing goes on, we'll have to get the fields ready right now, so we'll have food in the spring."

"What will we eat this winter?"

"We'll have to scrounge or trade for food, if we have anything to trade. With the food we have stored at the farm and what we're able to find in the next couple of weeks, we should be able to make it through the winter if we're careful, but it's going to be hard, very hard."

Henry hadn't thought of any of this, and by his mom's silence, he doubted she had either.

"If this lasts," she said quietly.

"Better safe than dead," Edgar said. "If we're ready, we're good either way."

"I really don't want to be out after dark," Marie said.

"Too late for that. If we left for the farm right now, we wouldn't be there until after dark. We could split up. You go with Stan and I'll pick up my guy alone. That would save some time."

"I don't want anyone out here alone after dark. It's too dangerous."

"I'll take Henry with me. All I'm doing is picking someone up. We'll be home hours before you and Stan. The warehouse Stan wants to check out is in Parkrose. When you leave there, it'll take a while to get to Wonderland on side streets."

"Perhaps we should go to the warehouse another day."

"That depends on how secure the warehouse is. It's first come, first served. The more time that passes, the less likely the stuff will be there."

"Let's ask Stan."

Edgar picked up the two-way.

"No," Marie said. "Pull over. Let's talk face-to-face."

They stopped on the Vista Bridge, overlooking the city, and got out. Gray smoke obscured the view and stung Henry's eyes.

"Discouraging," Edgar said, looking at the view.

Marie explained her thinking to Stan. He frowned during the

entire explanation. When she finished, he shook his head. "Forget it, Marie. We can't wait to go to the warehouse. In fact, it might already be too late. I'm not the only one who knows what's inside. One of those things is an ancient semi and trailer. I can't drive it and the flatbed back to the farm. Someone needs to go with me, and I guess that's you because Edgar has something else to do. I don't want to waste time stopping downtown." He looked at Edgar. "Any chance Marie can pick up your friend?"

"I doubt he'd go with her. To be honest, I'm not sure he'll come with me. He's kind of an oddball."

That's rich, Henry thought, *coming from the original oddball.*

"And we really need him?" Stan asked.

"We do."

Stan nodded. "That's good enough for me. What do you want to do, Marie?"

Marie looked out over the city for a moment before answering. "You and I will go to the warehouse."

CHAPTER TWELVE

It took Edgar and Henry forty-five minutes to drive the ten blocks to Broadway in the heart of downtown Portland. There were a lot of people wandering the streets, loaded down with junk. All of them stared at the Cadillac with surprise, and maybe a little envy.

"Grab the shotgun in the back seat and make certain people can see it," Edgar said.

Henry put it between his legs, barrel up. He knew all about shotguns. His uncle Chester had built a skeet range in the back of the house he and Aunt Ruth lived in. Henry had obliterated thousands of clay pigeons over the years.

Edgar slowly wove his way through the stalled cars on Broadway and came to a stop in front of a store called Gunderson's Fine Jewelry. The front door and window glass were shattered. There were three people lying dead by the entrance. One of them was a uniformed policeman.

"Why are we stopping here?"

"Because this is my friend's place. It looks like he's had trouble."

"Is he one of the dead guys?"

"No."

"Did your friend shoot the policeman?"

"Albert wouldn't shoot a cop."

"Albert?"

"Albert Gunderson. Former marine recon sergeant. This jewelry store has been in his family for almost a hundred years. Albert took it over when he got out of the corps." Edgar unrolled Henry's window, leaned across him, and shouted, "Are you in there, Albert?"

"I'm here," a voice answered from the dark interior. He was speaking through a bullhorn.

"You okay?"

"Never better."

"What about the three dead guys?"

"They've been better. The cop tried to stop the two perps from breaking in. They shot him, so I shot them. See the kid standing across the street with his hands in his pockets?"

There were several people standing across the street.

"He has dark curly hair. Twentysomething. Clean-shaven. Dressed in khakis, blue turtleneck sweater, and green down vest. Tall guy with the smart-ass grin."

"I see him," Edgar said.

"He was with the two perps, but he wasn't in on the shooting, so I let him go. The problem is, he won't leave. I'm not sure what his plan is. He probably doesn't know either."

"That kid can hear everything Mr. Gunderson is saying," Henry said.

"I think that's the point."

"I figure one of the dead guys is his brother, cousin, or best friend. Who knows? He's ticked off. He wants vengeance. I get that. But that's not going to happen. The reason he has his hands in his pockets is that he has a nine-millimeter automatic pistol tucked in the small of his back. I told him to put

57

his hands in his pockets after he refused to move on. I promised to shoot him where he's standing if he takes his hands out of his pockets. And he knows I can do it because I sent a couple of rounds a half inch from his left ear an hour ago. That's how the window behind him got shattered. He's waiting for it to get dark, thinking the advantage is going to shift in his favor. What he doesn't believe is that I have a nightscope and that I can put his eye out at a thousand yards."

"Can we come in?" Edgar asked.

"Who's the kid?"

"My nephew Henry."

"What's in his lap besides that shotgun?"

They were twenty feet from the front door. Henry was a little uncomfortable knowing that Albert was checking him out through the lens of a rifle scope. If his mother knew this was what they were going to encounter in downtown Portland, she would have never let him go. She probably wouldn't have let Edgar go either. Henry held Gort up so Albert could see him better.

"Good-looking heeler. What's his name?"

"Gort," Henry said.

"Klaatu barada nikto."

Henry decided right then and there that he liked Albert Gunderson a lot.

"The three of you can come in."

"I don't want to leave the car unattended," Edgar said.

"Don't blame you. It's a beauty. What happened to the door?"

"Elephant hit it."

"Nothing would surprise me. Not now."

Henry glanced over at the guy with the dark curly hair. His

smirk had turned into a wide, white-toothed grin for some reason.

"Don't worry about your car. I'll keep an eye on it." Albert Gunderson raised his voice so everyone for two blocks could hear him. *"IF ANYONE TRIES TO 'JACK THIS CAR, I WILL PUT A BULLET IN YOUR HEAD. That should do it. No one will bother your car. Before you come in, open the ragtop so I have a clearer view of the street."*

Edgar hit a button on the dash. As the top opened and folded in on itself, he said, "You probably shouldn't mention any of this to your mom. If you do, she may keep you on the farm until you're thirty."

Maybe longer, Henry thought.

"You go first," Edgar said. "I'll watch your back."

Henry slid out, cradling the shotgun, with Gort at his heels. He hesitated when he got to the dead bodies. He didn't want to look at them too closely and add to his dead-people memories.

"To your left," Albert said without the megaphone. "There's plenty of room to get by the corpses. Just be careful of the blood pool. It's slippery as snot."

Thanks for the imagery, Henry thought. He crept by the pool without getting too much gore on his white sneakers and stepped into the store. Gort wasn't quite so finicky. He had blood on all four paws and his muzzle because he had paused to sniff the corpses.

It was mostly shadows inside the jewelry store. One of those shadows was Albert. He was Edgar's age, gray hair, balding, over-weight. He was sitting on a tall stool behind a glass display counter filled with jewelry. He wasn't alone. Sitting next to him was a younger guy, maybe thirty years old, dark hair, heavy beard, lean and fit-looking. On top of the counter was a short tripod holding a long rifle with the biggest scope Henry had ever seen. The young guy was peering through the scope. Next to the tripod were half a dozen plastic water bottles and a package of Oreo cookies with one row missing.

Edgar stepped in behind him.

"Stand to either side of the door," Albert said, putting on a set of shooting earmuffs. "Cover your ears."

Bam!

The young guy fired a round. It sounded like he had set off a stick of dynamite in a confined space. The kid across the street started yelling, but Henry couldn't understand what he was saying because his ears were ringing.

Albert slipped his shooting earmuffs down around his thick neck. "That'll keep his hands in his pockets for a while. I wish he would give it up and move on." He leaned over and scratched Gort behind his ears. "Your dog didn't even flinch. Unusual."

"I thought you were alone in here," Edgar said.

"That's what I want everyone out there to think," Albert said. "This is my nephew, Derek. Ex–Army Ranger. Pretty good shot, but not as good as me. He's been bumming around the country since he got out. Swings through Portland a couple times a year. Came through at the wrong time this time, although I suspect this is what it looks like everywhere at the moment."

"Hands in pockets," Derek said, still peering through the scope. "Good boy. I really don't want to shoot this kid." He took his eye away from the scope and stretched. "My back is killing me."

"It's no wonder," Albert said, looking at his watch. "You've been sitting behind that scope for almost five hours."

In spite of his age, Albert was tough-looking, with sharp, alert blue eyes. The only soft thing about him was his delicate-looking fingers, which Henry guessed you had to have if you were a jeweler. Albert handed him a pair of binoculars.

"I need you to keep an eye on the street while we talk to your uncle," he said. "Let us know what the kid is doing, or if anyone approaches your car, or the store."

"Do I call you Al?"

"You can try it once, but I wouldn't recommend you try it twice. My name is Albert, not Al, not Bert. Your uncle is Edgar, not Ed. Now look through those binoculars while Edgar brings us up to speed."

Edgar gave them a brief summary of everything that had happened since the plane crashed in the lower field. When he finished, Albert said, "We're not two days into this thing and look what's happened." He nodded at the front door. "Pockets, across the street, is a customer. Well, not really a customer. He's never bought anything, but he's been in here a few times the past couple of years.

"He's a crow. He covets shiny things he can't afford. Thinks he knows a lot about high-end watches, gems, and gold. He doesn't. Not sure if knocking off the store was his idea, or his two unfortunate friends'. Guess he thinks that the power is going to reboot, like all the other looters. You can't believe what I've seen people carrying past the store. In a week or so they are going to realize what they really need are the essentials. Food, water, shelter, and power. You have all four things on your farm, assuming the wind turbine is cranking out juice."

"It is," Edgar said. "I'll cut right to the chase. I want you to come to the farm with us. We need your help."

"I figured that's why you dropped by in the middle of this hellish mess. Are you in charge of the farm?"

"No. My sister Marie is running the show. It's her farm, and I think she has what it takes."

"Did she want the job?"

"Nope."

Albert smiled. "I like her already."

"Do you think this outage is going to last?" Derek asked.

"I don't know," Edgar answered. "But even if it doesn't last, it will be a long time before things get back to normal."

"Is Derek part of the invitation?" Albert asked.

"If he wants to come," Edgar said.

"What would our jobs be?" Derek asked.

"Defense, reconnaissance, training, organization, help with the wind turbine, and probably a lot of other things."

"What's happening out on the street?" Derek asked.

It took Henry a second to realize that he was talking to him. "Nothing," Henry said. "The guy still has his hands in his pockets. People are looking at the car, but they are all across the street."

"Might as well start the training right now," Derek said. "How many people do you see?"

Henry counted them. "Eleven people."

"Describe them. Tell me what they are doing."

Henry guessed their ages and told him what they were wearing. "They're all just standing across the street watching us and other people walking by."

Derek looked through his scope. "There are two more people since I last looked. I think the guy standing to the right of Pockets is a friend. See how they keep glancing at each other?"

Henry hadn't noticed, but Derek was right. They were giving each other furtive looks.

"It's all in the details," Albert said. "You are going to have to learn to notice everything from now on. Derek and I will teach you."

"So, you're coming to the farm with us?" Edgar asked.

Albert looked at Derek. "What do you think?"

Derek shrugged. "It's either go to the farm, die here by being overrun, or being forced to leave after we run out of Oreos. I can't say I'll stick on the farm for long, though. You know me."

Albert laughed. "No one knows you, Derek." He looked at Edgar. "Derek is the black sheep of the family. Drives my sister crazy."

Henry looked at Derek. "Where does your mom live?"

"New York City," Derek answered. "If the power is out there, it's worse than it is here."

"You must be worried about her."

"Of course I'm worried, but there's nothing I can do about it. She might as well be on Mars. She'll be okay. The Gundersons are a tough bunch. Mom is a survivor."

"It's fortuitous you came along when you did," Albert said. "We're kind of in a pickle here. We were discussing our options when you pulled up. Derek doesn't own a car, and mine is parked six blocks away in a parking lot. As soon as the juice was cut, he jogged over to see if it would start. It was fried like all the other cars. I should have bought an old clunker. That left us with two options. Stick it out here or grab what we could carry and run.

If we stayed, we'd probably have to shoot more people, a prospect neither one of us was thrilled about. And if we ran? Well, where would we run to? As you know, I don't have a lot of friends, and the only people Derek knows in town, besides me, are street people," Albert said. He pulled an Oreo out and offered it to Gort, who gobbled it down like he was starving. "Gort has a sweet tooth. You think it's an enhanced, or super, EMP?"

"I don't know," Edgar said. "I've been out of the disaster loop for a long time."

"What's a super EMP?" Henry asked, still looking across the street through the binoculars.

"It's theoretical," Edgar answered. "A pulse that's big enough to shut down the entire country."

"I guess there's no point in speculating," Albert said, then looked at Derek. "Want to go to the farm?"

"Sure," Derek said. "Let's get out of here."

"Good," Albert said. "Here's the plan."

He explained what he wanted Edgar and Henry to do, then gave them a couple of headlamps. Edgar and Henry slipped them on and headed through the door behind the counter. Gort didn't go with them. Henry guessed he didn't want to stray too far from the Oreos.

CHAPTER THIRTEEN

Edgar spun the combination into the huge walk-in safe and pulled open the heavy door. The floor-to-ceiling shelves were filled with jewelry, watches, gems, gold, silver, ammunition, and guns. On the floor in front of the shelves was a stack of empty duffel bags.

"Wouldn't it be easier to just leave this stuff here?" Henry asked. "They'd need dynamite to blast this door open."

"Probably, but this stuff might come in handy down the road for trade when food gets scarce. Like Albert said, people like shiny things."

They started stuffing things in the duffel bags. Henry felt like he was robbing the place. He started pulling watch boxes off the shelf and came to a stack with Edgar's name on them.

"Your name is on these."

Edgar looked at the boxes. "So it is. I brought them in to be serviced a couple of months ago. Haven't had time to pick them up." He opened a green box embossed with ROLEX. Inside was a stainless steel watch with a black dial. He took it out. "Vintage Submariner in pristine condition." He wound the crown, then set the time by the watch he was wearing. "Strap it on. We'll call it a late birthday present. It's an automatic. No battery. Stays wound by the movement of your wrist. Electronic watches have been fried."

"Thanks." Henry put it on, and they got back to work.

Ten minutes later Derek walked into the safe. "How's it going?"

"Just about done," Edgar said. "How's it going out there?"

"Status quo. Pockets and his buddy are just standing across the street like a couple of vultures waiting for their turn to feed. We'll keep 'em at bay until we meet you in the alley."

He left them to their legal heist, which according to Henry's watch took them ten more minutes. When they finished, they started the hard work of dragging the heavy duffels through the maze of hallways that led to a small door in back of the store. The door led to a narrow alley. After the duffels were staged on the loading platform, they walked back to the storefront.

Albert was sitting behind the display counter, looking through the scope. Derek wasn't there.

"Where's Derek?" Henry asked.

"Look across the street," Albert said, nodding at the binoculars.

Pockets and his friend were still looking at the store. Derek was standing next to Pockets, posing as an onlooker. Pockets was saying something to him, and Derek was smiling as if he had found whatever Pockets said amusing.

"Derek exited through the alley. They have no idea who he is," Albert said, smiling. "If they try something when you get into the Cadillac, they're in for an unpleasant surprise. You guys ready?"

Edgar and Henry nodded.

Albert picked up the megaphone. "*MY FRIENDS ARE LEAVING! DO NOT APPROACH THEM. DO NOT APPROACH THEIR VEHICLE. IF THEY ARE THREATENED IN ANY WAY, I WILL SHOOT YOU.*"

These instructions were punctuated by the crack of two

bullets. One, inches from Pockets's feet. The other, inches from his friend's head.

"Go!" Albert told them.

Edgar went first, cradling the shotgun. Henry followed close behind, with Gort at his heels. The people standing across the street were frozen in place like store mannequins, including Derek, who was feigning shock even though he must have known the shots were coming.

Henry got into the front passenger seat. Edgar slid behind the steering wheel and turned the key. For a second Henry thought the car might not start, like in one of those predictable TV shows he had watched in Edgar's barn, but the engine roared to life. On the quiet street the sound was almost as shocking as the crack of Albert's rifle. Henry looked over at Derek. He wasn't looking at them. He was looking at Pockets.

"So far, so good," Edgar said, pushing the button to raise the roof. He put the car in gear and started down the street, slowly serpentining around stalled cars. "What time is it?"

Henry looked at his wristwatch. "Six twenty."

Bang!

Startled, Henry turned around, but couldn't see anything. They were already two blocks away.

"Albert's just letting them know that he's still inside and alert. We have fifteen to twenty minutes before sunset. I doubt they'll move on the store until after dark."

Henry hoped he was right.

Edgar put on his blinker, which was completely unnecessary as they were the only working car on the street at the moment. He drove two blocks, took a right, then did a clockwise circle to the alley in back of the store.

"Keep your eyes peeled. He said the alley was hard to spot."

"There!" Henry said.

"Are you sure?"

"I think so." The alley would have been impossible to see if Albert hadn't told them exactly what to look for. Henry wasn't certain it was wide enough for their car.

Edgar stopped the car, then put it into reverse.

"Why are you backing in?"

"So we don't have to back out. It's a dead end."

The alley was only a quarter of a block from the street Gunderson's Jewelry faced. They couldn't be seen on the side street, but there was a good chance the engine could be heard from that far away.

Bang!

"I guess Albert is still keeping the vultures at bay," Edgar said. He had to jockey the car back and forth several times to get it lined up with the entrance. "Keep your eyes open. If you see anyone running down the street toward us, let me know."

In seconds Henry's view vanished, replaced by solid brick inches from his face. The walls were so close they weren't going to be able to open the doors to get out.

Edgar was twisted around in his seat, concentrating on keeping the wide car centered.

"Watch the side mirrors," he said. "Let me know if they're going to scrape."

Bang! Another gunshot shattered the oncoming night.

"We just might be able to pull this off," Edgar said. "I should have grabbed the two-way from Stan before he and your mom headed east. That way we could have stayed in touch with Albert. It's little mistakes that will get you killed. Twenty more yards."

The driver's side-view mirror scraped along the bricks. It was loud.

Edgar swore and overcorrected. Henry's mirror scraped along the bricks.

Bang!

Bang!

Bang!

Edgar got back on track. "Albert must have heard the scrape too. The three shots were to distract the guys across the street. At least I hope that's what he was doing."

Henry hoped so too. It was nearly dark now.

"What time is it?"

Henry looked at his watch. "Six forty."

"Perfect." Edgar stopped next to the loading dock marked GUNDERSON'S JEWELRY.

Henry was about to ask him how they were going to get out of the car but didn't because Edgar answered the question by pushing the button to open the convertible top. Gort jumped into the front seat. It took a lot of shoving and pulling to get the heavy duffels loaded. By the time they had them inside, the car was pretty low to the ground.

"Go get Albert," Edgar said. "I'll rearrange the load to distribute the weight better."

Henry switched on the headlamp as he walked through the

back entrance into the maze of hallways. As he got close to the front of the store, Albert hissed, "Douse the light! I'm supposed to be alone in here!"

It's little mistakes that will get you killed, Henry thought, and switched off the light, feeling his way the last twenty feet. It was completely dark on the street. He couldn't see anything beyond the windows. He couldn't see Albert either.

"Your eyes will adjust," Albert's voice said from the darkness. "Are the duffels loaded?"

"Yeah."

"One of our guys disappeared after you scraped the wall. Derek followed him. Did you see anyone in the alley?"

"No."

"I'm going to squeeze off four shots."

Henry felt something touch his hand and nearly jumped out of his skin.

"Earplugs," Albert said. "Put them in. You need to cover your eyes so the muzzle flash doesn't blind you. As soon as you hear the fourth shot, head back to the dock. Don't turn on your headlamp."

"Got it." Henry fumbled with the earplugs in the dark. "You can see them?" He still couldn't see anything. He was worried about finding his way through the maze of hallways back to the dock.

"Clear as a bell. I switched to my nightscope. I can see Pockets as clear as day. I'm going to give him something to think about. Ready?"

"Yeah."

Bang!

Bang!

Bang!

Bang!

Henry ran . . . Well, it was more like tripping forward as he tried to remember the route to the back door. He lost track of how many turns he had taken. He was about to chance turning on his headlamp when he felt a gentle touch on his shoulder.

"You're doing fine," Albert said. "You can take the earplugs out, but don't turn on your lamp. We're almost there. That other guy might be in the alley."

Henry felt the cool air from the open back door. In a few seconds he stumbled through the opening, with Albert right behind him, clutching his rifle. Edgar was sitting behind the steering wheel with Gort next to him.

"Get Gort in the back seat," Edgar said.

Henry scooted Gort onto the duffels piled in back.

"I'll take the middle," Albert said, clambering past him. "I think they're onto us. We have a possible bogey in the alley. I'll scan with the scope as you drive. Go!"

Edgar drove down the alley. Something flashed in front of them.

Bang!

The windshield shattered.

"Get down, Henry!" Edgar shouted.

Henry got down. His shirt and jeans were covered with a thousand glass shards.

"It's over," Albert said. "Turn your headlights on. We're safe."

Henry sat up and looked through the shattered windshield. Derek was standing at the end of the alley, holding a pistol at his side.

CHAPTER FOURTEEN

Henry's nerves were as shattered as the broken glass all over his shirt and pants. He crawled into the back to make room for Derek. Edgar peeled out, fishtailing around the corner, nearly throwing Henry and Gort out of the car. Duffels stuffed with gold, guns, ammo, watches, and jewels were not comfortable to sit on. Henry put his arm around Gort's neck to steady him. The dog had finally lost his cool and was shivering. Or maybe Henry had lost his cool and was shivering. He couldn't tell.

Edgar raised the top.

"Did you kill him?" Albert asked Derek.

Derek shook his head. "No. But I should have. I didn't think he was going to take that shot. He didn't see me coming. I cold-cocked him with my pistol and dragged him out of the way so you didn't run over him like he was a speed bump."

Henry picked glass out of Gort's fur with trembling hands as they wove their way down the street. Albert had his sniper rifle poking through the broken windshield, keeping his eyes open for potential threats. There weren't many people out, and the few who were gave them shocked deer-in-headlights expressions as they drove by.

"They appear to be more afraid of us than we need to be of them," Edgar observed as he turned south onto Barbur Boulevard, which parallels I-5.

"You're probably right," Albert agreed, pulling his rifle back in and setting it between his legs. "I don't know how you're going to replace this windshield now."

"I have a spare at the farm," Edgar said.

They didn't see any more people on the streets until they drove past a Fred Meyer grocery store. The parking lot was filled with nighttime shoppers, or probably *theefs*.

"Looks like Freddy's held out longer than some of the other stores," Edgar said.

"Without a vehicle it takes people longer to get here, and they can't carry as much when they leave," Albert said. "It'll be stripped clean before dawn. How are your food supplies on the farm?"

"Food's going to be a problem this winter," Edgar said. "My brother-in-law Chester is in charge of scrounging."

Albert laughed. "Chester the freegan?"

Edgar nodded. "The one and only."

"You know my uncle Chester?" Henry asked. These were the first words he'd spoken since they had left the alley.

"Met him a couple of times during his rounds," Albert said. "I didn't realize he was married to a Ludd. He used to work the alley. There are two restaurants there. He said it was pretty good pickings midweek when the restaurants were slow."

Chester was a hard-core freegan, aka dumpster diver. Most of the food he and Ruth had at their house was outdated stuff grocery stores and restaurants had thrown out. He knew the exact day and time stores and restaurants dumped their food for a fifty-mile radius. Henry's mom and dad and several other Ludds refused to eat at Chester and Ruth's. Henry had no problem eating at their house. The food was delicious, and there was always a lot of it. Ruth worked for the school district, and Chester had been unemployed for as long as Henry could remember, but that didn't mean he wasn't working. He left his house early every morning to "find stuff," as he put it.

"Of course, my scrounging is going to be a little different now that there's no juice," Chester had explained at the meeting. "But I still know where a lot of stuff is."

"How far away is your farm?" Derek asked.

"Not far," Edgar answered. "But it will take a while to get there through the snarl."

Whomp . . . whomp . . . whomp . . . The wind turbine cranked away in the darkness.

They arrived back at the farm just before nine o'clock. Henry's mom and Stan were not there to greet them, nor was his dad, but a few more Ludds had arrived during their absence. They marched out of the house like a string of army ants carrying flashlights, led by Madeline. Henry didn't know it then, but this was the way it was going to be from now on when someone arrived on the farm. It wasn't so much the stuff brought in from the outside that interested them, but the information.

"Is Dad back?" Henry asked.

"Not yet," Madeline said. "Where's your mom and Stan?"

"They went to a warehouse on the east side of Portland to check out some old equipment."

"Oh, that's right. Stan mentioned he wanted to do that." Madeline looked at Edgar's car and frowned. "What happened?"

Before Henry could answer, Edgar said, "Elephant encounter. Most of the animals at the zoo are loose."

"And Tom?"

"He wasn't there. A keeper told us he was out stalking a couple of tigers yesterday and he hadn't seen him since."

"Good God!"

Edgar glanced at Henry. "I think there's still a good chance that he's okay."

"I'm sure he is." Madeline looked at Albert and Derek.

"I'm Albert Gunderson, and this is my nephew, Derek."

"Albert and Derek are going to be helping us at the farm for a while," Edgar explained. "They can bunk in the barn with me."

"Welcome," Madeline said, then looked down at Gort. "And who's this?"

"Gort," Henry said. "A birthday present from Dad."

"He looks exactly like Boomer!"

"Same parents."

She reached down and scratched Gort's head, then stood up quickly and shined the flashlight beam on her hand. "He's covered with glass."

"We all are," Edgar said. "When the elephant smashed the car, it must have done something to the windshield. It shattered while we were driving home."

"That's weird," Madeline said.

It's also a whopper, Henry thought. Clearly, Edgar didn't want anyone to know what had happened to them downtown, which was fine with him. He didn't want anyone to know either. It would just freak them out.

"Everything's weird right now," Edgar said.

"I'll brush you off before you come inside."

"You can brush Henry and Gort. We'll take care of ourselves down at the barn," Edgar said.

CHAPTER FIFTEEN

Henry stepped into the brightly lit house. The blinds were closed. Ludds were everywhere. One of his cousins asked if she could take Gort downstairs to show him to the other kids.

"Sure, but no roughhouse," Henry said. "He's had a tough night. If you upset him, he might bite."

He doubted Gort would bite anyone. He hadn't tried to bite Madeline when she brushed him off. But with blue heelers you could never tell. Gort happily followed the cousin downstairs.

"Go down and take a shower," Madeline said. "Change out of those clothes and put them to the side. I'm sure there's still glass in them. We have plenty of hot water. When you come back up, we'll feed you."

Henry was relieved to get out of there before she asked him any more questions. His aunts were good at asking questions. The problem was there were more aunts in the basement.

Ruth, Molly, and Maggie were sitting around the card table at the bottom of the stairs in the small library. Molly was married to Gino. They lived in Lake Oswego. Maggie was divorced and lived about ten miles away in Willamette. All of his aunts were at the Aunt Farm. He wondered how they had gotten there without cars. He gave them a brief, not very accurate, summary of what had happened at the zoo and downtown, then asked Molly where Gino was.

"Down at Ruth's house with Chester," Molly said. "I'm not sure what they're doing."

His aunts were sorting through scorched wallets, purses, briefcases, and backpacks. Hundreds of them. The little room smelled like burned cloth and flesh. A smell Henry was very familiar with now. Unfortunately.

"What are you doing?" Henry asked.

"Cataloging the dead," Molly answered.

Ruth frowned. "Don't be so morbid, Molly."

Molly shrugged. "Well, that's what we're doing."

Ruth looked at Henry. "Everyone is buried," she said. "Chester dug the ditch after the Olofs' internment. We saw no reason to wait. Here, I'll show you."

She flipped a few pages back in the notebook they were scribbling in. It was a map, or a diagram, of where everyone was buried.

"We were able to identify most of the people because their photo identification was in their pockets. For the others . . ." Ruth hesitated. "Some of their faces were, uh—"

"Gone," Maggie said.

Maggie had always been brutally honest, which put some people off. Henry kind of liked it because you always knew what she was thinking and where you stood.

"Those people are represented by question marks," Molly said.

"Chester dug the ditch next to the creek, rather than down the middle of the field," Maggie said. "The land next to the creek isn't arable. We can't use it for planting because he says he can't get the plow along there. If Edgar is right about the power not coming back on, we're going to need as much arable land as we can eke out.

"*If* Edgar is right," Maggie stressed.

A lot of people on their list were question marks.

"What did you do with the baggage and other stuff?" Henry asked.

"We didn't know what to do with it," Ruth said. "We piled it outside Edgar's bunker."

"Which was locked up like a bank vault," Maggie added. "Just like the barn, which is why we're stinking up your house sorting through this charnel. Edgar acts like he owns this farm. What does Edgar keep in that bunker? How big is it?"

For some reason his aunts had the mistaken idea that Edgar confided in Henry. He hung out with Edgar, and he had been in his barn more than any other Ludd, but Henry only got to see what Edgar wanted him to see. He hadn't seen the inside of the bunker.

"I don't know," Henry said. "I need to take a shower."

He left them to their grim task and went into the bathroom, locking the door behind him. He looked in the mirror and saw a haggard thirteen-year-old with wild black hair and green bloodshot eyes. He didn't like what he saw. He had a haunted appearance, which he guessed wasn't surprising considering what he had seen the past thirty-five hours. His reflection scared him.

He stripped out of his clothes and stepped into the shower. The hot water rinsed off the dirt and sweat of the past day and a half, but it didn't rinse off what he had seen and felt. Without warning he couldn't breathe. It felt like Indira was doing a headstand on his chest. He dropped to his hands and knees, hot water pounding on his back, puking his guts out.

Get ahold of yourself, Bucko! he heard echo off the bathroom tile.

Impossible, Henry thought. *It can't be.*

He looked through the steaming glass in panic, thinking one of his aunts had come in to check on him.

No one was there.

It must have been a panic attack from the crash, corpses, bullets, my dad, he thought. *That's it. A panic attack brought on by stress. It could happen to anybody.*

He managed to get to his feet and had to put both hands on the tiled wall to keep himself up. He stood that way until the shower turned cold.

That's better, Bucko.

Henry looked around in terror, but was still alone.

There was only one person who called him Bucko, and she was dead.

PART TWO

THE WONDERLAND

COMPOUND

February 10

Who would have guessed that writing things down could be so cathartic? (Caroline's word, not mine. I had to look it up. Her vocabulary has always been better than mine.) As I understand it, catharsis has to do with the sudden release of emotions, like a valve letting off steam so the tank doesn't explode. I am the tank.

Caroline has been inside my head, on and off, for over four months. I can't seem to shake her. I'm not sure I want to.

She claims she isn't haunting me. Just hanging with me like the good old days. I did hang out with Caroline when we were kids. She was smart, sarcastic, and funny. She was the first girl I knew to dye her hair pink, the first to get a tattoo, the first to get pierced. When everyone else started to do the same thing, she pulled her piercings, kept her tats covered, and let her hair revert to its natural auburn color, saying it was no longer alternative. A lot of kids and teachers didn't like her. Her sharp tongue, intellect, inappropriate honesty, and weird humor scared them. I always had a feeling that Caroline wanted to be liked more than she was but wasn't willing to give up who she was to achieve that.

Over the years we hung out less and less. She had her circle of friends and I had mine. We were always friendly toward each other, saying hello in school hallways or nodding when we passed on Wonderland Road, me on my bike, her walking.

She doesn't pop into my head every day. Sometimes a week will go by without her mouthing off and I think that she's moved on, then she comes back with a vengeance, making snide remarks about me or someone I'm with on the farm.

I fluctuate between thinking Caroline is a figment of my imagination and real. I miss her when she isn't here. I'm scared when she is.

CHAPTER SIXTEEN

Henry, Edgar, Albert, Derek, and Gort were gathered in the corner of the upper field, looking down at a dead cow. It was nine o'clock in the morning, four months after what they called the "switch." No one knew what had caused it, or who had caused it. Few talked about it anymore, because everyone was too busy trying to survive. Henry had told no one about Caroline haunting him, or whatever she was doing, because everyone was busy, and there was nothing they could do about it even if they had the time. They all worked eighteen-hour days, seven days a week. Henry had embraced the long days of hard work. He found that exhaustion was the only way he could sleep without being woken by charging elephants, blood splatter, broken bodies, and his missing father, who was presumed to be dead, or *gone*, which was the word most people now used to describe those who were unaccounted for.

It was cold, twenty degrees. Henry could see everyone's breath, especially Albert's, who looked like he might collapse.

"I told you to wait in the barn," Derek said to Albert.

"Let it go," Albert gasped. "I just have to catch my breath. I'm fine."

Caroline chimed in . . .

He looks like he's going to keel over. He's as pale as the frost sticking to the hay stubble. Thin. Brittle-looking. I bet he's dropped fifty pounds since he got to the farm. Don't ya think?

Henry didn't answer. He agreed with her, but he was afraid he'd respond out loud and everyone would think he was crazy, which he thought he probably was.

"This mutilated cow looks better than you do, Albert," Edgar said.

"Thanks for that."

"You know what the doc said," Derek reminded him.

"Doc" was Dr. Miles Hassle. He, his wife, and his five-year-old son had moved to the farm a couple months earlier after a gang of looters had come through their neighborhood and taken over their house. Chester and Gino had found them on the street with nowhere to go. Doc had turned the Carters' recreation room into a small medical clinic and Henry's bedroom into their bedroom so he could stay close to his overnight patients, although there hadn't been any of those yet.

"Let me go over it just in case it slipped your mind," Derek continued, counting Albert's maladies on his gloved fingers. "You have type-two diabetes, congestive heart failure, probably the onset of kidney disease, and glaucoma. Good news though: You'll probably die before the glaucoma causes you to go blind."

"Yeah, I get it. I'm circling the drain. We all share the same destiny. It's not a matter of if. It's a matter of how and when. At least I know what's going to kill me."

Elegant old fart. You ought to write that down.

Again, Henry ignored Caroline, but he decided that he would write it down in his notebook when he got a chance.

"From the womb to the tomb," Edgar said.

Another good one.

84

"That about sums it up," Albert said. "Now, what about this cow?"

"Here comes Steve," Henry said. "Maybe he saw something."

Steve Miller was their electrician. He'd been on the farm for about six weeks. Derek had found him in downtown Portland during one of his frequent forays outside. He was helping Edgar and Albert figure out how to get power to some of the other houses in the valley. Because shelter was tight on the farm, Steve lived inside the wind turbine.

Whomp . . . whomp . . . whomp . . .

Steve looked down at the dead cow. "I'm hungry enough to eat that raw."

Henry was too. It looked like someone had butchered the cow with a hatchet, hacking away large chunks of red muscle around its ribs and hindquarters.

"You didn't see or hear anything?" Derek asked.

"No windows in the tower," Steve answered. "All I hear anymore is that turbine cranking. I'm not kidding about eating this cow as is."

The Ludds had power, which was more than most people had, but you can't eat electricity. Rationing had started the first week after the switch, and the portions had gotten smaller and smaller every week. Henry had gained bulk because of all the work he was doing, but he was always hungry.

Doc was in charge of nutrition. He said their problem, aside from lack of food, was calorie burn. "You're all hard laborers now and are burning twice as many calories as you did in your previous lives. The only thing keeping you alive is Chester's scrounging."

Chester took the flatbed or semi out at dawn every morning,

with Gino riding shotgun. When Henry heard the truck return in the evening, he'd start salivating like a hungry dog.

"How did they take the cow down?" Steve asked.

"Bow and arrow." Derek pointed at the entry wound. "They retrieved the arrow so they can use it again."

Steve fingered the wound. "Smart rustlers."

"It's my fault," Edgar said. "I should have put the cows in the barn last night, but Albert and I were busy tinkering with stuff. I forgot all about them."

"We need to start posting sentries and patrols," Albert said.

"We won't have the manpower until Stan finishes his wall," Edgar said.

Stanley's Great Wall. The idea came to him a few days after the switch, while he was watching the kids play with LEGO bricks. He proposed that they build a twelve-foot steel wall around the property using dead cars. The concept caused a huge argument among the Ludds. Henry stayed out of most of the contentious debate, as he did most everything else except his daily chores, but it centered around the fact that the cars did not belong to them, and to take the vehicles without permission amounted to grand theft auto on an unheard-of scale.

"What if someone wants their car back?"

"How will you move the cars and stack them?"

"How many people do you need for the work?"

"We'll be arrested when the power comes back on!"

"We'll be sued!"

"We'll lose the farm!"

In the end Marie told Stan that he could build the wall, but the plan exploded when their neighbors got wind of it. Instead of trying to stop another monstrosity, they wanted the wall expanded to include the entire valley. This request was brought on by several break-ins and burglaries, some at gunpoint. Stan said he could expand the wall, but he would need everyone's *enthusiastic* help to get the wall up in a timely fashion. Henry wasn't certain how *enthusiastic* their neighbors were after several weeks of grueling work, but they had hung in with the project, and the Great Wall was nearly complete.

The reason your mom gave Stan the okay on the wall was to keep him out of her hair.

Henry thought Caroline was right about that. Stan was smart, but a bit of a control freak, second-guessing every decision Henry's mother made, usually after the fact. Since the wall started, Henry had barely seen him. He didn't think his mom had either, and she was much more relaxed because of it.

Stan started the wall by putting in three twelve-foot-tall sliding gates. One on Stafford and Wonderland, one on Gage and Stafford, and one on Homesteader and Mountain Road. The gates were made out of the aluminum skin from the jet that crashed. Once the gates were up, he started stacking cars using Edgar's crane. The tires were taken off the rims, and the rims were spot-welded to the roof of the lower car for stability. The street-side doors of the cars were spot-welded so people couldn't climb through, except for Volkswagen Beetles. This was supposed to be a big secret, but Henry suspected dozens of people knew about it, because there were nearly fifty neighbors working on the wall. Stan called the Beetles *Bug holes*. They were only to be used in an emergency, in the unlikely event that a member of the Wonderland Compound (as Henry's mother called it) could not enter through one of the locked gates. There were three Bug holes in each wall, located higher in the stacks.

The wall was four or five cars high, depending on the sizes of the cars. Stan or Chester, Henry didn't know which, scrounged or stole two car haulers. Each hauler carried eight cars and operated seven days a week. Once the dead cars were dumped along the wall, they were lifted into place under Stan's watchful engineering eyes, as if he were putting together a vertical jigsaw puzzle. The result was a sturdy, impregnable, very ugly wall that looked nothing like the LEGO bricks Henry had loved as a kid.

Henry couldn't see the wall from any of the Ludd houses because the houses had been built in the center of the valley. He felt a little sorry for the neighbors who had a junkyard fence obscuring their former view, but he hadn't heard anyone complain.

"Are you going to eat this cow?" Steve asked.

"We'll have to ask Doc," Edgar said. "They were none too careful when they hacked it up. You can see where the offal has contaminated the meat in places. But the cold weather has probably helped keep it fresh. By the way, how's that freezer coming along?"

Steve was wiring a walk-in freezer that Chester and Gino had dismantled and hauled back to the farm piece by piece.

"Probably three or four days out once they get the rest of the parts here," Steve answered. "Too late for this meat."

Most of Gino's and Chester's efforts were concentrated on scrounging food. They had a third truck on the road as well, smaller than the semi and flatbed, driven by one of Henry's aunts and someone riding shotgun for security. It went outside every couple days to pick up supplies that Chester and Gino couldn't get to before dark. Early on, Marie insisted that all vehicles try to return to the farm before sunset. Bad things happened outside after dark. Gang attacks. Carjackings. Arson. Kidnappings. Murder . . .

"You headed outside today?" Steve asked Derek.

Derek nodded.

Steve pulled a scrap of paper out of his pocket. "I have a list of things I could use. Tools and hardware mostly. Little things, none of them an emergency, but . . ."

Derek took the list, looked it over, then stuck it in his pocket. "The stalls downtown have a ton of this stuff. I'll see what I can do. I don't expect to be back for several days. But if I get your supplies, I'll try to get them to Chester and Gino, or on the other truck." He put his backpack on, started up the hill toward Mountain Road, then turned and shouted back at Henry, "The yurt is yours, kid!"

Henry gave him a wave and glanced at his watch. "I better go too," he said. "I have to deliver messages."

"Tell your mom about the cow when you get down to the house, and let Doc know that we need him up here to check out this meat," Edgar said.

"And be careful on those roads," Albert said. "They're slippery as snot."

Henry headed down the hill, thinking about the pool of blood outside Albert's shop the day he met him, which he sometimes had nightmares about. Gort was at his heels, as usual.

Are you leading Gort, or is he herding you?

Ha, Henry thought. *You should have been a comedian.*

CHAPTER SEVENTEEN

Edgar had managed to get some of the two-way radios he had taken from the zoo working, but they didn't transmit much beyond the farm, so one of Henry's many chores was to deliver messages up and down the valley. He also delivered a weekly newsletter put together by his mom and aunts called the *Wonderland News*, which was printed out on a machine Henry had never heard of called a mimeograph. Caroline said it was ancient technology that Chester must have traveled back in time to retrieve. The ink was blue and had a strange smell, but it worked.

Sometimes Henry did his deliveries on foot with a backpack, or he pulled a wagon if he had something big to pick up or drop off. Today, he was on his bike with his small go-pack (or bugout bag, as Albert called it). Most of the Ludds carried these packs wherever they went. The idea was that if the compound was over-run, or if they got stranded outside, they'd have enough essentials to keep them going for a day or two until they figured out what to do. But Henry hadn't been outside the compound since the day after the switch.

He rode his bike up their steep driveway to Wonderland Road, with Gort running alongside trying to keep up.

Delivering messages could take an hour or more depending on who snagged him to talk or do some chore for them. Most of the able-bodied people in the valley were working on the Great Wall. The old folks and little kids mostly stayed at home. Henry was hoping for a two-hour round-trip because that would give him an hour at the treehouse before he was missed at the farm.

He got lucky at the first three houses. No one was home. He jumped off his bike, ran up to the porches, put the messages where they would be seen, and quickly rode away. His luck ran out at the fourth house. Mr. and Mrs. Hoffer were in their front yard cutting up a tree with a chain saw. The Hoffers had lived in the valley almost as long as the Ludds. Every neighbor had been cutting down trees for their woodstoves, if they were lucky enough to have one. If it kept up, the valley was going to look like a desert by summer.

Mr. Hoffer switched off his chain saw and Mrs. Hoffer quit stacking wood and joined Henry on the porch. They were in their eighties.

"What do you have for us?" Mrs. Hoffer asked.

Henry had no idea. The messages were in sealed envelopes like regular mail. He pulled the envelope out of his pack and handed it to her. She put it into her pocket without opening it.

Let's go!

"Hold your horses," Henry said.

"What?" Mr. Hoffer asked, startled.

Henry was startled too. He hadn't meant to respond to Caroline out loud. "Nothing," he said. "I was thinking that it would be easier to deliver messages on horseback."

"If we had a horse, we'd eat it," Mrs. Hoffer said.

Which reminded him to tell them about the poached cow.

"What are you going to do with the meat?" Mr. Hoffer asked.

"Doc's checking it out to make sure it's not contaminated. We don't have a freezer big enough to freeze the meat. If the meat's good, Mom wants to have a compound barbecue at the church to celebrate the completion of the wall and talk about what we need to do next. If there is any leftover meat, we'll divide it up among those who need it the most."

He was sure the Hoffers were salivating by now. He was. "Is there anything you need?" Henry asked, which is what he asked everyone before he rode away.

"Electricity would be nice," Mr. Hoffer said.

"A working toilet," Mrs. Hoffer added. "Running water. Food. You know . . . the usual."

Henry smiled politely. This wasn't the first time he'd heard this and knew it wouldn't be the last. Every house in the valley was on a well, which was worthless without a pump to get the water up from the aquifer. Chester had found a stash of hand pumps on one of his forays outside, and they had installed them for several people, including the Hoffers. They still had to haul water in buckets into their houses and dump it into their toilet tanks so the toilets would flush.

"One thing I could use is some more gas for this chain saw," Mr. Hoffer said.

"You're welcome to all you need."

The gas was siphoned out of the cars before they were stacked and stored. Henry offered to bring him a can of gas, but thankfully Mr. Hoffer declined.

"We've been meaning to drop by and say hello to your mom," Mrs. Hoffer said. "The gas will give us a good excuse."

"Okay, see you later."

Henry got back on his bike and rode away, with Caroline sounding off in his head.

Old Hoffer's gas can was nearly full. They're going to the farm to find out if and when the meat will be on the menu.

Henry didn't care why the Hoffers wanted to go to the farm. He had six more messages to deliver, and he wanted to get it over with. Half the people were home, half were away working on the wall. As always, it took a lot longer than he thought. Everyone was very interested in the dead cow. By the time he finished, he would have less than a half hour at the treehouse, but a few minutes there was better than none.

CHAPTER EIGHTEEN

When Henry reached the Olofs' driveway, Caroline disappeared. She always did this. He wasn't sure why. Maybe she wasn't allowed to go home. Or maybe it was too painful for her. All he knew was that when he went to her house, she was no longer with him.

The Olofs' house had been broken into by *theefs* soon after the switch. They had taken all the food, the portable backup generator in the garage, and a lot of other stuff that was useless without power.

When he opened the kicked-in front door, Gort shot past him like a bullet. A family of raccoons had moved into the house a few weeks earlier. There was nothing Gort liked more than harassing them.

"Leave it!" Henry said.

Gort came to a sliding stop and looked back at him with a *you've-got-to-be-kidding* expression as the male raccoon bounded upstairs and disappeared into the Olofs' workout room.

"He would have kicked your butt," Henry said in his defense. "Heel!"

Gort followed him with his head at Henry's left knee but kept glancing back at the stairs as if he wanted to bolt. They crossed the trashed living room into the kitchen. The floor was scattered with pots and pans, utensils, and raccoon scat. They stepped through the shattered sliding door into the once beautifully landscaped back-yard. The lawn was knee-high and had gone to seed. Mrs. Olof's carefully trimmed rosebushes looked like small, thorny trees now. They climbed up the steep, moss-covered steps leading to the knoll behind the yard.

The knoll used to be the highest point in the valley until Edgar put up his wind turbine. Caroline had told him this was her father's chief objection to the wind turbine. Her dad liked being king of the mountain.

On top of the knoll was an ancient oak tree. The story was that when Caroline was little, her parents couldn't stop her from climbing it. She would sneak out at every opportunity and scale the oak's gnarly old branches. The Olofs were terrified she was going to fall and break her neck. The only solution was to make the tree safer. Mr. Olof hired an architect, an engineer, and an arborist to design and build a treehouse for her. It had insulated walls, a metal roof, and double-paned storm windows. Before the switch Henry had only been inside it a few times, because Caroline rarely allowed visitors into her private sanctuary. Henry took over the treehouse a few weeks after the switch and made it *his* private sanctuary.

It was virtually impossible to be alone on the farm now. You'd think that, growing up in a huge extended family, Henry would be used to being around people, and he was, as long as he could be by himself once or twice a day for a little while.

His father had been the same way. He would walk the fence line by himself or sit on the bank of Wonderland Creek to get away from what he called the Ludd Hubbub. The Ludds were a friendly bunch, but noisy.

When Henry got inside, he looked out the window and saw Gort staring up at him, no doubt wondering if he was going to pull him up. Mr. Olof had rigged a dumbwaiter system to haul up supplies. It was the only way to get Gort into the treehouse. Henry didn't have much time, but he lowered the platform and brought him up so he wouldn't go back into the house and get into a raccoon brawl. Gort plopped down onto the sleeping pad with his broad head between his front paws.

Henry walked over to the spotting scope. It was on a tripod pointed down at his house. He hadn't moved it since the day he took over the treehouse. He wondered if Caroline had watched them when she was up here, or maybe her dad had been watching Edgar's "monstrosity," now the envy of everyone for a hundred miles. Whatever the reason, there was no doubt that Caroline had been keeping an eye on them before she fell out of the sky.

Ruth and Madeline were standing on his parents' deck, holding steaming mugs of tea or coffee, which were both hard to find, like everything else. They were watching the front loader scooping up the cow in the upper field. Henry really hoped it was edible.

The car loaders had dumped their dead cars up on Mountain Road during the night. Stan was directing the crane operator where to place the next car on the wall. One good thing about the wall was that there were fewer fried cars snarling the roads, according to Gino and Chester.

Henry stepped away from the scope and surveyed his hideout, or squat, which was what the outsiders called the abandoned houses they had taken over. Several families had moved out of the valley in the weeks following the switch. None of them had returned. One by one, squatters moved into the empty houses. Mom stopped the practice because she was afraid that they would run out of places for their people to live. *Their people* meaning the Wonderland Compound people who were working to make the valley self-sustainable and secure. She did this by moving Ludds or people working for them into the abandoned houses. The Olofs' house hadn't been taken over yet, but it was only a matter of time.

People wanted to join the compound because they believed all the houses had electricity and there was plenty of food for everyone, neither of which was true. Their three houses were the only houses with electricity, but Edgar, Albert, and Steve were working on plans to power up more houses. Food was scarce, but they hoped that would change in the spring and summer when the crops came in.

Henry walked over to Caroline's small desk beneath the window and sat down in front of the old typewriter Albert had cleaned and oiled for him. He opened his notebook and started transcribing.

```
I've figured out that writing is a pro-
cess with thousands of little moves and
decisions. I guess I was told this in
school, but I'd forgotten, or I hadn't
paid much attention at the time. I jot
things down in the journal I got for my
birthday: things that happen, snippets
of conversation, descriptions, observa-
tions, dates, weather, stuff like that.
When I get to the treehouse, I use my
notes and type out a rough draft. When
I finish a section, I correct it with a
```

red pencil, retype a clean copy, then correct it again, then retype, and on and on, until I get out the scissors and tape and rearrange everything, then retype it again. Writing on a computer is a lot easier, with cut-and-paste and spell-check. One good thing is that I'm a better speller than I was because I have to look words up.

I'm not sure why I bother with this journal or diary, or whatever it is. I don't plan to show it to anyone, except for Dad, if I ever see him again...

Dad.

I'm looking at a photo of him pinned to the bulletin board behind Caroline's desk. I brought up a bunch of photos when I took over the treehouse. In this one he and two keepers are holding a huge anaconda, probably moving it to another cage. He has the anaconda's head. He once told me that animals have two ends. "One end can hurt; the other end can be messy." He usually grabs the end that can hurt.

Dad is still gone, but not forgotten, at least by me. After four months I realize there isn't much chance of him walking into the kitchen and asking what's to eat, but I still haven't given up hope. Chester, Gino, and Derek are still asking about him when they're outside and checking in with Gary Dulabaum, who is still working the zoo solo. A few weeks ago, they took Robert and Catherine (Bob and Cat) back to the zoo because they started shredding Mom's furniture.

I haven't left the valley since the day after the switch. Mom won't let me, and I haven't fought her on the idea. Sometimes I'm desperate to leave, other times I don't care if I ever get out of this little bubble, as Edgar calls it. Once in a while I wake up in the middle of the night unable to catch my breath, dreaming that an elephant is doing a headstand on my chest in front of Gunderson's Jewelry. During the day I'm haunted by Caroline. I wish Dad was haunting me instead of Caroline, but that would mean he's dead. I'm not willing to accept that. Not yet.

He pulled the sheet of paper out of the typewriter and put it onto the short stack with the other sheets. Gort got up, stretched, and walked over to the dumbwaiter, knowing it was time to go.

Caroline usually came back into Henry's head as he turned onto Wonderland Road, but not today. It was a silent ride down to his house. He walked through the back door into the kitchen and wasn't surprised to see a half-dozen people sitting around talking or working on various projects. It was like this all day and half the night. His mom glanced up from the kitchen table, gave him a weary smile, then got back to her conversation with Pastor Bob and his wife, Charity. It would be an hour before he could give her his three-minute report from his valley run. People dropped by to ask questions, complain, report on projects, borrow something, or argue. Marie listened attentively, thought carefully about what they said or asked, then commented or answered if she could. People left the kitchen satisfied, disappointed, and sometimes angry, but not for very long, because no one wanted Marie's job except for Stan, who was a firm believer that he knew more than everyone about everything. Henry wondered for the hundredth time what his mom was going to do about Stan when he finished the wall.

Send him downtown to build a wall around Portland! It will take him several years.

Henry was glad Caroline was back. She wasn't fond of Stan or anyone else except for his mom, Edgar, Derek, and Albert.

He walked out onto the deck to get away from the Ludd Hubbub while he waited for his mom to be free. The plowed fields still had frost sticking to them, glittering in the sunlight. Someone had put the cows into the corral and thrown them hay. He wouldn't be surprised if Edgar posted guards tonight to keep the poachers away. They had the dead cow strung up outside the barn and were gutting it, which could only mean that Doc had given the meat the okay; otherwise they would have buried it. Gort was watching every slice of the knife, hoping someone tossed him a bloody scrap.

Beyond the deck on a flat area were three fifth-wheel trailers, a portable building, and Derek's yurt, all found by Gino and Chester and hauled back to the farm to house people. Henry slept in one of the fifth wheels when he wasn't yurt-sitting for Derek.

His mother came out onto the deck. She looked at the butchering for a moment, then said, "What's the word in the valley?"

Henry passed on what he had heard, which wasn't much, then added that everyone was excited about the possibility of getting some meat into their stomachs.

"It's not a possibility," his mom said. "It's a reality. There will be a big barbecue at the church tomorrow afternoon. I was just working out the details with Pastor Bob and Charity. We'll see how long it will take two hundred hungry people to eat a cow. I'll save some for you."

"What?"

"Gino and Chester want you to go outside with them tomorrow."

"And you're going to let me?"

"Reluctantly. That is, if you still want to go outside."

"I want to go," Henry said, but he wasn't sure that was the truth.

"You'll miss the barbecue. Gino and Chester are taking the cow bones and inedible meat up to the zoo for the cats that are still in cages and to check on Gary. They haven't been there since they dropped off Cat and Bob. They saw that black leopard running around the parking lot, and I think it freaked them out. They're also a little disconcerted by Gary."

"He is a little strange."

You mean he's a wack job. The only job he could possibly do is work at a zoo. That's why he's stayed there by himself all these months. You have farm fever. You need to buck up, get out of the bubble, and see how others are enduring this. You never know what you might find unless you go out and look. You're cowering away here and working your ass off because you're afraid . . .

Henry wanted to put his hands over his ears to try to block her out, but couldn't because his mom was standing there. He was surprised Caroline knew about Gary. He didn't think she was inside his head when he was at the zoo.

I've been with you since you looked down at me strapped in the middle seat. It took me a while to find my voice.

Henry wondered if Caroline could leave the valley, then realized that his mother was waiting for an answer and looking at him curiously. A lot of people looked at him curiously now.

Yeah, like what the hell is the matter with you?

"I'll skip the barbecue," he told his mom. "Why the change of heart?"

"Your uncles have been bothering me about it for weeks. They think you're old enough to go with them. They want to train you. They're having to go farther out to get what we need. Eventually, they want to find more trucks and get them on the road, but they can't send people out on their own. It's too dangerous. Someone needs to ride shotgun with the drivers. I'm not thrilled with the idea, but it makes sense. We'll try it for a week or two and see how it goes."

Ruth opened the slider. "Mr. Hoffer is here. He wants to talk to you for a minute, Marie, if you have time."

"I'll be right in," Mom said, then looked back at Henry. "Are you sure you want to go?"

"As long as you save a T-bone for me."

She smiled. "I can't guarantee that. We have a lot of hungry people."

Henry hoped she was kidding and walked down to the yurt.

CHAPTER NINETEEN

Henry loved staying in Derek's yurt. The inside was simple, immaculately clean, and set up with scrounged furniture and other comforts: a single bed perfectly made; a comfortable chair with a reading lamp; a bookcase with about a hundred well-read books, mostly novels and a few philosophy books that might as well have been written in another language for all Henry could make out; a woodstove for heating and cooking; a sink, counter, and cupboards; a small refrigerator, virtually empty, of course. The only decoration was a framed embroidered picture that read *Nie mój cyrk, nie moje malpy*, a Polish phrase meaning "Not my circus, not my monkeys," which Henry thought summed up Derek's philosophy, and Henry's too now. He minded his own business. Life was a lot easier that way. Derek was friendly and helped out when asked, but he didn't get involved in any of the day-to-day farm drama when he was there, which wasn't often. He was Marie's eyes and ears on the outside. He stayed somewhere in downtown Portland gathering information that might impact the compound. Essentially, he was a spy. He had told Henry a few things about what was going on outside. It sounded pretty bad. Henry was surprised his mom was letting him go with Chester and Gino.

You mean worried.

"That too," Henry admitted out loud now that he and Caroline were alone.

He picked up the book he'd been reading, but he couldn't focus. He stoked the woodstove so he wouldn't freeze after the sun went down. He picked the book up again, but still couldn't get into it. He opened his notebook and stared at the blank page, waiting for the words, but none came. He looked at his watch and followed the second hand for a couple of revolutions.

What the hell are you doing?

It was a good question. There was always a lot to do on the farm, and sitting around not knowing what to do wasn't one of them. He left the yurt and walked down to the barn to see if they needed help with the cow. They didn't. Mr. Hoffer had joined the slaughter after talking to Marie. It turned out that he used to be a butcher and had brought his tools with him. He had the cow quartered in about twenty minutes, then started slicing out various cuts of meat and laying them on a plastic tarp.

This is gross!

Caroline was right, it was a little gross, but fascinating because of Mr. Hoffer's enthusiasm for the task. Henry always thought of him as an enfeebled old man, but there was nothing feeble about his knife and saw work. This was the first time Henry had seen a cow butchered. Edgar always had the cows hauled away first.

Henry tossed a bone to a grateful Gort, who ran off to gnaw on it in privacy. Edgar came out of the barn in his bib overalls, carrying a roll of plastic bags.

He looked at Henry. "Let's clean this offal up before it starts to stink."

It already stank. Most of the people watching Mr. Hoffer suddenly remembered they had to be somewhere else and hurried off.

Edgar snorted and said, "They won't be in such a hurry tomorrow when the meat's sizzling on the grill."

Pushing cow entrails into a bag is different from pushing steak into your mouth with a fork.

"I hear you won't be at the barbecue because you're leaving the bubble tomorrow," Edgar said.

"Mom will save some for me."

"I'm sure she will. I wish I was going with you. I hate these big get-togethers. It'll be the same questions and complaints for which there are no answers. People will leave with their bellies full, but strangely dissatisfied."

Edgar has lived his life strangely dissatisfied, grumbling about everything even when everything is going well.

Henry changed the subject. "How's Albert?"

Edgar shook his head. "Not good. Doc checked him out when he checked the dead cow. He said Albert should be in the hospital, which would work if there was such a thing as a functioning hospital. The only thing we can do for him is to keep him on the meds, providing Chester and Gino can find them. The walk up the hill nearly killed him. He's in the barn sleeping, which seems to help. We'll keep these bags of guts outside tonight to keep them cool. Gary has a small freezer hooked up to the generator we took up to him. We'll throw some fuel into the truck in case he's running low."

"I didn't know we were still supplying Gary with things."

"It's your Mom's idea, but it hasn't been much. If the cow meat was bad, we would have taken the whole carcass up to the zoo. The cats aren't too fussy."

"When was the last time you were up at the zoo?"

"Albert and I were up there a couple of weeks ago. Gary seems to be doing okay. He concentrates on keeping the animals alive, which keeps him from thinking about how miserable life has become. He's probably the happiest guy I know."

CHAPTER TWENTY

Henry was up before daylight, pacing the inside of the yurt like a caged animal.

Settle down! You're going to wear yourself out before you even get into the truck.

"Are you coming with me?"

Can't say. I never know until you go there. I don't even know where I am except when I'm inside you.

"Where are you when you're not inside me?"

Nowhere I can remember.

They'd had this conversation many times, and Henry was still confused. He thought Caroline was too. He looked at his watch.

You're always looking at that fancy watch. If you want to know what time it is, look out the window. It's sunrise.

She was right. Dim morning light was coming through the windows. He hurriedly made the bed, not as well as Derek, and straightened things up. That was Derek's only rule: "When you leave the yurt, it should look as if you have never been here."

By the time Henry and Gort got outside, the sun was just rising behind the wind turbine.

Whomp . . . whomp . . . whomp . . .

"I'm not sure they're going to let you come with me," he told Gort as they headed over to the barn.

Edgar was watching the cows in the corral, which were all

accounted for. "I need to borrow Gort for a minute to chase the cows into the upper field."

Moving the cows was Gort's favorite activity. Henry set him on them, and he started pushing them out of the corral.

"Now, if you could teach him to shut the upper field gate behind them, I'd be impressed," Edgar said.

"I'll walk up and shut the gate."

"Don't bother. I need to check on the wind turbine and roust Steve from his cot. We have a lot to do today."

"Albert?" Henry asked.

"He's better today. He's in the barn making breakfast, such as it is. Dry toast and a poached egg. There's one for you. Chester and Gino have already wolfed theirs down. They're loading the truck with junk they hope to trade today."

Everything was bartered now because cash was worthless. Henry suspected they would load some of the beef into the truck, because it was worth a fortune in trade. So were chickens. They incubated a third of the eggs on the farm and sold the chicks for backyard coops. He'd heard that some people even kept coops on the decks of their apartments and condos.

Henry walked to the other side of the barn. His mom was helping Gino and Chester load the truck.

"Good morning, sleepyhead," she said.

He pointed at the lightening sky. "It's the crack of dawn."

"The early bird catches the worm," Chester said.

"I hope you catch more than worms," Marie said, then looked back at Henry. "Albert has your breakfast inside."

Henry was so anxious about going outside he hadn't even

thought about how hungry he was. He walked into the barn, which didn't resemble the inside of a barn. It looked like a giant repair shop scattered with furniture. Most of the stalls had been taken down to make room for Edgar and Albert's various projects, everything from engine rebuilds to appliance repurposing. One of the workbenches was dedicated to reloading shotgun shells and bullets. Another bench was for jewelry and watch repairs. He hadn't been in the barn for weeks, and it was a lot better organized than it had been.

Albert was standing at the back of the barn in the makeshift kitchen.

"Grub," he said. "Not much, but it's fresh. Ruth made the bread and a chicken made the egg. All I did was poach and toast."

Henry sat down at the little kitchen table. He hadn't seen an egg in three days. Albert looked pretty good. He wasn't nearly as pale as he had been the previous day on the hill.

"Chow down."

Henry could have eaten it in two bites, but wanted to savor it. He cut off a little piece. It was delicious. "You've really gotten this place organized," he said in between bites.

"Far from it," Albert said. "But we're getting there. We'd be in better shape if Gino and Chester would stop trying to wheedle us out of everything we have in here. Make sure they don't try to trade you off for something when you're out there. I swear to God they'd do it if somebody had something they wanted. They're like a couple of squirrels. They just talked your mom out of half that cow and tried to talk her out of taking the guts and bones up to the zoo. But she was having none of that. Make sure the guts get to the zoo. Those cats need to eat too. I just hope that Gary Dulabaum character doesn't decide to eat entrails himself."

"I'll make sure." He finished the last bite, wishing for more. "Thanks for breakfast."

Henry didn't think Albert heard him. He had walked over to a bench and was working on a wristwatch with a jeweler's loop stuck to his eye.

Henry walked back outside. The truck was loaded. His mother was going over a list with Gino and Chester of the things she needed.

"And you better get something good for that meat," she said.

"We will," Gino promised. "Don't worry about that. We could trade the guts and bones too. People will make soup out of them. I know a guy who would love the hide."

"We've already been over that, Gino. Gary gets the guts."

"Fine."

"Henry will let me know if you don't give it to him. And if you don't come back with Henry, don't come back at all."

"Understood," Chester said. "We have a lot of stops today. We won't be back until well after dark. Don't worry about us."

"I'll worry about you every second of the day," Marie said. "Like I always do."

"It's nice to know someone does," Gino said, then looked at Henry. "You ready?"

"Can I take Gort?"

"Of course," Gino said. "Where is he?"

Henry whistled. "He'll be here in a second."

The old semi had a small sleeper in back of the driver and passenger seats. Henry sat on the bunk with his legs dangling, between Gino and Chester, looking through the windshield. Chester hopped out of the cab and slid open the gate, then closed it behind them once the truck was through and climbed back in. Henry was officially out of the bubble.

"There's a shotgun in back of you if you need it," Gino said. "And both me and Chester are carrying."

"Carjacking is a problem outside," Gino explained. "But so far they've stayed away from us because they know we're well armed. We're careful about the routes we take and vary them as much as possible so we don't drive into a trap."

"We never tell anyone if or when we'll be back next," Chester said. "If we're suspicious of someone, we don't come back."

"Unless they have something we really want," Gino added. "In that case we park the truck a few blocks away and one of us walks in on foot to check the place out before we bring in the truck. Edgar gave us a couple of two-ways so Chester and me can keep in touch. People are hungry and desperate. We're friendly and fair, but don't be fooled into thinking we trust people, at least not all the way. That's kind of how everyone is outside now. There are good people and bad, but even good people can turn on you if their circumstances go south on them."

"Sounds like you've been talking to Derek," Henry said. Derek had been lecturing him about this for weeks. He thought he was being a little paranoid, and wondered if Derek knew Gino and Chester wanted to take him outside.

"We hear from Derek, one way or the other, every day," Chester said. "We wouldn't be able to do this without someone like him on the outside. He's saved our asses a hundred times."

"A thousand times," Gino said. "He knows more about what's going on out here than anyone. Which gangs or groups are on the rise and which have seen better days. What they want and what their plans are. People think he's on their side, but his sole purpose is to protect the Wonderland Compound, which is getting more difficult every day."

"People don't know he's connected to the compound," Chester said.

Have you noticed that your uncles finish each other's thoughts and sentences like they're one person? It's kind of creepy.

This answered Henry's question about Caroline joining him outside the bubble. His uncles did finish each other's thoughts. He guessed that's what came from spending ten to twelve hours a day less than three feet apart.

"That wall Stan built is keeping people out of the compound," Gino continued. "But it is also attracting people. They want to know what's inside. They *want* what's inside."

"It's not much," Henry said.

They both stared at him like he had lost his mind.

Gino raised his voice. "Are you kidding?"

"We've got it made compared with most people," Chester said. "Sure, we're hungry, but we aren't starving like everyone else. We're not cold, we have working vehicles, we have electricity. When the crops come in, we'll have everything we need. People are starting to get organized. There are different factions, but they all want the same thing. Security, food, power, and—"

"Control," Gino said.

Henry stared through the windshield, wondering if the Ludds wanted the same things. Food and security, for certain. But control? He didn't think so. Not his mom anyway. All she wanted was to protect their family and help their neighbors.

"You notice anything different out here?" Chester asked.

A couple houses were burned to the ground. At several other houses, it looked like people were in the process of replacing their landscaping with vegetable gardens that wouldn't produce until spring.

"No stalled cars," Henry said.

Gino nodded. "You'll start seeing more dead cars the farther out we get."

Five miles north, the jam resumed, and they had to serpentine their way through the snarl, which wasn't easy to do while pulling a trailer. There were only a few people out this early in the morning. The world looked like it had been abandoned. Trash was strewn all over the streets and sidewalks. Garbage pickup was a thing of the past. The way they handled it at the compound was for people to put their garbage out on the road, and they'd pick it up once a week and haul it to the landfill in Edgar's flatbed. Henry had never been, but he'd heard it usually took two or three trips. A couple of his aunts were the garbage women. They liked it because it gave them a chance to go outside. The closer they got to Portland, the more garbage there was.

"Strange, isn't it?" Gino said.

"It's a mess," Henry said.

"You mean the garbage?" Chester asked. "That's nothing.

Wait till we get closer to Portland. Everything we've taken for granted the past hundred years is gone. The garbage is thrown into the streets because people don't want it in their houses and yards. Wonderland Road would look just like this if we hadn't gotten a jump on this thing."

And a couple of working trucks and the wind turbine and Edgar the former nutcase, now allegedly a visionary genius.

Up until that moment Henry hadn't really understood how good they had it in the valley or why people might want to take their compound over. Looking at all the garbage and chaos made him feel guilty and kind of stupid for not grasping what was going on outside. In his defense, people didn't talk much about the outside, even when you asked them, except to say that things were crazy. And they were so busy inside the compound working, there wasn't much time to dwell on what might be happening outside their little bubble.

Well, the bubble has popped, at least for you.

"We have a couple of stops to make before we go to the zoo," Gino said. "I want to get rid of this beef as soon as possible. It won't take long. We know what we need. The question is, will they trade it for the meat?"

"They'll trade," Chester said confidently. "As long as they haven't already unloaded the stuff we need."

"What stuff?" Henry asked.

"Meds and medical supplies that Doc wants, for one thing," Gino answered. "Hard to come by these days."

"Where do people get things like that?"

"We never ask," Chester said.

I bet no one ever asks, and no one ever tells.

And no one feels guilty about it either, Henry thought. You just hoped you had something that people wanted so you could get what you needed.

The way of the world now.

Gino left the main road, zigzagging through a neighborhood before coming to a stop in front of a ranch-style house that looked like all the other houses in the neighborhood.

"We'll wait for John to come out," he said.

Henry saw several neighbors looking through their windows at the truck. John stepped out of his house five minutes later. He was wearing a heavy coat, jeans, and red tennis shoes. He was in his early fifties, with longish brown hair peppered with gray. If he was armed, Henry couldn't see the gun, but both his uncles had put their pistols in their laps. He wondered if he should grab the shotgun, but he didn't.

Gino rolled his window down. "Hey, John."

"Gino . . . Chester," John said, then nodded at Henry and Gort, who had woken up and poked his head out of the sleeper to see what was going on. "You're all up early."

"We have a lot of places to go today," Gino said. "Do you still have the stuff we're interested in?"

"Yeah, but I have some other people stopping by this afternoon to look at it."

"What do they have to trade?" Chester asked.

John shrugged. "I'll see when they get here. What do you have?"

"Meat," Gino said.

John looked excited, then frowned to cover it up. "What kind?"

"Beef. Butchered last night. Two boxes. About fifty pounds, I'd say." Gino looked at Chester.

"Closer to sixty," Chester said.

I bet there's a hundred pounds of that bloody meat in the truck. What are they going to do with the leftovers?

Henry had no idea, but he was sure they would make a good trade for it.

"I should probably wait to hear from the other guy," John said.

"We can't wait," Gino said. "And we're not coming back today. The meat is perishable. You're our first stop. Someone down the road will be happy to trade for it."

"Do you have a freezer?" Chester asked.

John nodded. "And a small generator to run it."

"Lucky you," Chester said. "We can throw in a few gallons of gas along with the meat."

John thought about it for a minute. "I'll need to see the meat."

Chester reached under his seat and pulled out a plastic bag. Gino handed the bag through the window to John. He pulled the meat out of the bag and gave it a sniff. "I guess we have a deal. I'll get the med supplies." He started back into the house.

"Give me a hand," Chester said.

Henry told Gort to stay and followed Chester to the back of the trailer. He unlocked the padlock and swung the door open.

"How do you know the medical supplies are any good?"

"Everything he has is still sealed and inventoried. Doc looked the list over and said we could use all of it. Jump up there and hand down three boxes of meat. The gas is in the back of the truck. Grab a five-gallon can."

Henry passed him the meat and gas. John came back outside, pulling a hand truck stacked with boxes. He checked the meat while Chester checked the medical supplies.

"Nice doing business with you," Chester said, shaking John's hand. "Keep an eye out for that other stuff we're looking for, and we'll do the same for you."

"When are you coming back?" John asked.

Chester answered with a smile and a shrug.

And this is how it went the rest of the morning. Pickups, drop-offs, and trades. Gas for sacks of flour. A sack of flour for a couple boxes of fruits and vegetables. A box of vegetables for five gallons of milk. A gallon of milk for a box of old engine parts. The transactions were all quick, without a lot of haggling or conversation. Make the deal and move on seemed to be Gino and Chester's technique. Everyone was friendly, but businesslike. People appeared to get along with Gino and Chester, but it was clear they didn't completely trust them. Some of the people they talked to wouldn't trade; others had already traded the stuff Gino and Chester wanted. The beef was a popular commodity. There was only one small box left by the fourth stop. Henry wondered if the people who got it were going to eat it or trade it for something else they wanted that day, because it wouldn't last long without being refrigerated.

Some of the people carried guns, some didn't. They stopped at individual houses like John's, and neighborhoods that had been barricaded and were guarded. They stopped at indoor and outdoor trading malls to see what people had. Gino and Chester took turns trading. One of them always stayed with the truck.

At one trading mall Gino found a pair of binoculars he

wanted, but the woman who operated the stall was a tough bargainer. She had a list of things she was willing to trade for them, but Gino didn't have anything on her list.

Gino has met his match.

Maybe, Henry thought.

"How about WC coin?" Gino asked.

"You have WC coin?" the woman asked in surprise.

"Some," Gino answered.

What is WC coin?

Henry had no idea. He'd never heard of it before.

"Where did you get them?" the woman asked.

"Here and there. Trading. I'll give you two silvers for the binocs."

"Three."

Gino shook his head. "Two is all I can do."

The woman shook her head. "Sorry."

"That's okay."

They started to walk away, but she stopped them before they had taken five steps.

"I'll do it," she said.

Gino fished out a couple of small silver coins from his pocket and handed them to her. She looked them over carefully, then handed him the binoculars.

"I've been looking for a pair of these for a long time," Gino said as they headed back to the truck.

"What are WC coins?" Henry asked.

Gino looked at him in surprise. "You don't know about them?"

Henry shook his head.

I've told you that the not-my-circus-not-my-monkeys thing was not a good philosophy.

Several times, Henry thought.

"Coin of the realm," Gino said. "Well, our realm anyway."

"I still don't know what you're talking about."

"I'm surprised you aren't carrying some of them in your bug-out bag. But I guess there was no need, since you haven't been outside. Wonderland Compound coin is money. Silver or gold in different weights or denominations. We aren't the only ones that make coins, but ours are the most trusted currency on the outside."

"We make money?"

"We *mint* money, or coins. It was Albert's idea and his silver and gold. He and Edgar make them in the barn and give them to us and Derek, or whoever has business outside, to buy things we need at WC that we can't trade for. But they're kind of stingy with them."

"I wasn't told about them."

"It's kept quiet, but it's not exactly a secret. US currency is worthless. Gold, silver, and jewelry have intrinsic value and are portable. We try not to use them very much, but some people on the outside only trade for coin. Chester and I would much rather trade for things, but it's not always possible. Most of the downtown stores and stalls only accept coin."

They climbed into the truck.

"What did you get?" Chester asked.

"A pair of binoculars for a couple of small silvers," Gino answered. "Better than the ones we have. They'll come in handy to check things out before we drive the truck in."

"Smooth day," Chester said, looking at the watch Albert had given him. "If this keeps up, we might be back in time for the barbecue."

"Are we going downtown?" Henry asked.

Gino shook his head. "We only go downtown if there's something we need that we can't get anywhere else. Derek sets it up for us and makes sure it's safe. The prices are twice as much downtown as they are out here."

"Good place to get 'jacked," Chester added.

Gino gave Henry a handful of coins. "Emergency cash," he said. "Put them in your bugout bag. The zoo's next."

He started the truck.

CHAPTER TWENTY-ONE

"What happened?" Henry asked as Chester pulled up to the curb in front of the administration building.

"What are you talking about?" Gino asked.

"The perimeter fence is gone. It was up the last time I was here. The poles were still standing, but the chain link is gone."

"I never noticed," Gino said. "It's been that way since we've been coming up here, hasn't it, Chester?"

"I'm not sure," Chester said. "We're usually in and out of here pretty fast. Sometimes we don't even see Gary. We just leave stuff at the curb for him."

Gino laughed. "I see the poles now where the fence was. We should have taken the fence ourselves. It would have been a lot easier to string fence around the compound than stacking cars."

"I don't think there was enough fence to go around the compound," Henry said. "The zoo's only sixty-four acres."

"Good point," Chester said. "And Stan's wall got the local roads cleared."

"They must have had a truck," Gino said. "No other way to move it."

"How many times have you been to the zoo since the switch?" Henry asked.

Chester shrugged. "At least a dozen times. Your mom asked us to check on Gary whenever we could."

"We came to the zoo regularly the first few weeks," Gino said. "We thought your dad might show up." He hesitated uncomfortably. "As you know, he didn't."

Up until a few weeks ago, Henry would have corrected him by saying *hasn't*, which left open the possibility that he might still show up. Now he knew his dad was not going to show up ever again.

"What do you think happened to him?" Henry asked.

He had asked a lot of people this same question, but not Gino and Chester. They were rarely at the farm, and when they were, they were busy getting ready to go out again.

Chester stared through the windshield. Gino shook his head. "I don't know, Henry. He's just gone, like so many others. Accident? Jumped by someone because he had something they wanted? It's impossible to say. I don't think we'll ever know."

"That's why we stopped coming up here as much," Chester said. "We only come when we have something Gary might need, like the cow parts. A couple of months ago Edgar and Albert came up and managed to get a tractor and two small generators working. We came across a water tank that he could use to haul water to the animals. We bring up hay and gas from time to time. Things like that."

"So, where is Gary?" Henry asked.

Gino hit the air horn three times. "We stay in the cab until Gary comes out and gives us the all clear. If he doesn't show, we dump the stuff out quickly and get out of here. There are still big cats hanging around."

"And the elephant that smashed Edgar's Cadillac," Chester added.

A couple of minutes later Gary rode his bicycle through the

front entrance. His bicycle was painted with black-and-white zebra stripes. He was wearing a stiff pair of bib overalls covered by a ratty down vest. His straggly gray beard looked like it had been trimmed with a chain saw. He was at least twenty pounds lighter than when Henry had seen him last, and he was thin to begin with. He got off his bicycle and smiled. His front teeth were missing.

Chester rolled down his window.

"I think we're good!" Gary said. "The lions are in the park on a deer kill. I think Bathsheba is over in the Arboretum hunting birds, rabbits, and stray dogs. That's kind of her turf now."

"What about the polar bears?" Henry asked. Of all the animals at the zoo, they were probably the most dangerous. His dad had told him polar bears didn't care if it was a seal on an ice floe or a human standing on a path. Anything that moved was fair game.

"The polar bears are long gone," Gary said. "Who's that?"

"Henry," he said.

"Wow. For a second I thought it was Tom. You sound just like him."

Henry leaned forward so Gary could see him better.

"You sound like your dad, but you look more like your mom," Gary said.

Chester got out of the truck, and Gort and Henry followed him. Gary squatted down and scratched Gort's head. "Who's this?"

"Gort."

"Klaatu barada nikto," Gary said.

I'm not surprised. Gary is a geek.

That's another reason I like him, Henry thought.

"I sure do miss watching movies," Gary said, standing up. "What do you have for me?"

"Three bales of hay, gas, a bag of cow guts, skin, and bones, and a box of old lettuce and cabbage."

"Beggars can't be choosers," Gary said. "It'll take four wheelbarrow loads to move it. The barrows are down the hill in the ungulate paddocks."

"Henry will help you bring the wheelbarrows up," Gino said. "Chester and I will stay up here and get your stuff off the truck."

Which means there is no way in hell they're stepping one foot inside the zoo. That's one of the reasons they brought you along.

Henry and Gort started down the hill with Gary.

"It's been four months," Henry said.

"Four months?"

"Yeah, since I saw you last."

Gary looked confused, then said, "That's right! Flat tire. I put the pump back in your dad's office. I've used it a few times since, but I always put it back."

"The next time you need it," Henry said, "just keep it."

"How will Tom find it?"

Henry stopped walking. "Have you heard from my dad?"

Gary continued walking. "No. What's he up to?"

Talking to Gary is like having a conversation with the wind. Whoosh . . .

"I haven't seen him in four months. None of us have."

"Wow. Where is he?"

Whoosh . . .

"Remember? Mom and I came up here looking for him. We didn't find him."

"Oh yeah. He was chasing Niki and Nuri."

"Have you heard anything about Niki and Nuri?"

"Nope."

They reached the ungulate paddocks. Gary unlocked the gate. Gort and Henry followed him inside. The alleyway behind the exhibits was freshly swept and immaculately clean.

"I heard that my uncle got your tractor and a couple of generators working."

"Yeah." Gary picked up a wheelbarrow and flipped it into another wheelbarrow as if it were as light as a wicker basket.

Pretty strong for a skeleton.

"I saw that someone took down the perimeter fence."

"Wild Bunch," Gary said.

"You mean the animal rights protesters?"

Gary nodded, combining two more wheelbarrows. "The same ones that shut the power down. I'm surprised the police haven't caught them yet."

Whoosh . . .

There was no point in telling him that the Wild Bunch were not responsible for the switch or that there was no such thing as the police anymore.

"They took it down months ago," Gary continued. "I tried to stop them, and that's where I got this." He pointed at his missing teeth. "Robin hit me in the mouth with a fence post."

"Robin?"

"He's the ringleader."

"They had a truck?"

"An old clunker. My granddad had one just like it. Took 'em

days to get the fence down and haul it away." Gary let out a gap-toothed laugh that sounded more like it had come from a hyena than a human. "Didn't do them no good. I had the animals locked up in their exhibits. Nothing got away."

Whoosh . . .

"How many animals are left here?"

"Don't know exactly. I lost some of them. Couldn't feed 'em. I let some of 'em go. Buffalo, zebra, animals like that. They're doing okay foraging in the park. Cats are still out, but the prey have gotten wise to them. They have to work for their food now. Bathsheba wanders through the zoo once in a while. Same with the elephants. I let 'em out to browse. They come back to the elephant barn almost every night, except for Indira. She's off her rocker. The snakes are okay. They only eat every couple of weeks or so. There's plenty of rats and mice running around. I have traps set up all over the zoo."

"What do you eat?"

"Peafowl eggs when I can find them, rabbit, squirrel, rats, and mice. You hungry?"

"I'm good. Thanks though."

"Let's get these 'barrows up top."

Gary closed the gates and locked them, even though they were presumably coming right back down with the loaded wheelbarrows. Keepers always locked doors if they didn't need to be locked. Henry's dad had been a keeper before he became a curator and zoo director. He locked everything behind him, even when he was home. He might forget his wallet or cell phone, but there was always the jingle of keys in his pocket.

They started up the hill. "Tell me more about the Wild Bunch."

"Not much to say. Robin comes up once or twice every couple weeks with some of his people."

"Is he trying to set the rest of the animals free?"

"No. He eats them."

Henry stopped. He thought he had heard him wrong. "What did you say?"

"He and his gang come by for what they call a harvest. They were here this morning and said they were going to harvest a yearling elk calf."

"When?"

"Didn't say. Maybe in a day or two. They left in their pickup."

"The elk are still here?" There was a large elk pen at the back part of the zoo.

"They didn't take the elk fence down. Robin said if I opened the gate and let them out, he'd kill me, and I believe him. The guy's bad news. I don't mind losing a tooth or two, but I don't want to get killed. Who would take care of the animals?"

It appears that the Wild Bunch have changed their animal rights stance into animal bites.

Henry laughed.

"It's not funny," Gary said. "We better get going. The guys in the semi are always in a hurry."

The guys? I wonder if Gary even knows they are your uncles.

They continued pushing the wheelbarrows up the hill.

"You don't have to stay here, Gary. You can set the rest of the animals free, and come live with us. You'd like the farm. We could use your help. There are animals to take care of, and no one is going to knock your teeth out or threaten to kill you. In fact, there's a dentist in the neighborhood, Dr. Rask. He could probably replace the teeth you lost."

Gary shook his head. "I don't think the primates would make it through the winter. I already lost the penguins and seals because I didn't have enough fish to feed them."

Henry wondered if there was a way to move some of the animals to the farm. He was sure there was a way, but he doubted people in the compound would want them running around.

Gary glanced at Gort. "I'd keep a close eye on your dog. He's edible."

Gort moved a little closer to Henry, as if he understood, then started growling, which was strange. He barked once in a while, but Henry had never heard him growl. He put the wheelbarrow down and grabbed him by his collar. "What's the matter?"

He stopped growling, but he was still acting nervous. Gary dropped his wheelbarrow and looked at the top of the hill. "There might be a cat up ahead. Bathsheba or the pride. Or it could be Indira. I hope the semi guys are smart enough to get back into the cab."

"Have the cats attacked people?"

Gary shook his head. "Not that I know of, but they might if they felt cornered or were hungry enough. And I think they're getting hungry. They wouldn't hesitate to snatch Gort. I'd put a leash on him if I was you."

Gort sticks to you like paint on a wall.

Caroline was right. If Gort wandered away, all he had to do was give him a little whistle and he'd be back at his side in seconds. He didn't like leashes.

"Let's go," Gary said.

Every step Henry took, he thought a pride of lions was going to pop up over the rise and rush down on them, but when they reached the top of the hill, there were no lions or any other animals. Why had Gort growled?

Gary put his wheelbarrow down and turned in a complete circle. "No lions. Bathsheba could be out there. She's sneaky. But I'm not sensing her vibe. I can usually feel her before I see her. She's stalked me a couple of times, but she's never pounced."

Lucky for him.

Gary stood looking around for another minute before he started pushing the wheelbarrow again. Henry had to trot to keep up with him all the way to the administration building.

"Nice," Gary said. "They got everything unloaded for us."

Henry put his wheelbarrow down and stared.

The supplies were at the curb, but the truck was gone.

So were Gino and Chester.

CHAPTER TWENTY-TWO

Gary separated the wheelbarrows and started loading them, while Henry gawked at the empty curb.

"Aren't you going to help me load up?" he asked.

Henry ignored him and stepped off the curb and into the street. There was no sign of the semi. It would have been easy to see among the dead cars.

"I could use a hand!" Gary complained.

"I can't see the truck," Henry said, walking back over to him.

"At least they left the stuff."

"They also left me."

Gary dropped the first bag of guts into a wheelbarrow. "Why would they do that?"

"They wouldn't do that!"

"I'm not sure what I'll do with these cow parts. I let most of the cats go to fend for themselves. I still have Bob and Cat. I guess I can dump some of it in the park for the other cats to feed on. Maybe boil the bones for broth and soup. Eat some of it myself."

"What about the missing truck?"

"Must be playing a joke on you. The other keepers are always doing things like that to me."

I bet they do.

The Ludds were all practical jokers, but there hadn't been

much of that since the switch. Henry began looking at the ground where the semi had been parked.

"I guess I'll wheel this load down . . ." Gary said loudly.

Henry didn't look up. There were wet spots on the asphalt. He put his finger in one of them. It looked like blood.

". . . that is, unless you want to take it down while I fill another wheelbarrow up. I wish they'd left some gas. I'm getting low on fuel. I don't like leaving stuff on the curb. The Wild Bunch might steal it before I get a chance to hide it."

Henry swiped his finger through another spot. No color. He smelled it. Gas.

"Do you think the Wild Bunch came back while we were in the zoo?" Henry asked.

"I didn't see them. Did you?"

It was all Henry could do not to scream at Gary. He closed his eyes and took a deep breath, remembering how his mom had handled Gary's weird leaps of thought.

"No, I didn't see them," he said slowly. "But I was wondering if the Wild Bunch might have dropped by and gone someplace with my uncles?"

Meaning, did the Wild Bunch 'jack the semi and kidnap your uncles?

Exactly, Henry thought.

Gary considered his question for a full minute before answering. "Are the semi drivers friends with the Wild Bunch?"

Oh my God!

"No, they're not," Henry said.

"Then why would they go with them?"

Deep breath. Henry reminded himself that Gary had been

strange before the switch. Four months of living at the zoo alone, getting his teeth knocked out, and a diet of rats hadn't helped. He didn't know if the Wild Bunch had 'jacked the truck or not. All he knew was that his uncles were gone and there were drops of blood on the ground where the truck had been.

"Does anyone come by here besides the Wild Bunch?"

Gary shook his head. "Not really. Sometimes people walk up from Sunset Highway, looking for a place to spend the night. The roads aren't safe after dark. I let them stay in the admin building, because it's not safe in the zoo after dark either, with the cats prowling around. The next morning, the overnighters are gone. I never see them again. It gets a little lonely here sometimes. One thing though: I taught myself to play the guitar."

"Guitar?"

"Yeah. Found one up in the education building with a stack of how-to-play books. I miss listening to music. Now I make my own."

"That's great."

"Maybe I can play something for you."

Henry felt bad for Gary, but he had a lot more important things to think about than his loneliness and guitar playing. "Maybe later. So, no one really comes up here but the Wild Bunch?"

"Pretty much. And I think they're here even when I don't see them."

"What do you mean?"

"Just a feeling I get. I think they're watching me. I find signs of them out in the woods. Old campfires, rodent bones, garbage, things like that."

"Okay," Henry said. "I'll load the other wheelbarrows while

you take the full one down." Henry needed to be alone for a few minutes to think. His mind was spinning out of control.

Gary nodded and picked up the wheelbarrow. "You know, I don't think the Wild Bunch could have taken that truck. The drivers have guns. The Wild Bunch use bows and arrows like Robin Hood."

"Is that where Robin got his . . ."

But Gary had already trotted off with the wheelbarrow and was too far away to hear him.

Robin and his merry men and women. The cow was killed with an arrow.

"Hundreds of people have bows and arrows," Henry said quietly. "I saw people carrying them the first time I was outside, along with baseball bats, guns . . . I even saw a guy with a sword. That doesn't mean the Wild Bunch poached our cow."

He stepped back onto the road and tried to piece together what might have happened. He took a closer look at the asphalt and found a few more blood spots. If it was an arrow, wouldn't there be more blood? Maybe they had remembered something they had to do and had driven away, thinking that he was safe enough at the zoo with Gary. What were the odds of someone driving by and 'jacking a truck from two guys with guns without a shootout? With the exception of Derek and Albert, Gino and Chester were the two best shots on the farm. Someone driving up would have put them on high alert. They would have drawn their guns. If for no other reason than to let the drivers know that they were armed. Maybe they thought someone was going to 'jack the truck and had driven it somewhere safe.

Nice theory, but what about the blood? What about Gort's growl?

134

Henry looked over at the administration building. It was the only cover for a hundred feet in every direction. If someone had been waiting to ambush the truck, that's where they would hide. All the windows were broken. If they were standing inside, a foot or two back from the windows, his uncles would not have been able to see them.

He walked into the building and nearly gagged. It smelled like a septic tank. He took his headlamp out of the bugout bag and put it on. The floor was ankle-deep in moldy paper, garbage, animal or maybe human feces, and other unidentifiable squalor.

I'd rather risk getting devoured by a lion than sleep in this toxic waste dump.

"Lions don't eat mental illnesses, or ghosts, or whatever you are."

You don't know that.

There was a skittering noise in the corner of the room. Before he could get his light on the sound, Gort shot past him. There was a loud squeak, then a crunch. Gort had a rat the size of a kitten in his mouth.

"Good boy," Henry said.

Gort dropped the rat. He never ate rodents.

Henry continued down the hall, paying particular attention to the offices on the right side that had windows facing the curb. All the rooms had a perfect view of where the truck had been parked. Ten people could have been inside, and his uncles wouldn't have seen them.

The last room was the veterinarian's office. The door to the drug safe looked like it had been torn open with a crowbar. Everything inside was gone. He shined his headlamp around the office, trying to remember the last time he had been in there. It was with his dad. He was going to tranquilize an animal, and all the equipment was kept in the safe. At first, his dad grabbed a CO2 pistol, then rejected it, saying he needed to go lighter. So, he pulled out a . . .

"Tranquilizer blowgun," Henry said.

They used blowguns for close shots on animals like small primates so they didn't damage a muscle or break a bone.

Henry looked out the window. It wasn't more than thirty feet to the curb where the truck had been parked. An easy shot. Tranquilizers don't work as fast as they appear to in movies and TV shows. It usually takes a few minutes for the drug to take effect. He'd watched his dad and the veterinarian dart animals several times. The animal jumps at the initial impact, as if stung by a bee. After a few minutes it starts to wobble, then finally falls asleep. He had no idea if Gino and Chester had been darted, but he tried to imagine what their reactions might have been if they had been . . . Two tranquilizer darts. *Ssst . . . Ssst . . .* Shocked, they yank out the darts, but it's too late. The drug is already in their systems. They pull their guns and take cover behind the truck. But they don't know where the darts came from. They think about jumping in the truck and driving away. But they have a problem. Henry is not with them. The drug starts to take effect . . .

Or they could have driven away to pick something up or drop something off so you can get to that barbecue on time.

Caroline might be right, Henry thought. But he had a bad feeling.

Gort grabbed another rat, gave it a violent shake, then dropped it.

"You're killing Gary's main source of protein," Henry said.

Gort ignored him and started digging through the trash beneath the window for another rat, or at least that's what Henry thought. Instead, he picked up an empty drug vial.

"Drop it."

Gort dropped the vial. Henry picked it up and read the label.

KETASET KETAMINE HCI INJ.

"Injectable ketamine."

Henry had seen the tranquilizer used on several different animals. He'd even helped his father fill the darts. There was a tiny amount of liquid in the bottom of the vial. He kicked through the rubbish under the window and found a syringe with the needle still attached. He pushed the plunger. A drop of liquid came out of the needle. This would not have happened if the syringe had been old. If his uncles had been tranquilized, there would have been a little blood from the darts, just a couple of drops like he'd found on the pavement.

Gort let out a low growl and turned toward the door. Henry knew better than to dismiss it this time. Gort's growl became deeper and more menacing. Henry looked around for some kind of weapon. He picked up a small chair and held it over his head. He heard a rustling noise in the hallway. Too loud for a skittering rat.

"Who's there?" Henry yelled.

The noise stopped.

"I have a gun!"

Which looks a lot like a chair.

The noise started again, louder, as it drew closer to the room. Henry's arms started shaking. He glanced at the window. It was broken in several places, but none of the holes were big enough to squeeze through without shredding him to pieces.

The noise got louder.

Henry wasn't sure how long he could hold the chair above his head.

The strum of a guitar.

"Gary?"

Gary appeared in the doorway with a guitar around his neck.

"Why didn't you answer me?" Henry shouted.

Gary played a chord. "I wanted to surprise you."

"I was about ready to bean you!"

"Why are you holding that chair over your head?"

"Because you didn't answer me!"

Just hit him.

Gary played a complicated riff on the guitar, then gave him a gap-toothed grin.

Henry set the chair back on the trashed floor and took a deep breath in an attempt to calm down.

"Pretty good," he said, to humor the grinning scarecrow, then pointed at the safe. "Who tore the door off?"

"Not sure. It was a couple weeks after the power went off. I heard the noise at night, but I didn't check. Too many animals running around in the dark. I sleep down at the paddocks. When I got up here the next morning, everything in the safe was gone."

"Blowguns?"

"Everything. CO2 pistols, trank rifles, blowguns, drugs. I don't know what the heck they think they're gonna do with that stuff."

"Do you think it was the Wild Bunch?"

"I already told you they have bows and arrows. Did you load the wheelbarrows?"

Henry shook his head.

"What are you doing in here?"

Don't tell him. Who knows where that will lead?

"Just looking around," Henry said.

"Sorry about your dad's office."

Here we go again.

"What about it?" Henry asked.

"The fire."

"What fire?"

"The campfire the overnighters started in the middle of Tom's floor. They broke up the shelves for kindling. It was cold that night, but they shouldn't have burned his books. It's bad luck to burn books."

"I better go down and take a look."

"What about the wheelbarrows?"

"I'll help you with them when I come back up."

Henry and Gort walked down the cluttered stairs. Henry was not sure why he wanted to see his dad's office. It wasn't going to help him find his uncles. The office smelled worse than upstairs. All the windows were broken; the walls were scorched from the fire and moldy from where the rain had gotten in. His dad had never cared much about his office and spent as little time as possible there, but he did love his books, most of which were now a pile of sodden black ash.

Seen enough?

Henry had seen more than he wanted to see. He left the office. Gort bounded up the steps in front of him, grabbing another rat on the way outside. He dropped the rat on the sidewalk. Gary eyed it hungrily.

"I guess you'll be spending the night," Gary said.

"I don't think so." Henry put a bale of hay into a wheelbarrow. "I need to find out what happened to my uncles."

"How?"

It was a good question, for which Henry had no answer. He loaded another bale, then started putting the rest of the stuff into the last wheelbarrow. Gary played some more chords on the guitar while Henry worked. By the time he finished, he knew what he was going to do.

"Three trips to the paddocks," Gary said. "Two if you take one of the wheelbarrows down."

"I'm afraid it will be three trips," Henry said. "I need to get going. I was wondering if I could borrow your bike."

"Where are you going?"

I'm curious too.

"Home," Henry said.

"What do I tell the guys in the truck when they come back for you?"

Henry didn't think they were coming back. "Tell them I went to the farm."

"That's a long walk."

"That's why I'm hoping to borrow your bike."

"I don't know," Gary said. "Except for my feet, my bike is the only way of getting around the zoo. I only use the tractor to haul water and the manure trailer. Gotta conserve fuel."

"I'll bring it back." They had several bikes on the farm. His plan was to bring him a better bike than the piece of junk he had. Henry picked up the bike. "Are you attached to this bicycle?"

Gary laughed. "No, I'm standing here."

"I meant do you like it?"

"Of course I like it. I just painted it."

"I could bring you a better bike from the farm. We have a bunch of them."

If your uncles haven't traded them off.

"When?" Gary asked.

"Within a couple of days. I'll bring your zebra bike back too. That way you'll have two bikes."

"Can't ride two bikes."

"But if something happened to one of the bikes, you'd have a backup."

Gary thought about it for several seconds, then nodded. "I guess that would be okay."

Henry adjusted the seat and swung onto the bike before Gary changed his mind. As he was riding across the parking lot with Gort trotting next to him, he glanced back. Gary was holding the neck of his guitar in one hand and the tail of the rat in the other.

CHAPTER TWENTY-THREE

There were a lot of people on Sunset Highway. Some were walking, some were riding bicycles, a few were in old cars and pickup trucks, all swerving through the stalled cars. Many of the bicycles were painted with wild colors, carrying impossible loads strapped to the frames. Henry blended right in with them on the zebra-striped bike, although all he was carrying was his bugout pack.

To get downtown on Sunset he had to pass through the Vista Ridge Tunnel. Before the switch the inside of the tunnel was as bright as daylight. Now the opening looked like the entrance to a mine shaft. As people approached, they slowed down, as if they were entering the maw of a monster. At first, he thought people were slowing down because the tunnel was dark. When he got inside, he saw it was because people were living in the tunnel. They were camped twenty feet deep on either side, leaving only ten feet for walkers, riders, and drivers to get through. The only light came from campfires and lanterns. The smoke stung his eyes. He worried that someone might grab Gort. He kept to the middle, swerving around trash and people who had stopped to trade or talk to the occupants. As he got near the end, the tunnel brightened and he was able to get a better look at the people living inside. They were thin and ragged-looking, with a hungry gleam in their eyes.

The tunnel's probably as good a place to live as any. It can't be burned to the ground, it's close to downtown, and they have a chance to steal or trade stuff before it goes to market.

Just before he got to the end of the tunnel, a man jumped out from the edge and grabbed his handlebars.

"What's the hurry, sonny boy? What do you have in the pack?" Gort growled.

Henry met his eyes just like Derek had taught him and spoke slowly and clearly. "Let go of my handlebars."

"This is a toll tunnel," the man said.

"My dog doesn't like you."

To accent this point, Gort let out a deeper growl and bared his teeth, which Henry had never seen before.

Henry held the man's eyes. "Fair warning."

The man released the handlebars and smiled with bad teeth, nervously glancing down at Gort. "Can't you take a joke?"

Henry moved on without answering, without looking back, but with a triumphant grin on his face.

It was Gort, not you.

Not even Caroline's snide remark could take his smile away. When he was clear of the tunnel, he stopped on the shoulder to give Gort a rest and calm himself down. Derek had told him that when you're outside you needed to have a swagger that telegraphs to those around you that you are not to be messed with. He now knew what that felt like and remembered the other thing Derek had told him: "If you ever go outside, keep in mind that people don't have much. They want what little you might have. Don't wear shiny things that can be traded. Don't act like a victim."

What made the guy choose him from all the others heading into town? He had nothing strapped to his bike, and Gary's bike was a piece of junk. Did he look like a victim? He got his water bottle out and took a drink. He found a hubcap and poured a little water for Gort. He checked the time. The sun glinted off the stainless steel wristband.

A shiny thing.

Chester and Gino had traded several of Albert's watches for things they needed on the farm. What good does a watch do if most people don't know what time it is? He took the shiny thing off his wrist and put it in his pocket, then joined the stream of people heading into the city, with Gort loping beside him.

CHAPTER TWENTY-FOUR

Henry took the Market Street exit off Sunset, because that's what almost everyone else was doing. His plan, which he had to admit wasn't much of a plan, was to ride through downtown on his way back to the farm. It wasn't the most direct route, but he had this wild hope that he might see Derek on the way. Derek would know what to do and could probably get him back to the farm faster than he could on a bicycle.

His hope vanished when he reached the top of the exit. He got off his bike. Gort sat. They both stared. There were throngs of people buying and trading at sidewalk stalls and inside stores that hadn't been burned out. It was like a street festival.

This is just the edge. It's thirteen blocks to the Willamette River. Imagine what it's like the deeper you get into the city.

Caroline knew the city better than he did. She hung out downtown on weekends, or at least she used to. The smart move was to get back onto the freeway and head south, pedaling as fast as he could back to the farm. But the busy scene across the street intrigued him. The people were nothing like the people living in the tunnel. There was a lot of hand shaking, laughing, and smiling. It was almost like the farm. The switch was horrible, but it hadn't really altered their fundamental cheerfulness. "The world is what it is," his mom was always saying. "We do not panic. We respond. We deal with it. We adjust." The people across the street appeared to have adjusted.

He watched a half-dozen cyclists jump off their saddles and walk their bikes into the crowd because there wasn't enough room to ride through it. Two old cars exited the ramp and turned left, as if they weren't allowed to drive onto the street where the stalls were.

Henry decided to cut through the market and make his way down to the river. If he didn't spot Derek, or Derek didn't spot him, he could catch Interstate 5 from Front Street and head south to the farm. He pushed the zebra bike across the street, with Gort nervously bumping his left leg. He wasn't used to crowds.

Neither are you.

He squeezed his way through the crowd, ignoring the people trying to sell him everything from toilet paper to gold necklaces.

"You need a dog collar? Only one silver!"

"Books here! Books here! No mildew! Read 'em and weep!"

"Aspirin! I got aspirin! Sealed bottle! Fifty count!"

"Disposable razor! Good shape! Twenty shaves! Maybe more!"

Every fourth or fifth building was more or less intact, meaning it wasn't a burned-out husk. The street floors had been turned into shops, and he guessed the upper floors had been turned into living quarters, because there were a lot of people hanging out the windows, shouting down to people on the street.

"Anybody got a roll of toilet paper for sale?"

"We need candles and matches!"

"We have apples and pears up here!"

A couple of blocks in he started to get a little panicked. There was so much noise and activity. His heart was pounding. It was like the day after the switch when he was in the shower and Caroline popped into his head. He wanted to retrace his steps and get out of there. Instead, he pushed the bike into a nook between two buildings and tried to calm down. He was determined to reach Front Street.

You're never going to find Derek down here.

"You don't know that," Henry said.

Gort stared up at him as if he was talking to him, then turned his attention to the street and let out a low growl. There was a little kid standing ten feet away from them.

"Don't know what?" he asked.

His clothes were filthy. He was seven or eight years old, with wild red hair and a pale, freckled face. He had a SpongeBob SquarePants pack slung over his skinny shoulders.

"Don't know what?" the kid repeated.

"Nothing. I was just musing out loud."

"What's funny?"

"Huh?"

"You said amusing."

"Musing," Henry said. "No *A*. It means thinking."

"Really?"

"Yeah, really. How old are you?"

"Seven."

This was not a place for a seven-year-old to be running around alone.

It's not a place for a thirteen-year-old either.

"Where are your parents?" Henry asked.

"Gone."

147

Gone like your dad and uncles?

It was a good question. "Do you know where they are?"

"They're dead."

"I'm sorry."

He shrugged. Henry asked him what his name was.

"Sprint."

"Is that your real name?"

"No."

"What's your last name?"

"Just Sprint. What's your name?"

"Henry."

"Is that your real name?"

"Yes."

"Henry what?"

"Just Henry. Where do you sleep?"

"Here. You're a newbie."

"What's that?"

"I been following you and your dog. You look lost. You haven't been here before. I would of seen you."

"I guess I am."

"What you looking for? I can find what you want."

Henry thought about this for a moment. Derek didn't use his real name downtown and didn't tell people he was connected to the Wonderland Compound. His cover was that he was looking for his little brother, which gave him a chance to question strangers without making them suspicious. A lot of people were looking for loved ones who were gone.

"I'm looking for my brother," Henry said.

"What's his name?"

"T-Rex."

"Tyrannosaurus Rex? I love dinosaurs."

"T-Rex is his nickname. Like Sprint. Do you know T-Rex?"

Sprint shook his head. "A lot of people here. Don't know everyone. I'd remember a guy named T-Rex. Is your dog safe?"

"He's friendly. You can pet him. He won't bite." Although Henry wasn't sure of that after all the growling.

Sprint tentatively put his hand out, then touched Gort's head. "A lot of dogs here bite. What kind of name is Gort?"

"Just a name. Do you know what happened to your parents?"

"They never came home," he answered.

"What did you do?"

"Walked down here to find 'em. Didn't. Couldn't find my way back home."

"They might be waiting there for you."

"Nah. Someone took me back home a few weeks after. The house was burned down. Gave up looking for 'em."

"My dad is missing too."

"Gotta move on. That's what some guy told me. He was right."

Henry didn't want to get into this with him, or anyone for that matter. He needed to *move on* to Front Street and get back to the farm.

"So, you haven't heard of T-Rex?"

"Nope."

Henry looked at his wrist to check the time and remembered he wasn't wearing his watch.

"What happened to your watch?" Sprint asked.

"I don't have a watch."

"There's a wrinkle on your wrist."

He was right. Henry hadn't taken the watch off since he put it on.

"I got rid of my watch. It didn't work."

"I know a guy that fixes watches."

"Too late," Henry said, reaching for his bike. "I better get going."

"Your bike's painted like a zebra."

Whoosh . . . Sprint reminds me of Gary.

Henry smiled and pulled the water bottle out of his bugout pack. There was only a gulp left.

"You need water," Sprint said.

"Where can I refill it?"

"From the water people. I'll show you. Do you have coin?"

"A couple."

Henry pushed his bike next to Sprint as he led him deeper into the city, pointing things out he thought Henry might be interested in. His anxiety attack, or whatever it was, seemed to have vanished for the most part. Sprint greeted several people as they passed shops and stalls. He was obviously well known and liked by everyone he waved to.

"Hey, Sprint!"

"How's it going, Sprint?"

"Good to see you, Sprint!"

Too bad he doesn't know T-Rex.

No kidding, Henry thought.

"What do you do here, Sprint?" Henry asked.

"For work?"

It was hard to think of a seven-year-old working, but it was a different world now. "Yeah, for work."

"Clean shops. Help unload. Show people around. But mostly I carry messages. That's why they call me Sprint."

Same job you have. Maybe we should give you a nickname.

Henry ignored her. "Is this where we get water?" They were coming up on a shop with a tank in front. It was called the Quench.

"Nah, they have bad water. It comes from the river. If you drink it, you get sick. You notice nobody's buying water there?"

"There are a lot of people going in and out."

"They're buying hooch. You know, booze, moonshine. It can make you sick too. Least that's what I hear. They use dirty river water to make it. You need to buy Bull Run water. It's clean. I only drink Bull Run."

Bull Run was a reservoir in the foothills of Mount Hood. Before the switch it was the main water source for the city.

They passed a bookstore that had so many books stacked outside Henry wasn't sure how people got through the front door. Next to the store was a bulletin board that stretched half a block down the street. On it were hundreds of photographs and information about missing loved ones. After a while he stopped reading the notices and just looked at the faded photos taken during much happier times.

"This is my mom and dad." Sprint pointed at a photo of a young couple at the beach with a toddler crouching down looking at a tide pool.

"Is that you?"

"When I was a little kid. See the red hair? We used to go to the beach all the time. This picture was about the only thing left after the house burned."

Underneath, in carefully printed block letters, it read:

```
JUDY AND PAUL GLAZE. MISSING. THEIR 7-YEAR-
OLD SON, JACK, IS LOOKING FOR THEM. JACK
LIVES DOWNTOWN NOW AND GOES BY THE NAME
OF SPRINT. IF YOU HAVE ANY INFORMATION
ABOUT SPRINT'S PARENTS, PLEASE LEAVE A
MESSAGE HERE OR AT ONE OF THE STALLS
OR SHOPS. SPRINT IS WELL KNOWN DOWNTOWN.
JUDY AND PAUL WERE LAST SEEN ON OCTOBER 6.
```

Sprint's parents had disappeared the day the earth stood still, like so many others.

"So, your real name is Jack," Henry said.

"Yeah, but I want you to call me Sprint. I like it better."

"Who helped you put this poster up?"

"A girl I know. Rebecca. You'll meet her. She works at Bull Run. She prints good."

"Has anyone responded to it?"

"Nope."

Henry watched the people walking by. None of them even glanced at the photos. "Do people ever look at the photos?"

"'Course. That's why they're put up. I check two or three times a week."

"It would take hours to look at all these."

Sprint shook his head. "I just check Mom and Dad and the

new ones people put up. Doesn't take long. We need to get going before the water runs out."

"You go ahead. I want to see if there is anyone I know here."

Sprint gave him an exasperated sigh. "I'll wait. You don't even know where Bull Run is."

"Thanks. It won't take long."

Henry walked along slowly, scanning the hundreds of photos. He didn't recognize anyone until he came to a photo that made his knees buckle. The photo was one of the bigger photos on the board. His dad standing next to Indira with a crooked smile on his face. Henry didn't remember seeing the photograph before. His mom must have found it in his office. It was covered in plastic to keep the rain off. The information below the photo had been typed with a manual typewriter, no doubt by his mother. He wondered how many of these had been posted around the city.

"That's one of my favorites," Sprint said. "The man is standing next to an elephant. What's it say?"

It hadn't occurred to him that Sprint couldn't read, or if he could, he probably couldn't read well. Henry read it out loud.

```
TOM CARTER. ZOO DIRECTOR. LAST SEEN IN
WASHINGTON PARK PURSUING ESCAPED ANIMALS
ON OCTOBER 6. IF YOU HAVE ANY INFORMATION
ABOUT TOM'S WHEREABOUTS, PLEASE LEAVE A
NOTE OR COME TO 2000 SW WONDERLAND ROAD,
WILSONVILLE, OREGON, ALSO KNOWN AS THE
WONDERLAND COMPOUND. WE ARE OFFERING A
```

SUBSTANTIAL REWARD FOR INFORMATION ABOUT
HIS DISAPPEARANCE.

"That explains the elephant," Sprint said. "I always wondered about that. The picture gets changed every few weeks. I've
seen the man holding a big snake and a monkey. Most people
down here call the Wonderland Compound the WC. I hear they
have plenty of food and electricity. But if you go there, you'll be
murdered."

"Who told you that?"

Sprint shrugged. "It's just something everybody knows. We
really gotta get going."

"Okay." It seemed pointless to look at more photos after seeing
his dad.

They headed deeper into the city. Several blocks later Sprint
pointed. "That's Bull Run!" He hurried ahead.

The place was packed with people waiting in six different
lines, carrying plastic jugs, bottles, buckets, and canteens . . . anything that would hold water. The line led to a huge stainless steel
tank hooked to an old semi tractor. Two people manned each
spigot, one taking money, the other filling the containers. On top
of the tank were several guards carrying rifles, scanning the crowd.

Sprint got into the longest line. Henry joined him and pointed
out that there were shorter lines.

"This is the best line," Sprint said. "That's why it's longer."

"You mean the spigots have different water?"

"'Course not. Different fillers."

Henry didn't understand, but let it go. "How do they get the

154

tanker in here?" The surrounding streets were blocked by stalled cars, shops, and people.

"Some of the streets are open at night," Sprint explained. "Shops and stalls are closed. Not safe after dark."

"Why are there guards on top of the tanker?"

"People get thirsty. Don't have coin." He pulled an empty bottle out of his pack, finished off what was left in the bottom, then shook out the residue.

There were two girls working their spigot. The younger girl was filling the containers; the other girl, who looked a few years older than Henry, was collecting money.

"Hi, Sprint," the older girl said as they stepped up with their containers.

"Hey, Rebecca."

So, this is his friend Rebecca. Pretty.

Rebecca looked at Henry and smiled. "And who are you?"

Her bold, frank stare threw Henry into confusion for a moment. She had straight black hair reaching almost to her waist, large, beautiful brown eyes, perfect teeth, and . . . He wasn't sure what it was about her. Assuredness? Fearlessness? All he knew was that it was something he didn't have. It nearly took his breath away.

Ha. Henry is smitten!

"This is Henry," Sprint said. "He's a newbie." He handed his bottle to the younger girl, and she started filling it.

Rebecca looked at Henry's empty bottle. "One liter. That will be a small silver, and we'll give you script for a couple of refills."

Henry doubted he would ever be back for a refill, but he handed her the smallest silver coin he had.

She looked the coin over, then scratched it with her fingernail. "Wow, a WC. We don't see many of these down here."

"You can use one of the scripts for Sprint's water," Henry said.

"We don't charge Sprint for water. He brings new people here like you and runs errands for us."

Sprint took Henry's water bottle and gave it to the spigot girl. "Henry's looking for his brother," he said.

"What's his name?" Rebecca asked.

"T-Rex," Henry said.

"I know T-Rex."

Henry was overjoyed. "Really? Do you know where I can—"

"So, he's your brother?" Rebecca interrupted.

"Yeah. My older bro—"

Rebecca smiled. "Obviously." She put his coin into the fanny pack belted around her slim waist. "He's been looking for you too, but I don't think his little brother's name is Henry. He was here this morning getting water. Early, like always. He doesn't like the dregs."

"Me either!" the guy behind them shouted. "Can we get moving here?" He had two five-gallon buckets in a wagon.

"Settle down!" Rebecca shouted back, then tapped the side of the tank. It sounded hollow. "I'll catch up with you and Sprint after I've finished here. It won't take long."

Henry turned and looked at the crowd. There had to be a hundred people still in line.

"You better get going," Rebecca said. She looked at Sprint. "Go to Granddad's."

CHAPTER TWENTY-FIVE

As they walked farther into the city, Henry checked his wrist again to see what time it was. Sprint noticed the movement.

"How long since your watch busted?"

"Not long."

Everyone down here notices everything. They're friendly enough, but they're as alert as coyotes.

Henry hadn't noticed, but he was sure Caroline was right. He needed to be more alert. This was not the WC.

"Tell me about Rebecca," Henry said.

Sprint shrugged. "Just a girl. Her granddad has a shop over on Taylor. They have an apartment on top. He's old. He used to be some kind of science guy. He's always looking in one of those microscope things. Rebecca works at Bull Run until the tanks go dry, then helps him at the shop. They sell things like bird books, pictures, pens, pencils, cards . . . things like that. The shop didn't get hit after the lights went out 'cause they didn't have anything anybody wanted. Oh yeah . . . and the mirrors."

"Mirrors?"

Sprint nodded. "He has a million of them in the shop. I bet he don't sell many. People don't like lookin' at themselves anymore."

"Where are Rebecca's parents?"

"Gone, I s'pose. Never asked."

I s'pose people never ask now. Churns up bad memories.

Mom would have a field day with Sprint's grammar, Henry thought.

They had only walked a few blocks when they heard someone call for them to wait. It was Rebecca. She jogged up carrying a gallon jug of water.

"That didn't take long," Henry said.

"The tanks were just about empty when you left. We go dry every day. People get mad, but there is nothing we can do except to write their names down so they can cut to the front of the line tomorrow when they show up."

"Let me carry that jug," Henry said.

"A little awkward while you're pushing a bike. I carry water back to the shop every day. Sometimes I carry several jugs." She leaned down and scratched Gort's head. "What's his name?"

"Gort."

"Klaatu barada nikto."

Why am I not surprised?

"What's your last name?" Rebecca asked.

Henry wasn't ready for the question. He assumed that Derek's last name was Gunderson, but he didn't want to blow Derek's cover by telling her that. He didn't think she would associate his last name with the compound because it wasn't Ludd.

"Carter."

"That's not T-Rex's last name."

"We're step-brothers."

"Really?" Rebecca smiled. "T-Rex, or I should say Derek Gunderson, didn't mention that. In fact, he said his brother's name was William."

"Isn't Carter the last name of that zoo guy?" Sprint asked.

Busted.

Henry had forgotten that he had read the missing poster out loud. Sprint may not have been able to read, but he had a remarkable memory.

"Everyone has been looking for Tom Carter for months," Rebecca said.

"They want the reward," Sprint added.

"More than that," Rebecca said. "They think finding him might get them an invitation into the WC. If you want me to help you, you'll have to tell me who you really are and why you want to find Derek."

"It's a common last name," Henry said lamely. He had to get them onto a different subject. "How well do you know Derek?" he asked.

"Well enough. Like I said, he gets his water from Bull Run. I see him on the street once in a while. He's a good guy. Bad people stay clear of him . . . most of the time. A couple of weeks ago I had to work the tank replacement shift at night. That's not a good time to be out and about. Derek walked me home after the tank was set up. On the way there we ran into a night gang. Derek hurt two of them badly. The others ran. If it weren't for Derek, I'd be dead, or worse."

She doesn't have to explain what worse *means.*

Derek had told him that the days belonged to the shopkeepers. The nights belonged to the gangs.

"I always suspected that Derek was connected to the WC or some other big compound," Rebecca continued. "He always seems to have coin, even though I've never seen him trading or working for anyone down here."

"Do you know where he lives or hangs out?"

"I have a good idea, but I won't tell you until I know why you want to talk to him."

Henry thought about his options. He could head to the farm, or spend the night somewhere downtown and try to catch Derek at Bull Run in the morning, or he could tell the truth.

"If you're worried about me or Sprint spilling our guts, you can relax," Rebecca said. "We're very good at keeping secrets. Aren't we, Sprint?"

"Loose lips sink ships," Sprint said.

I doubt Sprint knows what that means, but you have to trust somebody.

Henry took a deep breath and began spilling his guts. "Tom Carter is my dad . . ."

CHAPTER TWENTY-SIX

"That's it," Henry concluded.

"That's quite a bit of *it*," Rebecca said.

They hadn't heard of Robin, or the Wild Bunch. They didn't know that the zoo still had animals in it. Henry was the first Ludd they had met, even though he was really a Carter. They said the Ludds were famous. They weren't surprised that Gino and Chester had been kidnapped.

"Abducting wealthy people and holding them for ransom is common now," Rebecca said.

"Wealthy?" Henry protested. "We're struggling to get by like everyone else."

Really? After what you've seen today?

"Shut up!" Henry said.

Rebecca and Sprint looked shocked.

"I'm sorry," Henry said, embarrassed. "I sometimes blurt weird things out that I don't really mean. I'm not sure why."

Because you're an idiot.

If Henry could have fled, he would have. Instead, he swallowed his embarrassment and forced himself back on track. "Where can I find Derek?"

"He lives on the river," Rebecca said.

"On Front Street?"

"No, *on* the river. He has a boat."

Derek hadn't mentioned this.

"Lots of boats on the river," Sprint said. "Thousands."

Rebecca smiled. "I don't think there are thousands, but there a lot of them. It's the only way to get to the east side without getting hassled."

"Or charged," Sprint added.

"The bridges across the Willamette are blockaded," Rebecca explained. "You have to pay a steep toll to cross. If you live on the east side, or have business on both sides, it's best to use boats. No toll, no tariff."

"They charge for hauling stuff across the bridges?"

"By weight and estimated worth. It can take hours to get across a bridge."

As interesting as this was, he didn't have time for it. "So, you'll help me find Derek?"

"I guess so," Rebecca said. "But first I have to drop this water off and check on my grandfather."

The shop was only half a block away. Henry leaned his bike near the door and followed Rebecca and Sprint inside. It was dusty, cluttered, filled with bird books, bird prints, bird greeting cards, stationery supplies, and, as Sprint said, a lot of mirrors. Rebecca's white-haired grandfather sat on a tall stool behind a glass case with stuffed birds and articulated bird skeletons. He was peering into an old-fashioned microscope, seemingly unaware that they were there.

The mirrors aren't for sale. He uses the reflected light to illuminate the mirror on his microscope.

Rebecca put the water jug on the counter next to her oblivious grandfather.

"Do you need my help?" Rebecca asked.

"No. No. I'm good here. Slow day."

One might wonder if this shop has ever had a busy day.

"These are my friends, Henry and Sprint. This is my grandfather, Dr. Brandon O'Toole."

"Good to meet you," Dr. O'Toole said.

He still didn't look up.

"Nice to meet you too," Henry said, but he wasn't sure if he had actually met Dr. O'Toole or not. The wall behind him was covered in university degrees and honors. Beneath one of the honors was a large gold medal.

The Nobel Prize. I've never seen one of those.

Henry hadn't either, and he was about to ask Dr. O'Toole about it, when Rebecca spoke up.

"We're going to be out and about," she said. "Don't worry if I'm not home for a while."

"Okay. Have fun."

Rebecca quickly herded them out of the shop.

"Is he always like that?" Henry asked.

"Pretty much. Before the power went out, he had two modes: binocular and microscopic. He watched birds and microorganisms. Bird-watching is a thing of the past, at least down here, because people kill the birds and eat them. I haven't seen a pigeon in months. Gramps is a bit more conversational at night because there isn't enough light to use the microscope. But he only talks about things that another scientist can understand."

"I saw that he won a Nobel Prize."

"A long time ago in molecular biology."

"Your bike's gone," Sprint said.

Henry stared at the empty spot in disbelief. They hadn't been inside for more than three minutes.

Apparently, Henry Carter is not going to win a Nobel Prize anytime soon.

"That was quick," Sprint said.

"I should have told you to bring it inside," Rebecca said.

"I should have known better," Henry admitted.

"Probably be painted like a cheetah soon," Sprint said.

It looks like Gary isn't getting his bike back.

Henry's bigger problem was that he would have to walk back to the farm, which would take him ten times longer. He'd be lucky to get back there by tomorrow morning.

If you don't get jumped or murdered on the way.

Henry pulled his watch out of his pocket.

"So, it isn't busted," Sprint said. "What time is it?"

"Three thirty-five."

"You better put the watch away," Rebecca said.

"Someone'll swipe it," Sprint said.

Rebecca looked at Sprint. "My grandfather seems more out of it than usual. I'm wondering if you can do me a big favor."

"Maybe."

"I need you to stay here and keep an eye on him."

"Like a babysitter?"

"A grandfather sitter. I'll give you a coin. The only thing you need to do is to keep a glass of water next to him and a little food, which you'll find upstairs in the kitchen. There isn't much. He'll eat and drink eventually. When it gets dark, lead him up to the apartment and light the lantern near the recliner. He'll read until he falls asleep. Put a blanket on him and wait until I get back."

"How long ya going to be?"

"I don't know. It shouldn't be too long. But you need to stay with him no matter how long it takes. I don't want him left alone. Don't let him leave the shop. There's enough food to last for a couple of days if you're careful. Lock the shop door when you go inside."

Sprint thought about this for a moment, then nodded. "Okay, I'll do it. What if he asks what I'm doing there?"

"Tell him I asked you to stay there until I get back. I've had people watch him before. He's used to it."

"See you later." Sprint walked back into the shop and locked the door behind him.

"Maybe you should stay," Henry said. "I can find Derek on my own. Just tell me which boat he's—"

"Gramps has been like this since I was a little kid. Mom and I moved downtown to take care of him because he refused to give up the shop. He'll be fine. Sprint will be able to handle him. He may not have a lot of education, but he makes up for it in street smarts. He's an amazing kid."

They started walking.

"What happened to your parents?" Henry asked.

Didn't I warn you not to ask this?

The question didn't seem to bother Rebecca.

"Mom went blind the year before the power went out. She'd always had trouble with her eyes. A month after the outage she got pneumonia. There were no antibiotics to treat her. She was gone in two weeks."

"And your dad?"

You're pushing your luck.

"He died when I was five years old. Brain tumor."

"I'm sorry."

"Thanks. My parents were both a little odd. I guess they got this from Gramps. But they were great fun. My dad made his living teaching kids how to tap dance."

"Seriously?"

Rebecca tapped a few steps out on the sidewalk.

She's pretty good.

Henry thought so too.

"I told you my parents were a little odd," Rebecca said, continuing toward the river for half a block in silence. Then she slowed and said, "I'm sorry about your dad."

"Thanks," Henry said. "Do you have any other relatives living here?"

Rebecca shook her head. "Just my uncle Pat. He's an FBI agent in New York . . . or he was. That's how I know this thing is nationwide. He and my parents were very close. If he were alive, he would have made his way out here by now. But let's talk about happier things. Tell me more about the WC."

Henry gave her the rundown for about five blocks until they reached Waterfront Park, on the Willamette River, where he was struck speechless. He hadn't been down to the river in at least a year. He didn't recognize it. They were near the Steel Bridge, one of twelve bridges that spanned the Willamette, linking the east and west sides.

The river was choked with boats, floating houses, and log rafts with shelters built on them. For as far as Henry could see, the muddy riverbank was covered with tents and dilapidated structures pieced together from whatever people could find. Wooden planks crisscrossed what used to be a lawn, to keep people out of the slimy mud, but they didn't appear to be working well.

"You can walk across the boats to the other side of the river," Henry said.

"Not quite. You can't see it from here, but there's a narrow channel in the middle for boats to pass through."

"I've been wondering about that," Henry said.

"The channel?"

Henry shook his head. "Not just the channel. Everything. Who decides that a channel needs to be kept open? In the market, who decides how much room is needed to walk down the street? Who decided that the side streets need to be open at night so big rigs like your tanker can set up in the market? Who decided to put the boards down here to keep people out of the mud? Is someone in charge?"

"Not really. I mean, there have been a few attempts at some kind of government, but all of them have failed. The leadership would disagree and split off from one another. There were fights and murders. Right now, we're in between. There have been better times and worse times. I think people just adjust to things where there's no leadership."

Henry had to smile at this. *We adjust*, his mom had said.

"I don't know how Bull Run managed to get the tankers in at first," Rebecca continued. "They probably plowed their way into where they wanted to park and told people they would be back every night and to keep it clear. Same thing for the shops and stalls. If someone puts a stall in the middle of the street, the other stall keepers make them move it, or move it themselves. These mud boards? Who knows? Someone got sick of sloshing through the mud and laid down some boards. More were added, and now everybody uses them. Who's in charge of the WC?"

"My aunts and uncles, but Mom makes the final decisions." He looked out across the filthy flotilla. "Which boat is Derek's?"

Rebecca pointed. "It's in that general vicinity."

"You don't know?"

Rebecca shook her head. "I've watched him boat-step to shore a couple of times. I couldn't tell which boat he came from, but I think it's one of those two sailboats next to the channel."

Both sailboats were white and thirty-five to forty feet long. Henry didn't see anyone on either deck. He wished he had the binoculars Gino had bought.

"Do we wait here or walk out to the boat?"

"It's going to get crowded soon."

"More than it is?" There were hundreds of people standing onshore as if they were waiting for something.

"Thousands of people live on the boats. The river is the only relatively safe place at night. The gangs have a hard time sneaking up on victims across the boats. The shop and stall owners usually sleep at their stores with a security detail to protect them." She looked up at the sky. "In a few minutes a tidal wave of people are going to start boat-stepping and tuck in for the night. There's an unspoken rule that everyone boards about the same time so people aren't disturbed later by people coming and going. I'm not sure Derek will be among the throng. Like I said, I don't know what he does or where he hangs out. For all I know, he might work on one of the nighttime security forces."

Henry watched the two sailboats. Their masts rocked gently back and forth from the channel wake.

"Look!" Rebecca pointed at the Steel Bridge.

A small herd of cattle and horse-mounted cowboys were on the east side of the bridge.

Henry proactively grabbed Gort. "Stay!"

"The butchers are going to be busy tonight," Rebecca said. "And the market is going to have a big day tomorrow."

"How much does beef cost?"

"I have no idea. I haven't had any since the lights went out. A fortune, I'm sure. Most people eat chicken when they can find it. We keep a few on our rooftop for eggs."

Henry thought about Gary Dulabaum. "Rats and dogs?"

"Not me, but some people aren't so picky, or can't afford to be picky, about where their protein comes from. We're lucky I earn a few coins from Bull Run. I buy fish caught in the river a couple times a week."

The cows started across the bridge, mooing, bellowing, and snorting. The cowboys whistled, shouted, and slapped lariats on their backs to keep them moving. Gort could hardly contain himself. The crowd below was looking up at meat they would probably never eat. People were starting to step onto the mass of bobbing boats.

"Time to go," Rebecca said.

CHAPTER TWENTY-SEVEN

The boats teetered, wobbled, swayed, and dipped as Rebecca and Henry made their way across. The boats closest to shore were connected by slippery planks, but the planks soon disappeared, replaced by gaps they had to straddle or jump. Gort was a lot better at negotiating the gaps than they were. He hopped from boat to boat like he was a kangaroo, sticking to the decks like he had suction cups on his paws rather than pads.

Rebecca and Henry got separated. She and Gort were four boats to Henry's right and three boats ahead. He stopped to catch his breath on a battered fishing boat. There was an old man sitting on a chair in the stern, drinking clear liquid out of a jar. Henry didn't think it was water. The man didn't say a word as Henry paused, inhaling the polluted river fumes. While he was standing there, two other people crossed the old guy's deck and jumped to the next boat. Henry looked back to shore. Hundreds of people were scrambling over the derelict flotilla like panicked monkeys.

As he got closer to the channel, the boats got bigger and were better kept. He ran up against a couple of big yachts that he had to go around because the decks were too high to reach. There was also more space between the boats, making it difficult to move forward. He had to backtrack several times and pick a new route. There seemed to be some kind of unwritten rule that the boats near the channel were to be given enough space so they didn't ding one another. He looked back at the shore again. People were still coming, but most of them were disappearing into the boats behind him.

He worked his way around yet another yacht and found himself within shouting distance of Rebecca and Gort, who were on the deck of one of the sailboats. Derek was not with them.

Rebecca cupped her hands around her mouth and shouted, "Slowpoke!"

He wished it was Derek making fun of him.

Rebecca pointed. "To your left!"

Henry saw what she was talking about. There was only one way to get to the sailboat. Five more boats and he was there.

Rebecca gave him a hand up to the deck. "Derek's not here."

"I noticed. Are you sure this is his boat?"

"No. But he came from somewhere around—"

"Wait a second." Henry hurried over to the starboard side and looked at the other sailboat. "We're on the wrong boat."

"How do you know that?"

"Because the sailboat next to us is the *Osprey*, which belonged . . . I mean belongs to my uncle Gino. About a week after the switch, his restaurant on the Willamette near Lake Oswego was torched. I figured his boat had gone up in flames. He used to take us sailing on it."

"It's too far away for us to jump."

"But it's tied to this boat. We should be able to pull them together. This must be how Derek boards."

They hauled on the line and managed to pull the boats to within three feet of each other, just close enough for them to clamber over the gunwale.

The *Osprey* was shipshape, as Gino would say. The teak decks were oiled, the brass was shimmering, and the furled sails looked to be in perfect order. Derek must have spent every spare moment he had working on the sleek boat.

Henry looked at Rebecca. "You probably need to get back to your grandfather. I can't thank you enough for your—"

"Gramps will be fine," Rebecca said. "I spend a couple nights a week working for Bull Run and a lot of time out scrounging for food. Sprint's a good kid. He'll stick with him as long as necessary."

You know you want her to stay.

Henry did want her to stay and felt his face warm a little at the thought.

"The cabin door's locked," Rebecca said. The hatch wasn't just locked, it was covered with a steel plate locked in place by two heavy-duty combination padlocks. "Looks like we'll have to wait for Derek up here."

"Not necessarily," Henry said.

For as long as Henry could remember, the Ludds had used the same combination on every lock and alarm on the farm. It was the last four digits of his long-dead grandparents' phone number. Admittedly, not a very good security measure, but easy to remember. Derek wasn't a Ludd, but there was a good chance the padlocks belonged to Gino. He dialed in the numbers and both locks popped open.

"How'd you know the combinations?" Rebecca asked.

"Lucky guess. Give me a hand with this plate."

It took both of them to lift it off and set it to the side. Henry opened the hatch, put on his headlamp, and climbed down the companionway. Rebecca followed. Gort remained on deck, looking worriedly through the opening.

"Should we carry him down?" Rebecca asked.

"He'll figure it out."

Henry lit a lantern. The cabin was as neat as the deck. The galley dishes were washed, all the surfaces wiped down, the bed made, everything stowed away tidily, as spic-and-span as Derek's yurt. Gort made his way down the steep steps like he was walking a tightrope backward. He lay down at the base of Derek's bunk, knowing better than to jump up on it. Rebecca and Henry sat down at the small galley table.

"Almost dark," Rebecca said. "I guess we just wait for Derek to show up."

Henry looked through the port. "I hope it's soon. I haven't done a single thing to help my uncles."

"If you're right about your uncles being tranquilized, they're probably okay," Rebecca said. "They could have just as easily been murdered."

"I hope you're right, and I hope Derek comes back tonight."

"I think he will."

"What about the unwritten rule about people boarding at the same time?"

"I don't know if it's a rule. It's probably more like a guideline. I doubt anyone would complain. People like having Derek around. He's a good guy to have close when things go bad, which they often do. If anyone knows what to do about your uncles, it will be Derek. You made the right choice trying to find him down here."

Unless he's on his way back to the farm.

Henry didn't think this was likely. Derek had only been outside a couple of days. He was usually out for a week or more at a time.

"There are a lot of rumors about the Ludds," Rebecca said, changing the subject.

"Like what?"

She laughed. "They're pretty wild. Some say you're Satan worshippers. Others say you're cannibals. Let me think . . . Some say the Ludds shut the power down. That those who don't follow the WC rules are hanged. That you have enough electricity to power the whole state, and that slaves do all the work in your compound."

"It's all true," Henry said, smiling. "And worse. Doesn't anyone have anything nice to say about the Ludds?"

Rebecca shook her head. "Not really."

"Like I told you, we have a wind turbine, but we have to ration our power, just like we have to ration our food. We're a lot better off than people down here, but it's far from easy. We work eighteen-hour days, seven days a week. If we get extra food, which isn't often, we share it with our neighbors. A couple of days ago someone killed one of our cows. Right about now we're having a community barbecue for a few hundred of our neighbors. Otherwise, the meat would go bad. We have a handful of old working vehicles that allow us to go out and scrounge and trade for things like food, medicine, and seeds for our fields, which won't start producing for months. The big worry now is that everything we've worked for will be taken away from us by people who are more desperate than we are, which is just about everybody."

"Why do you think the power went off?" Rebecca asked.

"We call it the switch at the compound."

"Good name. What do you think happened?"

"My family's convinced it was some kind of an EMP, electromagnetic pulse. The cause could have been a nuclear explosion in the upper atmosphere, or an unheard-of solar event. We don't talk about it much anymore. We're too busy trying to survive."

"I guess that's the way it is down here too. Can anyone join the WC?"

"We've let a lot of people in, but mostly people with skills we need. A doctor, an electrician, an agricultural expert, a couple of teachers, although school hasn't started up again, but they're working on it. It's getting kind of crowded, and there is only so much room."

A look of disappointment crossed Rebecca's face, and it dawned on him why she might have asked the question. There was nothing more he wanted to do than to tell her that she and her grandfather were welcome to come live at the WC, but it wasn't up to him.

"My mom, aunts, and uncles decide who can join us," Henry said, so she wouldn't get her hopes up.

There was a light footstep on the deck. A second later Derek jumped down the companionway with a pistol in his hand.

"Freeze!"

They froze.

When Derek recognized them, he cursed, then shouted, "I might have shot both of you! What are you doing here?"

CHAPTER TWENTY-EIGHT

Henry told Derek about Gino and Chester's abduction. Or at least what he thought had happened.

"I'm not convinced that's how it went down," Derek said when he finished. "But it doesn't matter. The bottom line is that Gino and Chester are in trouble. You were right to come down here and find me." He looked at Rebecca. "And you were right to bring Henry to me."

A series of gunshots sounded in the distance.

"What now?" Derek said wearily. "Let's go topside and see what's going on."

They followed him up to the deck. The gunshots were coming from the west end of the Steel Bridge. It was hard to see in the dark, but it looked like a lot of people were gathered there.

"The cows," Derek said. "I told them it was a bad idea to herd them into the city. They should have butchered them before they crossed the river."

"You talked to the cowhands?" Rebecca asked.

Derek nodded. "I rowed over and tried to buy a cow. They wouldn't sell. The herd was already paid for. They were herding them to a farm near the coast. Now they're going to be butchered by the mob, which means getting to Forest Park will be dangerous tonight."

Forest Park was a five-thousand-acre urban forest northwest of downtown. "Why would we go there?" Henry asked.

"Because that's where Robin and his merry band of men and women live. If they grabbed Gino and Chester, that's where they would take them and stash the truck until they can paint it. The truck is well known. They might as well have hijacked Air Force One. We've spread the rumor that the Ludds are bloodthirsty maniacs and to attack them is a death sentence. It's better protection than Stan's fence."

"If you mess with a Ludd, you'll pay for it," Rebecca said.

She didn't share that rumor with you.

Henry was glad Caroline was still with him. *Maybe it isn't a rumor,* he thought. *Maybe it's true. Who knows what the Ludds will do when they find out about Gino and Chester.*

We'll see.

"We need to get to the park," Henry said. "I don't care how dangerous it is."

"You two aren't going," Derek said.

Before Henry could protest, more gunshots cracked out. People were running toward the Steel Bridge along Front Street and boat-walking in droves back to shore.

"They're slaughtering the cows," Derek continued. "Probably the cowboys too. To get to Forest Park I'll have to walk through that mess. People will be up all night fighting for scraps."

"We could walk around," Rebecca said.

"You are not going," Derek said adamantly. "I'm probably not going either. If I left right now, I wouldn't get there until morning.

I need to get there at night so I can reconnoiter and see what their setup is without being seen." He looked at Henry. "Tell me everything you know about the Wild Bunch."

"The only thing I know about the Wild Bunch is what Gary told me, and Gary's a little strange."

"Who isn't a little strange these days? Tell me what he said."

It didn't take long. When Henry finished, Derek started pacing the deck. There were a couple more gunshots in the distance. A few people jogged back down Front Street empty-handed and began boat-walking to their floating homes.

As Henry watched, he thought about the barbecue at the church that was probably still underway. His mom would be getting worried about him by now, but not panicking . . . yet. Chester and Gino had warned her they might be late. They sometimes didn't roll in until after midnight.

Which means they aren't going to start looking for you until then. Why do you think Derek is pacing back and forth on the deck like a nervous ship captain?

Henry had no idea. Every once in a while, Derek frowned, shook his head, and mumbled something he couldn't understand. He wondered if Derek had someone jabbering inside his head like he did.

I don't jabber.

Derek finally sat back down with a grim expression. "I screwed up," he said. "I underestimated Robin."

"How can you underestimate someone you've never met?" Henry asked.

"I have met him. More than once. I didn't realize that he was with the Wild Bunch."

"What are you talking about?"

"Pockets," Derek said.

Henry was still confused.

"Across the street from the jewelry store."

"The guy with the gun?"

Derek nodded.

"It's not an uncommon name. Did he say he was from the Wild Bunch?"

"No. I thought he was just another looter. As soon as he figured the juice was cut, he must have hustled downtown to see what he could grab. Picked the wrong place to loot. I've talked to him a few times since then. He tried to recruit me. He has a camp up in Forest Park. Calls it the Rabbit Hole. Something to do with *Alice in Wonderland*. I thought he was just another wacko."

He should have called his camp Sherwood Forest.

I don't think he steals from the rich and gives to the poor, Henry thought. *And it's hard to believe that Pockets is the same Robin from the Wild Bunch.*

"He took over an old homestead," Derek continued. "It used to be a farm. There's a cabin and a barn they fixed up and turned into a dormitory. He made it sound like paradise, but I've heard it's a disaster and Robin is a tyrant. His people are sick and half-starved most of the time."

Derek got back up and started pacing again, obviously angry and agitated. "I wonder why Robin didn't move his tribe into the zoo," he said. "It's a better location, close to downtown, plenty of shelter, food, and it was defendable until he took down the perimeter fence. But Robin isn't the brightest bulb, or so I thought." He pounded the gunwale with his fist. "Which is what I meant when I said I underestimated him. He might have started out as an animal rights leader, but that was thrown out when the juice went out."

I've never seen Derek angry.

Neither had Henry.

"Robin is charismatic," Derek said. "I don't think it was ever about the animals. It was about being in charge of a group of people. But to stay in charge you have to feed your people or force them to follow you. I hear he has six or seven goons that take care of that part for him. Probably some of the same bunch he took up to the zoo minus the guys we took out in front of the jewelry store. He has four-person squads he calls *foragers*, and an old pickup truck to drop them off and pick up supplies. Their job is to find stuff they need for the Rabbit Hole and recruit followers. Robin has the final say about who can join. I hear that new people have to stay in camp for weeks before they're allowed outside."

"Sounds like a cult," Henry said.

"Probably is, but there are a lot of cults now. Mostly religious. I don't think Robin's cult has anything to do with religion. He has a military air to him, like he's an ex-soldier. I wouldn't be surprised if he washed out of the Rangers or SEALs. He has the posture, the crispness, of a soldier. But he's carrying a chip on his shoulder. Someone did him wrong, and he's trying to prove to the world they made a big mistake."

Derek sat back down, but he was still agitated, bouncing his knees, pursing his lips, and shaking his head in disgust.

He may have found his circus and his monkeys.

"I think Robin has been targeting us for a long time," Derek said. "Right under my nose. He may know that I'm connected to the WC. I've seen his people hanging around the waterfront, but I didn't think anything about it."

"Are you saying they were watching you?" Henry asked.

"I don't know."

"A lot of people loiter around Front Street," Rebecca said. "It could be a coincidence."

"Doubtful. Robin is a good actor. When he *bumped* into me at the market, it was as casual as anything I've ever seen. He said he recognized me but couldn't remember from where, then remembered that it was across the street from the jewelry store. I asked what had happened after I left. He said the owner snuck out the back door with most of the valuables, had a car waiting for him. He said he managed to grab a few things. Not exactly shy about being a thief."

No one is anymore.

"He bumped into me four days later," Derek continued. "Again, it appeared to be random, but I realize now that it wasn't. He must have been asking around about me, because he tried to recruit me. He had just dropped off one of his squads and offered me a ride to the Rabbit Hole to check it out. I told him that I had some other things to do but that I'd head up there when I could. That was three weeks ago."

"I guess if I suspected that you were working for the WC,

others might too," Rebecca admitted. "You know how rumors fly around down here."

"I spend half my time running rumors down, most of which turn out to be untrue. Up until now, I thought my cover was pretty good. But like I said, I think I underestimated Robin. There's a better than even chance that he's been ghosting Gino and Chester, which wouldn't be hard to do. The semi and the flatbed are well known. I'm sure Gary has told him they drop things off at the zoo. It wouldn't be hard to tail your uncles from the WC, figure out when they were heading up to the zoo, beat him there, and set up an ambush."

What about the poached cow?

Henry explained Caroline's cow theory to Derek, without saying where it came from. He thought Derek would laugh it off, but he didn't.

"Interesting idea," he said. "You might be right. Robin could have sent one of his squads to check the WC out. That's what I would have done if I was thinking about taking it over. I can see them sitting up on the hill with binoculars, looking down at the houses. A cow wanders by and no one's around. They put an arrow into it. I've seen a couple of squad members with compound bows and bowie knives. They hack off what they can carry away. I'm certain Robin didn't condone it. If his people killed the cow, it was off mission. Risky. You don't leave evidence like that behind, even if we weren't smart enough to figure it out."

This got Derek back on his feet and pacing again.

"Snatching Gino and Chester gives Robin a lot of leverage," he said. "To say nothing about the semi, which, after the wind turbine, is our most valuable asset. The chances of replacing it are zero. I haven't seen more than three working semis since the switch."

"We still have the flatbed and the Cadillac," Henry pointed out.

"I know, but Stan wouldn't have gotten his wall up without the semi, and we wouldn't have been able to haul in half the stuff we needed for the compound. We need to get it back."

Henry was a lot more concerned about getting Gino and Chester back than he was about the semi.

"Why didn't they snatch me?" Henry asked.

"Robin may not have recognized you, or he may not have been there when they 'jacked the truck," Derek answered. "He spends most of his time in his truck checking on his squads and moving them from place to place. He gives orders, but I don't think he gets his hands dirty."

"What does he want?" Rebecca asked.

"I think Robin wants to stay in charge," Derek said. "In order to do that he has to give his followers food, shelter, and security."

"Doesn't he have that in the Rabbit Hole?" Henry asked.

"I doubt it. He certainly doesn't have electricity. Do you think your mom would trade the farm for Chester's and Gino's lives?"

It was a good question. Henry didn't know the answer. The choice, if it came to that, wouldn't be just the farm; it would be the entire compound. It was all one place now. A couple hundred people and everything they owned.

"Maybe she'll just pay him off with coin," Henry said.

"She could try, but I doubt it would work."

The sound of another gunshot carried across the water. More people were returning to their boats.

"Then what do we do?" Rebecca asked.

Henry was glad she said *we*.

Derek looked at Rebecca. "I think it's too dangerous for you to go back to your grandfather's tonight. You can spend the night here and go back when it's light." He looked at Henry. "You need to head to the farm and tell them what's going on. You'll be safe enough on the freeway heading south. I'll go to the Rabbit Hole tonight and see what I can learn."

"You said that it would take all night to get there," Henry pointed out. "That getting there in daylight wouldn't work."

Derek shrugged. "I don't have a choice. I'll have to risk a daytime recon. I don't know what kind of security they had before they 'jacked the semi and your uncles, but if Robin is smart, he's probably hardened it."

It was dark out now. If Henry left for the farm right then, he wouldn't get there until morning. By that time, they would already be out looking for him. "How do you get in touch with Gino and Chester?" he asked.

"We have a mailbox on Front Street. I check it once a day. If I had scored a cow on the east side, I would have left them a note about when and where to pick it up. I usually make my own way back to the WC, but if I need a lift, I leave a note."

"Do Albert and Edgar have the combination to the mailbox?"

Derek nodded. "Your mom too."

"Seven seven eight eight?" Henry asked.

Derek grinned. "The magic number."

"What are you talking about?" Rebecca asked.

"Family joke," Derek said.

"Mom's going to send people out looking for me," Henry said. "They're going to come here to see if you know anything."

"That's a good point. I guess you should stay here too until they show up. I have a map to the Rabbit Hole. You should probably take a look at it so you can tell them where I am."

They went below, and Derek spread the map out on the galley table. *The Rabbit Hole* was written along the top. The map was very detailed and looked to have been drawn to scale.

"I don't know how many of these maps Robin has made, but it must have taken a long time to draw them up," Derek said. "The fastest route to the Rabbit Hole is through Northwest Portland along here to Route Thirty, then cut up to the park. But that's where the cows are. I'll have to go around that mess, which is going to add two or three hours."

Henry pointed to a spot along the Willamette River. "Why don't we just sail down here?"

"What are you talking about?"

Henry moved the map closer to the lamp. "We could tie up just past the St. Johns Bridge and walk up. It looks like Robin's camp is only a couple miles up from the river. We'd get there several hours before daylight."

"I have no idea how to sail. Gino brought the boat downriver, and I haven't moved it."

"I know how to sail," Henry said. "At least enough to get us downriver. And we may not have to sail; we can motor down."

"There isn't much fuel," Derek said. "We talked about filling the tank, but it wasn't a priority. I wasn't going anywhere."

"It shouldn't take much fuel, because we'll be going down-river. If we run out, I'll unfurl the sails. What if you get up there and see an opportunity to spring Gino and Chester? How are you going to get them to safety? They might be injured. We could sail all the way up to Lake Oswego and walk to the farm."

Derek stared down at the map for a while, then said resign-edly, "I guess that's a better plan than mine. Let's see if the engine starts."

The engine did not start, at first anyway, because Gino, and probably Edgar, had disconnected the battery cables so they didn't drain the charge.

"Were you on board when Uncle Gino sailed down?" Henry asked as he attached the cables.

"No."

"So, you don't know if the engine was working."

Derek shook his head. "Gino said the boat was made in the fifties. It's all wood. He restored it from the hull up with original components when he could find them."

"I'm surprised he let you have it."

"He didn't have much choice after he and Molly moved to the farm. It was either take it down here or have someone steal it."

Henry climbed back up to the deck and flipped on the power switch. The running lights came on. Good sign. He turned the ignition key. The engine coughed and died. He gave it a little more gas and tried again. Same results. He waited a minute, then tried again. The engine fired up. It was rough, but it was running. Black diesel smoke billowed from the exhaust pipes.

"Better let it warm up for a while," Henry said. He looked at the fuel gauge. There was less than an eighth of a tank. "We have plenty of fuel to get us downriver."

"How about up to Lake Oswego?" Derek asked.

"I'm not sure."

"While we're waiting, I'm going to hop over to the mailbox and leave a message," Derek said.

Henry watched him head to shore, moving from boat to boat as easily as if he were playing a casual game of hopscotch.

Agile booger.

Henry adjusted the gas until the engine noise smoothed and the exhaust lessened, then went below. Rebecca had stayed down there with Gort. She was studying the map.

"It looks like this is the best place to tie up," she said, pointing. "It's almost a straight line up to the Rabbit Hole. It shouldn't take us too long."

What makes you think Derek's going to take either one of you up to the Rabbit Hole?

I'm going up to the Rabbit Hole whether he likes it or not, Henry thought. He got his journal out and jotted down a quick entry as they waited for Derek to return.

PART THREE

THE RABBIT HOLE

February 11

Dad grew up on the Puget Sound near Seattle. He had a small sailboat when he was my age and spent as much time on the water as he could. His dream was to sail around the world solo, until he got interested in animals. He promised that one day he would sail up to Puget Sound with me. This may be as close as I ever get to that dream . . .

CHAPTER TWENTY-NINE

They headed downriver. Derek and Rebecca were at the bow, pushing away flotsam and jetsam with boat hooks so the hull wouldn't get punctured. Henry was at the wheel, slowly guiding the boat along the narrow channel. His first moment of panic was when he remembered that the Steel Bridge was the lowest bridge on the Willamette. Their mast might not clear it. The lower span was for trains. Before the switch, you'd radio ahead and the bridge tender raised it so you could get underneath. There were no bridge tenders anymore and no power to raise the span.

They had motored only a hundred yards, and Henry thought their trip was over, at least until daylight so they could see what they were doing. He reversed the motor to stop their momentum.

"What are you doing?" Derek shouted. "The channel is clear."

"The span," Henry shouted back. "I'm not sure the mast will clear."

Derek shined his headlamp on the bridge, which wasn't more than fifty feet in front of them. It looked like the train span was in the down position. He shined his light to the top of the mast.

"I can't tell from here," he said. "Bring the boat a little closer to the bridge."

Henry did. Slowly.

"That's enough!"

Henry held their place by alternating between forward and reverse.

"Hello, the bridge!" Derek shouted.

After a few seconds a bright light shined down on them from the upper span.

"Hello, the boat!" a woman shouted.

"We're not sure if our mast will clear!"

The woman shined her light on their mast. "It'll be close, but I think it might make it under. Who's in the boat?"

"T-Rex," Derek said.

"Hi, T! It's Pam. Where are you going this time of night?"

"I have to get to Scappoose to pick up some supplies. Tomorrow morning might be too late. Can you keep an eye on the mast?"

"Yeah, okay, but you have to give me some of that tuna you have the next time I see you."

"You have my word."

"I'll climb down to the train span where I can see better. Just line the mast up with my light. I'll let you know if you're going to crash. Go slow."

Derek walked back to the wheel. "Did you get all that?"

"Yeah. Tuna?"

Derek smiled. "Your mom's tuna is a delicacy down here. You okay at the helm?"

"No problem. If we sneak under the Steel Bridge, we'll be okay."

"I hope you are right."

So did Henry. Derek walked back to the bow and joined

Rebecca. Pam moved to the center of the train span and flashed her light three times. Henry adjusted his headlamp so he could see the top of the mast, which looked impossibly tall as he inched the boat toward the bridge.

"Hold it!" Pam shouted.

Henry put it into reverse.

"It's going to be close," Derek said, staring at the top of the mast.

From where Henry was standing, it looked like the mast was ten feet higher than the span.

"I think it's going to clear," Pam shouted. "Not by much, but I think you're going to make it."

What's the worst thing that can happen? Henry thought.

You could tear out the mast and sink Gino's boat and Derek's home.

Henry ignored the mast and Caroline and started forward, waiting for Pam or Derek to scream at him to stop.

"You made it with four inches to spare," Pam shouted. "Bon voyage!"

Henry looked up, surprised to see they were past the bridge. He let his breath out, unaware that he had been holding it. Sweat trickled down his neck in the nearly freezing night air. He turned to look at the receding bridge. Pam was waving with her flashlight.

There were fewer boats on this side of the bridge. Henry opened the throttle a little. Gort walked back to him and lay down behind the transom, out of the wind. They passed the dark Union Station. Rebecca and Derek continued to push debris away.

As they passed under the Broadway Bridge, Rebecca joined him at the wheel.

"Not much debris ahead," she said. "Derek told me there was some food in the galley and to help myself. Do you want anything?"

Now that she mentioned it, Henry realized that he was hungry. He hadn't eaten anything since Albert's poached egg on toast. It would be interesting to see what Derek had stashed away. Rebecca went below and came back ten minutes later with a couple of sandwiches. Tuna, from the smell. Henry nearly gagged. He hadn't smelled tuna since the plane crash. Bad association, he guessed.

"Tuna!" she said. "Derek has a half-dozen jars. He even had mayo."

"I think I'll pass."

"Eat. Who knows when we'll get another chance."

Henry held his breath and took a tentative bite, hoping he didn't projectile vomit in front of her. He managed to get it down. The second bite was easier.

"The bread probably came from my mom or one of my aunts," he said. "They also canned the tuna. I don't know where he got the mayo."

"I see an odd jar in the market from time to time. It's pretty expensive. People usually don't waste their money on it because there's no way to refrigerate it."

"There's a propane refrigerator in the galley. Did Derek say anything more about us going to the Rabbit Hole with him?"

Rebecca shook her head. "I'll ask him when I get back to the bow."

"I wouldn't," Henry said. "I learned a long time ago not to ask questions that can be answered with *no*. On the farm, *no* ends the discussion. Best not to get to *no* before we have to."

Rebecca laughed. "That sounds like something my dad would have said. He had a strange way of looking at things. So do you."

She doesn't know the half of it.

That's interesting coming from you, Henry thought.

Rebecca likes you.

Henry felt his face redden, and he was glad it was dark so Rebecca couldn't see it. He changed the subject.

"You must be worried about your grandfather," he said.

"A little, but I'm always worried about him." She finished her sandwich and didn't say anything for several minutes, then said, "Can I be honest with you, Henry?"

"Sure."

"Okay, here it is." She took a deep breath. "I didn't tag along with you and Derek because I thought I'd be useful. I could have easily gone back to the shop in the dark. It wouldn't have been dangerous. It would have been far safer than usual, because the night gangs follow the action, which was several blocks from the shop. I hung with you because I thought it might help me to get into the WC even though I don't have any useful skills."

"You know how to tap," Henry said, smiling. "You make a good tuna sandwich, and I don't even like tuna."

"I'm serious," Rebecca said. "I don't have anything to offer except my gratefulness. Things are getting worse downtown. Gramps has wandered outside the shop three times in the last month and couldn't find his way back. The last time, it took me four hours to find him. I thought I had lost him for good."

She probably has more useful skills than you have.

Henry agreed.

"Regardless of how this comes out tonight, I'll talk to Mom about it," he said. "I'm sure Derek will talk to her too. The compound would be perfect for your grandfather. We have plenty of birds for him to watch, and electricity so he doesn't have to rely on mirrors to look through his microscope. He can wander around all he likes. The gates are locked. We don't have a Nobel Laureate."

"St. Johns Bridge just ahead," Derek shouted.

CHAPTER THIRTY

They tied up to a rickety dock just beyond the bridge.

Derek went below and came back up with his bugout bag slung over his shoulder. Henry was ready with his rather weak argument for them going with him, but he didn't have to use it.

"Ready?" Derek asked, handing Rebecca a headlamp.

Henry hid his surprise. Rebecca did the same, putting the headlamp on.

"You need to do exactly what I tell you to do," Derek said. "No arguments." He looked at Henry. "Gort is not going. You can either lock him in the cabin or tie him on deck. I don't want him following us up to the Rabbit Hole."

Henry thought Gort might tear up the cabin trying to get out. He found a short length of rope and tied Gort to a deck cleat, then fetched a bucket of water for him. Gort was obviously unhappy about it.

They crossed Route 30, walking past dark houses and businesses, then entered the thick woods traveling single file, with Derek in the lead and Henry in the rear. It was uphill and hard going through the thick brush over uneven ground. They were off-map heading up to the dirt road that led to the Rabbit Hole. Henry thought Rebecca would not do well in the woods, being a city girl, but she appeared to be managing the rough ground better than he was.

It must be her nimble tap-dance feet.

Henry had wondered whether Caroline would accompany him into the forest. He was beginning to think that she had suggested he go outside hoping he would die so he could join her wherever she was. To reinforce this belief, he tripped over a root and fell flat on his face. Derek and Rebecca kept moving, with their lights dancing on the frosty fir branches, unaware he had fallen. He got up, brushed himself off, then hurried ahead to catch up with them, which took a while. He finally caught up as they reached a narrow dirt road. They were looking at the map. He put his hands on his knees to catch his breath.

"I'm not sure this is the right road," Derek said.

"The map doesn't indicate there are two roads," Rebecca said.

As Henry was bent over gasping, he saw fresh tire tracks in the mud along the shoulder. After he had recovered, he followed the tracks for a few yards.

"Where are you going?" Derek asked.

"I think this is the right road," Henry said. "Look at these tire tracks."

They came over and looked.

"They're semi tracks, all right," Derek said. "This is a narrow road for a big truck." He looked at the map again. "I can't tell where we intersected the road. Their camp might be close. We better go dark."

They switched off their headlamps and walked down the road. When they had gone about half a mile, Rebecca stopped and said, "We're getting close."

"What makes you say that?" Derek asked.

"Don't you smell it?"

Henry and Derek sniffed the air. There was the unmistakable scent of meat cooking.

"When the truck was 'jacked, was there meat on it?" Derek asked.

"A little," Henry answered. His stomach grumbled. He wasn't sure if it was caused by the savory scent or nervousness because they were close to the Rabbit Hole.

"No more talking," Derek whispered.

They continued down the road silently. The smell of cooking meat got stronger. Derek came to a sudden stop and waved them down. Fifty yards ahead was a chain-link gate. It was difficult to see in the dark, but it looked like there were people standing behind it. Derek led them back the way they had come until they rounded a bend out of sight of the gate.

"Time to go off-road," he whispered.

They followed him to the left into the trees along a narrow trail for maybe a quarter of a mile until he finally stopped.

"We almost blundered right into them," he said, sitting down next to a tree. "I guess we know what they did with the zoo perimeter fence. The question is, how much of it did they use and is there another way inside?"

"There were three gates and enough fence to enclose sixty-four acres," Henry said. "It was twelve feet high, topped by razor wire to keep intruders out."

"I saw the razor wire on top of the gate," Derek said. "Hard to get over without getting sliced to pieces. According to Robin's map, the road is the only way into their compound. The fence wasn't on the map. We'll have to find an opening, or dig under."

They sat down next to him.

"Give me the map," Rebecca said.

"I already told you the fence isn't on it."

"I know. I think I can use it to get through the gate."

"What are you talking about?" Derek asked, irritated.

"I'm not digging under a fence. I'm walking through the gate."

Derek looked at her like she had lost her mind. Henry thought she might have.

Hahahahaha.

It was the first time Henry had heard Caroline laugh since she had crawled into his head. It startled him. She had never laughed much, but when she did, it sounded like it was coming out of someone else. He had forgotten how musical her laugh was.

You go, girl! Rebecca's wonderful. There's a lot more to her than meets the eye.

"We need to split up," Rebecca said. "Divide and conquer. I'm going to walk through the gate. The map is my golden ticket. Your cover may be blown, but mine isn't. I don't have a cover. I'll tell them someone gave me the map, or that I found it at Bull Run and picked it up. I heard they were looking for recruits. I'd make a great recruit. I know a lot of people downtown. I lived downtown before the power went off."

Going down the rabbit hole like Alice, but her name is Rebecca. I really, really like this girl. Wish I'd met her when I was among the living.

"If the rumors are true," Derek said. "They won't let you out of the Rabbit Hole until they trust you. That could take weeks, and they may never come to trust you."

"I'll make them trust me," Rebecca said. "But I am worried

about my grandfather. If it turns out that you decide to abort because you can't get inside, or Chester and Gino aren't there, I need your promise that you'll take Gramps to the WC. When I get out of the Rabbit Hole, I'll have more information about Robin and his gang than you'll ever get tonight sneaking around."

And her grandfather will be her ticket into the WC. Edgar and Albert are going to love Gramps. He's won a Nobel Prize.

In microbiology, Henry thought.

I bet he knows a lot more than that.

"It's too risky going in alone," Derek said.

"I agree," Henry blurted out. "I'm going with her."

Derek threw his hands up in the air. "You're as crazy as Rebecca. Robin saw you outside the jewelry store. He'll recognize you."

Henry was nearly as shocked as Derek at his outburst. He could hardly believe he volunteered. He wondered if Caroline had been speaking through his vocal cords. But now that he had committed, he wasn't going to back down.

"He saw a kid wearing a hoodie from thirty feet away," he said.

"What do you think you're going to accomplish inside?"

"Find out if they have Chester and Gino. Help you get them out of there if we can. Take away Robin's leverage. It's our only choice. I think Mom would trade the farm for them."

Henry felt the same confidence he had when the guy grabbed his handlebars. He liked the feeling.

"I don't know about that," Derek said angrily, "but if you get caught, she'd certainly trade for you, which is another reason you shouldn't even be here, inside or out. I should have left both of you on the boat. I'm going to find a way inside and check it out on my own. You two stay here. If I'm not back in a couple hours, make your way back to the boat and sail it to Lake Oswego."

Without another word Derek got up and walked off into the dark, leaving them behind.

"I didn't expect that," Rebecca said after a moment.

"Derek can be a little edgy."

"Think he'll change his mind?"

Henry shook his head. "Derek doesn't change his mind."

"Neither do I," Rebecca said, holding up the map.

CHAPTER THIRTY-ONE

Rebecca and Henry followed the trail back to the road.

"I think there's a chance they'll search us when we get inside," Rebecca said quietly. "Better go through your pack and get rid of anything that might identify you as a member of the WC."

Henry removed the handful of WC coins Gino had given him, his pocket journal, and his watch. He put them all in a spare sock and stashed it under a small log on the side of the road in case he got a chance to retrieve it. They had concocted a story on the way up to the road, which Rebecca went over again.

"I'll be using my real name," she said. "There's a good chance that some of the people will know me because of Bull Run, at least by sight. You're Caleb Brown. Robin might remember your real name because he heard it outside the jewelry store."

"Got it," Henry said.

"We barely know each other," Rebecca continued. "We just met tonight during the food riot caused by the cows. You were walking by my shop while it was being vandalized and helped me get out of the city. I heard that the Rabbit Hole was safe, and you asked to go with me. Your backstory is up to you. I would say that you were just passing through Portland to Canada, where you have relatives or something. Your kit got stolen, which explains why you don't have much with you. I'm going to say that I didn't have time to grab anything except my daypack when I ran out of the shop."

"What do we do about Derek if we get inside?"

"There's nothing we can do. He's on his own. I just hope he's not too pissed at me to pick up Gramps if he decides to leave us here."

Derek will be pissed at both of you when he finds out you went into the Rabbit Hole, but I doubt he will leave you, whether Gino and Chester are there or not.

"I guess there's no point in stealth anymore," Henry said. "Might as well turn on our lights."

They switched their headlamps on and headed toward the gate. When they were about twenty feet away, someone shined a dim light in their faces.

"Who are you?" a man shouted. He was carrying a compound bow.

"Is this the Rabbit Hole?" Rebecca asked.

"Yeah, what of it?"

"I heard it's a safe place and you're looking for people to join."

"Who told you that?"

"I have a map." Rebecca took it out of her pocket and held it up.

"Step closer."

He shined his flashlight on it. It looked like the battery was about to go dead. "What's your name?"

"Rebecca O'Toole."

"And you?"

"Caleb Brown."

"Where are you from, Rebecca?"

"Downtown. Been there since before the power went out."

"And you, Caleb?"

"Ashland. Just got to Portland yesterday.

"What's your connection to Rebecca?"

"Just traveling together."

A woman stepped out of the shadows. She too had a bow. "Boyfriend girlfriend?" she asked.

"No, nothing like that," Rebecca said. "Safer traveling with someone. I told Caleb about the Rabbit Hole and he said he wanted to check it out. Do I smell meat cooking?"

"Yep," the man said.

"Did you get some of that cow meat downtown?"

"What are you talking about?"

"That's what caused the riot," Rebecca said. "Some cowboys took a herd of cows over the Steel Bridge and people went crazy. They started tearing everything apart downtown. That's why we got out of there."

"Didn't hear about that," the woman said.

"Think we should take them to Robin?" the man asked.

"I guess. The girl has a map. Open the gate."

The man unlocked the gate and swung it open.

"One at a time. We're going to have to search you."

They looked through their packs and patted them down.

"I'll take them down to camp," the woman said.

"If there's any meat left over, bring some back to me," the man said.

"This is Hector," the woman said. "I'm Janet."

Hector was in his forties, with a scraggly gray beard and long hair tied in a ponytail. Janet was a little younger, thin but fit-looking. Henry couldn't tell what color her hair was because she had it tucked under a sock cap. Hector and Janet were far from cheerful, but pleasant enough.

"How does it work here?" Rebecca asked.

"You mean the setup? It's pretty simple. There are about a hundred of us. A guy named Robin is in charge. He's kind of strict."

"How long have you been here?"

"A couple of months. We go out and scavenge for things in what Robin calls squads. I'm not officially in a squad, but I've filled in a couple of times. Mostly I walk the perimeter, man the gate, and do whatever else needs to be done. I drew that map you have."

"It worked perfectly," Rebecca said. "We had no problem finding you."

"It would have been easier in the light."

"We thought about waiting until morning, but that didn't seem like the best thing to do. A lot of people were killed downtown. We didn't want to join them."

"This place is safe enough, although we've had some bad times. Today was good because we scored some protein. Everybody's happy. I better not answer any more questions. Robin doesn't like us talking to new people before he talks to them. He'll fill you in on everything you need to know."

Janet led them off the road down a steep trail. Campfires were flickering through the thick trees. As they drew closer to the fires, they saw several tents. After a short walk they came to a clearing with a small log cabin and a huge barn with closed doors. The road they had come in on was to the left up a steep embankment. It looked like it swung around to the back of the barn. There was no sign of the semi, but it could have easily been hidden inside the barn. A half-dozen people were sitting around three campfires, cooking meat. They stopped talking when Henry and Rebecca came into camp.

"Where's everyone else?" Henry asked.

"Asleep," Janet answered. "No one stays up this late unless you have gate or perimeter duty. Robin wanted the meat cooked so it didn't go bad, which is why there are still people around the fires."

"It smells delicious," Rebecca said. "Where did you get it?"

Janet didn't answer. "This is Robin's house."

They followed her up onto the cabin porch. She knocked on the door. A tall, muscular man yanked it open. He was bald and dressed head to toe in camo. Standing next to him was a pit bull.

"What do you want?" he asked gruffly.

Janet took an anxious step backward.

Obviously, it's not as cozy in the Rabbit Hole as Janet made it appear.

"Two recruits showed up at the gate," Janet said nervously.

"At this time of night?" the giant growled.

"I didn't invite them, Sam."

"Did you search them?"

"Yes. They're clean. They weren't carrying much."

Sam glared down at them.

"What do you want me to do?" Janet asked.

"Stay here. I'll let you know." Sam slammed the door closed.

"What does Sam do here?" Rebecca asked quietly.

"Anything he wants," Janet said. "He's one of Robin's lieutenants, or looies, as we call them. Stay as far away from him as you can. That goes for the other looies as well. They're all badasses."

More like loonies.

The door opened. It was Robin. He was clean-shaven and dressed nicely in khaki pants, a sky-blue turtleneck, and polished boots. His brown hair was carefully combed, as if he was about to go out to a party. His eyes were pale blue, the color of glacial ice. He smiled with perfectly white teeth.

"What do we have here, Janet?" he asked, staring at Henry and Rebecca.

As clean-cut as he was, he was somehow more menacing than Sam.

Sam might kill you, but Robin would roast you over the fire and laugh.

"The girl had a map," Janet answered. "She said she was a recruit. She picked up the kid on the way. Her name is Rebecca O'Toole. His name is Caleb Brown."

"Any ID on them to verify the names?"

Janet shook her head. "They didn't have much on them at all. Traveling light. Running from a riot downtown caused by a bunch of cows."

Robin nodded, still staring at Henry and Rebecca without a glance at Janet.

"What do you want me to do with them?" Janet asked.

"I'll take care of them," Robin said. "Go back up to the gate, and don't let anybody else through."

Janet left immediately and didn't stop at any of the fires to grab meat for Hector.

"Sit down," Robin said politely, but it was clearly a command, not an invitation. "I'll only be a minute." He went back into the cabin and closed the door.

There was a small wooden table with four mismatched chairs around it. They sat down.

"What do you think?" Henry whispered.

"This place gives me the creeps," Rebecca whispered back. "Chester and Gino must be here. The barn is plenty big enough to hide their semi truck. I hope Derek finds a way through the perimeter fence."

A minute later the door opened. Robin and Sam stepped out. Sam was a foot taller than Robin, but it was clear who was in charge. Robin had an automatic pistol tucked into the front of his pants that looked like the one Gino carried. Sam was holding a revolver at his side that looked like Chester's pistol. They also had two-way radios clipped to their belts. Robin set a kerosene lantern on the table and turned to Sam.

"You go check on things while I talk to these two. Make sure everyone is being vigilant. You can go to sleep after that, but keep your ears open."

Sam nodded and walked off with his pit bull at his side toward the barn, tucking the pistol in the back of his pants. Robin adjusted the lantern wick so he could see them better, then sat down across from them.

He looked at Rebecca. "Explain again how and why you came up here."

Rebecca repeated her story.

"Where did you get the map?"

"I found it," she said. "A guy dropped it when he was rummaging through his pack looking for coin. I work at Bull Run."

"I thought I'd seen you before," Robin said. "I never forget a face."

Hope he doesn't remember your face.

As Robin grilled Rebecca, Henry watched Sam. When he got to the barn, he opened a small door next to the big door. A light shined for a moment as he and his dog walked through, but it was too far away to see inside.

"What do you know about the Rabbit Hole?" Robin asked Rebecca.

"Just what I've heard on the street," Rebecca said. "The rumor is that it's safe and people are friendly."

It was clear to Henry that Rebecca was much better at this than he was going to be when it was his turn. He started thinking about what he was going to say.

"I named this place the Warren after a book called *Watership Down*," Robin said. "Not *Alice in Wonderland*, but the Rabbit Hole stuck and there's nothing I can do about it now. Tell me more about what happened downtown tonight."

"Things went crazy after the cow massacre. I live over the top of a shop. Looters trashed the place and were going to set it on fire. I'd been thinking about getting out of town, and the Rabbit Hole seemed as good a place as any to move to. Someone told me that you were looking for people to join your compound. I thought I'd check it out."

Robin turned his disturbing blue eyes on Henry. "What's your story?"

Henry tried to meet his stare like Rebecca had, but it was difficult.

"Not as interesting as Rebecca's," he said. "I got to Portland a couple days ago. I walked up from Ashland, which took me more than a week. Got there at night and slept in a park. When I woke up, my pack was gone with all my gear. I traded my sleeping bag for the pack I'm carrying now and a few other things."

"Like your headlamp?" Robin asked.

Henry shook his head. He hadn't seen any headlamps in the shops or stalls. "The headlamp was in my sleeping bag. They didn't get it. A lot of people wanted to trade for it, but I couldn't let it go. When I walked from Ashland, I traveled mostly at night. I wouldn't have made it up here without my headlamp."

Robin looked back at Rebecca. "What about your headlamp?"

"I've had it in my go-pack since I put it together."

Robin shifted back to Henry. "What was your plan when you came to Portland?"

"I didn't have a plan. I thought it would be better than Ashland."

"Your parents?"

"Gone," Henry said. "Along with almost everyone else I know. Nothing in Ashland for me anymore. I have an aunt in British Columbia. I thought I might work my way up there. I hear it's better than it is in the States."

"I doubt it," Robin said. "Here's how it works. You're welcome to stay as long as you pitch in and do what I tell you to do. If you refuse, you're out. If you leave without my permission, you'll never get back in, and I mean never. There are punishments for people who don't toe the line, which I think are better than being tossed out forever. We'll give you food when we have it, shelter, and something to do. There are going to be a lot of hard chores. In exchange we give you safety. You don't have to worry about your gear getting ripped off. We deal with thievery harshly."

"Sounds like we can't come and go as we please," Rebecca said.

Robin gave her an unfriendly smile. "You're right. No one comes and goes as they please. If you don't please *me*, you're out. It's as simple as that. I have several lieutenants. You'll do what they tell you to do as if I'm telling you to do it. You'll know who they are because they all wear camo. I send out squads of four or five people led by one of my lieutenants with specific missions. If it works out, I might put you on a squad someday. The squads stay out until their mission is completed, or until they need to come back for further instructions. They're usually out for two or three days at a time."

"Sounds like the military," Rebecca said.

Sounds more like a dictatorship to me. Or a cult.

"I guess it is like the military in a lot of ways," Robin said. "In a few days you'll figure out that this is a good place. Once here, few people leave."

That sounds ominous.

"How long have you been here?" Henry asked.

"Since before the power went out. We were set up a little differently back then. Different needs. Most of my lieutenants were with me back then. They bunk in the barn, which is off-limits to you. You're pretty much useless to me, being new to Portland, but you look healthy enough and there's a lot of manual labor in here."

Robin looked at Rebecca. "You might be a little more useful

to me than Caleb. Were you downtown before the juice was cut?"

"Years before."

"Good. I'll be picking your brain over the next few weeks to find out if you know anything that I don't. In the meantime, you can join the people at the fires. Tell them I said it was okay for you to have some meat. I'll send someone over later to tell you where you can bunk for the night."

Robin stood up, stretched, then walked back into the cabin, closing the door behind him.

CHAPTER THIRTY-TWO

Henry and Rebecca started across the clearing.

"I don't want to stay here any longer than necessary," Rebecca said quietly.

"I guess we're stuck until we find out if Chester and Gino are here," Henry said.

Everyone had gone to sleep except for two people sitting at the farthest campfire. A man and a woman. Rebecca and Henry walked over to them. There were two plastic tubs near the fire. One contained raw meat. The other cooked meat. Henry recognized the tubs. Both had been in the back of the semi.

"I'm Rebecca and this is Caleb. Robin said it was okay for us to have some meat."

"Well, you'll have to cook your own," the man said grumpily. "We've been cooking for hours and we can't go to sleep until the meat is all cooked. My name's Terry Patent, and this is my wife, Patty."

They were white-haired and had to be in their seventies or eighties. They didn't look like they should be out in the cold at two in the morning roasting meat.

"We were given three times as much meat as the others," Patty said. "Which seemed like a good thing at the time."

"Until we got full," Terry said. "And realized that we had to cook all of it before they let us go to our tent. You're new recruits?"

Henry and Rebecca repeated their stories.

"Big bovine day downtown," Patty said. "I'm sure it was a nightmare."

Terry gave them sharpened sticks and told them to grab a piece of meat. Henry and Rebecca skewered a couple of hunks of raw meat and sat down across from them.

"How long have you been here?" Henry asked.

"A little over two months," Terry said.

"Did Robin give you his spiel?" Patty asked quietly.

"He did," Rebecca answered. "Sounds kind of regimented."

"That's not the half of it!" Terry said.

"Keep your voice down," Patty warned him.

Terry glanced nervously at Robin's cabin. "Sorry," he said in almost a whisper. "Did Robin mention that you aren't allowed to voice your opinion unless it coincides with what Robin or his thugs want to hear?"

"It's not that bad," Patty said. "You're just tired and cranky."

Terry let out a little laugh. "You're right, but what I said is true, and you know it. Just this morning you were talking about leaving."

"And then the meat showed up," Patty said. "It's always like that. We'll be at our wits' end, starving and sick, then food will show up, or some other comfort."

"And we'll decide to tough it out for a few more days."

"Robby always seems to come through in the end," Patty said.

"And the other problem is that we don't have anywhere to go," Terry said.

Whatever impact the switch was having on me, Henry thought, *it's worse for them, camped out in the forest in the dead of winter cooking meat over a campfire. People their age should be living someplace safe and comfortable.* He wondered why Robin had let them into the Rabbit Hole. What possible use could they be to him?

"You call Robin Robby?" Rebecca asked.

Patty chuckled. "Well, not to his face. And please don't tell him that I called him that. He'll just get mad. Old habits are hard to break."

"Old habits?" Henry asked.

"I used to take care of Robby, or Robin, when he was young. He was an only child of a neighbor of ours on the east side. He was a nice enough boy, but a little cruel and willful. His parents were wonderful neighbors and a good couple."

"Until they got divorced," Terry said. "I always thought he was a little hellion, but I was out working while you were babysitting him. Maybe you saw some sides to him that I didn't."

"I lost track of him when Terry retired and we moved downtown," Patty said. "I understand from his mother, who passed away several years ago, that he joined the army, but it didn't work out. He never did like being told what to do."

"Still doesn't," Terry said bitterly, and skewered another piece of meat.

"He was in charge of a big animal rights organization," Patty said.

"The Wild Bunch?" Henry asked.

"Yes! I think that's it. How did you know?"

"Just a guess," he said. "They're pretty well known around Portland."

Patty looked at Terry. "I told you that Robby was a big deal."

Henry hadn't heard about the Wild Bunch until his dad mentioned them on his birthday. If they had been a big deal, he would have heard of them before that.

Terry spitted another hunk of meat. "I guess Robin has changed his tune about animals."

"Where did you get this meat?" Rebecca said, blowing on her skewer to cool it down so she could eat it.

"We're not supposed to say," Patty said.

"And why not?" Terry asked. "Because they probably stole the truck that was carrying the meat."

"You're forgetting that Robby let us in when we had no place to go," Patty said. "The least we can do is abide by his rules."

"He barely let us into this hellhole."

"And gave us a nice tent, sleeping bags, pads, and a kerosene heater."

"Which doesn't work because we ran out of kerosene three weeks ago. Although I notice that Robin and his thugs seem to have plenty. Yesterday you were ready to kill him. It's amazing what a bellyful of meat can do for one's attitude."

He's got that right.

Like you were ever hungry when you were alive, Henry thought.

I went on a diet once. Ask them about the truck.

Henry didn't have to ask them about the truck. It was clear it was there because of the tubs, the meat, and the tracks in the road.

He took a bite of meat. It was good, but he wasn't very hungry after gagging down the tuna sandwich.

"What's in the barn?" Rebecca asked casually.

"It's off-limits," Patty said.

"Robin mentioned that," Rebecca said.

"Rule number one," Terry said. "We've never even peeked inside. The looies sleep in there. For all we know, it's filled to the rafters with food and supplies. They guard it like it's Fort Knox. The road leads to the back of it, not that we're allowed back there. It's under guard twenty-four seven. There are always one or two looies inside, sometimes the whole bunch of them."

"They come and go," Patty said. "I think most of them are in camp tonight."

The door to the barn opened and someone stepped out.

"Better shut our traps," Terry warned.

The figure walked over to them. It was a woman in her twenties with blonde shoulder-length hair and wearing camo and a sheathed machete belted around her waist. She looked in the tubs.

"Hi, Julie," Patty said.

"Looks like you still have a lot of cooking to do," Julie said, warming her gloved hands over the fire.

"We'll get it done," Terry said, almost cheerfully in contrast to his griping of a second ago.

Julie reached into a tub, pulled out a piece of cooked meat, and took a bite out of it. "You're overcooking it," she said as she chewed.

"Doing our best," Terry said. "Hard to get it exactly right over an open flame. Better to overcook than undercook. Don't want people getting sick."

Julie tore off another bite and looked down at Henry and Rebecca. "You're the new recruits," she said.

They nodded.

"Well, help Patty and Terry get the rest of this meat cooked and we'll find you a place to bed down."

Julie walked away and knocked on Robin's door, then disappeared.

"She's one of the lieutenants," Patty said.

"Also called an 'original' because she's been with Robin from the beginning," Terry added.

"She's one of the nicer ones," Patty said.

"She didn't seem that nice to me," Rebecca said.

"That's because you haven't met the others," Terry said. "Probably counted the pieces to make sure we didn't eat any more." He picked through the tub of raw meat. "We only have seven more pieces to cook. Shouldn't take us too long."

After this Patty and Terry went silent, as if they had already said too much or were too exhausted to talk. A half hour later they finished cooking the last piece of meat. Terry covered the tubs and stood up.

"We'll probably see you tomorrow," he said, helping Patty to her feet.

They hobbled to a tent near the edge of the clearing and disappeared inside. Before Henry had a chance to ask Rebecca what she had thought of the conversation, Julie came out of the cabin and walked back over. She opened the tub and counted the pieces of meat.

"That went fast. Not much left. Pretty soon we'll have all the food we need."

"What do you mean?" Rebecca asked.

"That's not your business. Follow me."

She led them over to a shelter made out of sticks and tarps the size of a big doghouse. She lifted the ratty tarp covering the entrance, and they were assaulted with a noxious odor.

"I'd leave the flap open and let it air out," Julie suggested. "The people who lived here left a couple weeks ago."

They might have died in there two weeks ago.

"You can straighten it out tomorrow," Julie said.

By torching it.

You're lucky you can't smell it from where you are, Henry thought. *Or can you?*

No smells here, which is an unpleasant sensation.

"There's a latrine in the woods about fifty feet in back of here. You'll smell it before you see it. Don't do your business anywhere near camp. It's not sanitary and it's against the rules."

Julie walked away. They crawled inside.

"It's hard to believe that this place smells worse than the latrine," Rebecca said.

"I'm not sleeping in here," Henry said.

"Me either," Rebecca agreed. "But let's stay inside for a while so we can talk. We'll pull the sleeping bags and pads outside when we're finished."

They turned off their headlamps and spoke softly, even though they were in the only shelter for thirty feet or so.

"Thoughts?" Rebecca asked.

"The semi is here. Robin is nuts and dangerous. I'd like to get Patty and Terry to the WC where they'll be safe."

"As long as Robin doesn't take over the WC."

"There's that. We need to get into that barn, or at least get a better look through one of the doors. I guess we can start figuring out how to do that first thing tomorrow morning."

"I wonder if Derek got past the perimeter," Rebecca said.

"I'd be surprised if he hasn't."

"How do we find him?"

"He'll find us."

CHAPTER THIRTY-THREE

Derek found them just before daylight. They had dragged the sleeping bags and pads to a flat spot a few feet behind the shelter. Henry didn't think he'd be able to sleep in a damp, stinking bag, but he had and didn't wake up until he felt Derek shaking him.

"It'll be light soon," Derek whispered.

Henry blinked the sleep away and looked over at Rebecca, who was sitting up, picking leaves and twigs out of her tangled black hair.

When they were alert enough to comprehend words, Derek said, "We can be out of here in twenty minutes."

"The truck's here," Henry said.

"In the barn?"

"Yeah."

"You saw it?"

Henry shook his head and told him what they had learned.

"Does Robin stay in the cabin or the barn?"

"The cabin, I think."

The sun was coming up. They could see their breath in the cold air.

"What do you want us to do?" Henry asked.

"I want you to get out of here and go to the sailboat."

Henry shook his head. "I'm not leaving until we find Gino and Chester."

"They must be in the barn," Rebecca added. "We're going to try to get a look inside."

"Forget it," Derek said. "It's too risky. Who are the guys that come and go into the barn?"

"Robin's lieutenants," Henry said. "Some of them have been with him since he got the Wild Bunch together. They're called originals."

"And they're not all guys," Rebecca added. "There is at least one woman lieutenant. They call them looies here. They all wear camo."

"Good," Derek said. "Easier to ID. How many lieutenants are there?"

"Six or seven," Henry said. "Maybe more. We'll figure that out today."

Derek shook his head. "You're both going back to the sailboat."

"We are not," Henry said adamantly. He looked at Rebecca. She was nodding in agreement, which he was happy to see.

Derek frowned. "Do you think Robin bought your cover stories?"

"He wasn't exactly welcoming," Rebecca said. "But he didn't seem suspicious. He made it sound like we could do whatever we wanted when we aren't doing chores, whatever those are going to be."

"Did he say you could leave the compound?" Derek asked.

"He didn't say we couldn't leave," Rebecca answered. "But he told us that if we leave without permission, we'll never be let back in."

What a tragedy.

Good morning, Caroline, Henry thought.

"Well, if you want to leave, we have a back door now," Derek said. "There was no way to get over the top with razor wire. They buried the bottom of the fence underground. I had to tunnel under." It was light enough now to see that he was covered in mud. "I guess you're safe inside for now, but don't take any chances. I better get going before someone wakes up and heads to the latrine. I'll be around, keeping an eye on you as best I can. If you get in trouble, just shout out. How many people are here?"

"A hundred or so," Rebecca said.

"Good. If I get spotted, they might assume I'm one of them."

"I think the lieutenants know everyone," Henry said.

"I'll stay away from them," Derek said, and got up. "Don't push for information. Just let people tell you what they know."

"What about the barn?" Rebecca asked.

"Stay away from it," Derek said, and walked back into the forest, disappearing from view in less than a minute.

CHAPTER THIRTY-FOUR

Henry and Rebecca spent the next hour pulling everything out of the shelter to air it out in case they had to spend another night in the Rabbit Hole, which seemed likely. When they finished, people started to emerge from their shelters, rubbing sleep from their eyes, stretching kinks out, brushing teeth, heading to the latrine. No one paid much attention to them. It appeared that the twenty or so people wandering around believed that they were just a couple of new recruits. There was no sign of the Patents, which didn't surprise them. They probably wouldn't have been up either if Derek hadn't woken them so early.

"What do you want to do?" Rebecca asked after they had everything from the shelter laid out.

"I guess we spend the day keeping an eye on the barn and talking to people," Henry said. "Not much else we can do at this point."

Eventually people started stoking the campfires in the clearing, trying to get warm. Henry and Rebecca walked over to the side of the fire with the best view of the barn, joining a woman in her mid-twenties with braided black hair. She was wearing jeans, heavy boots, a thick sweater, and a down vest.

They introduced themselves.

"I'm Lani," the woman said. "When did you get in?"

"Last night," Rebecca said.

Lani gave Rebecca a closer look. "You're one of the water girls, aren't you? I've seen you downtown. Why would you leave that cushy job to come up here?"

Rebecca gave her the story.

"I have half a mind to go downtown and ask them for your job," Lani said. "I tried to get on with Bull Run a couple months ago, but they said there was a long waiting list and no turnover."

"They've probably already filled my position, if they were able to get the water truck through the mess."

"People need water," Lani said. "I'm sure it got through. If it didn't, there would be another riot downtown."

"What do you do for water here?" Henry asked.

Lani pointed. "There's a stream that way. It's probably a hundred yards. You can only use it to get water. No washing, bathing, or brushing teeth. If Robin catches you doing anything besides filling your containers, he'll probably have one of the looies drown you."

"Oh, wow, um, we don't want that. Sounds like avoiding the looies is the best choice. How many are there?" Rebecca asked.

"I don't know. Eight or ten. You can't avoid them completely. They're the ones who portion out the food. They'll probably have breakfast with them when they come out of the barn. They brought in a big truck yesterday afternoon. I don't know what was inside it except the meat. Hopefully, more supplies."

"We heard about the truck," Henry said. "Did you see it drive in?"

"I was standing right here when it came roaring down the road. It was humongous. They swung it around to the back of the barn and drove it inside."

"I hear the barn is off-limits," Rebecca said.

Lani laughed. "It's the looies' private clubhouse. I don't know anyone who has been inside."

Henry had been taking furtive glances at the small barn door Sam had gone through the night before. He shifted his gaze upward and noticed that the hayloft doors were open and there was someone sitting back from the opening in the shadows. He looked over at their shelter and saw that there was a clear view of it from the hayloft.

Lucky you were sleeping behind the shelter when Derek showed up.

No kidding, Henry thought.

Lani must have noticed him staring at the loft. "Sentries," she said. "They have someone up in the loft on the back side of the barn too. They watch everything we do. You get used to it."

Henry shifted his gaze to the campfire.

"We were told there were a hundred people here," Rebecca said. "It doesn't look like there are enough shelters and tents for that many people."

"There are several camps inside the compound. Robin calls them warrens. That has something to do with rabbits, I guess. Anyway, when you first get here, they make you stay in the inner ring, where Robin and the looies can keep an eye on you. In a week or two you'll be able to pitch a tent wherever you like."

"What are we supposed to do here?" Henry asked.

Lani shrugged. "You wait. You'll find out there's a lot of that in the Rabbit Hole. The looies will come out soon and give us our assignments. In the meantime we get the fires going, straighten out our tents and shelters. Sometimes they don't have anything for us to do. If you're bored, you can go out and gather wood, but don't bring any live wood in. Robin doesn't like that. You gotta pick up deadwood from the ground. Most of the deadwood near the circle has already been snatched up. The best place to look is along the perimeter fence, where they had to cut down trees to get the fence up."

"How far is that stream, again? We should grab some water while we wait."

"Past the latrine," Lani said. "It's quite a hike."

Henry was perfectly fine standing next to the fire, but Rebecca said enthusiastically, "Let's go, Caleb!"

CHAPTER THIRTY-FIVE

"I guess we're not going to be sauntering into the barn anytime soon," Rebecca said when they were far enough away from the campfires.

"I guess not," Henry said. "Maybe we can find a vantage point after dark and at least get a look through the door when the looies are coming and going."

"That might be worth a try. We can look for a place when we get back."

When they reached the stream, they filled their water bottles, hoping the water was free of nasty organisms.

Henry took a sip. "Tastes okay."

"You can't taste shigella, giardia, or salmonella," Rebecca said. "I'll wait to drink mine until I'm sure you're okay."

"Thanks a lot."

Henry took a sip and waited a beat.

"I'm still here," Henry said.

"We both are," Rebecca said, taking her own drink. "Let's make our way over to the fence to check it out. We can grab some wood on the way back. The looies will think we're already pitching in."

Lani was right, there was no deadwood closer to the circle.

The fence was about a hundred yards beyond the stream. They could see immediately why Derek had so much trouble. It was formidable.

"Plenty of wood for the campfires," Rebecca said.

"I wish we had a wheelbarrow. It would be a lot easier to haul it back."

They started picking up the easier-to-carry pieces.

"Tell me what the girl said," Derek hissed.

Henry startled so badly, he dropped his armful of wood. He looked around, but couldn't see anyone.

"Quit rubbernecking," Derek said. "There are people in the woods not far from you. Just have a conversation between yourselves about what the girl told you."

Rebecca and Henry had a strange conversation between them that began with "Lani seemed nice . . ." and ended with "Did you hear her say that they have sentries in both haylofts with binoculars twenty-four seven?"

"I spotted them this morning before I woke you up," Derek whispered from wherever he was. "I'm outta here. You better get back before you're missed."

Henry listened for movement but heard nothing.

The invisible man. Must have learned that in the army.

A lot more people were hanging out in the inner circle when they returned. Again, no one seemed particularly curious about them, nor did they offer to help with the heavy loads of wood.

"Must be fifty people here," Henry said, dumping his pile near one of the fires.

"More," Rebecca said.

"At least someone is being productive this morning," a man said.

They turned around. It was Sam. He didn't look any less violent in the daylight than he had in the dark the night before, nor did his pit bull.

Henry guessed Sam had just given them a compliment, but he would have been happier if he had ignored them. Without meaning to, they had made everyone else standing around doing nothing look bad, which was not a good way to make friends.

Sam was holding a clipboard. "We'll bring some food out in a minute, but I want to give you your work assignments. We're going to do heavy perimeter patrol today. These are the people on the patrol." He read off a long list of names, including Henry's and Rebecca's and the Patents'. "You'll work in teams, but you'll walk solo, spaced fifty yards apart. If you see or hear anything, you're to let one of us know; we'll be around. Just give us a shout."

Everyone looked a little bewildered, as if it was the first time they had been asked to do this.

"It's not complicated," Sam said, irritated. "You walk in a circle, fifty yards apart. When you reach your partner they do a circle and you rest. Nothing could be simpler."

"Why?" Terry Patent asked. He and Patty had just walked into camp and joined Henry and Rebecca.

"It's a security drill."

"How many laps?" Terry asked.

"That depends on how the drill goes. If you screw it up, you'll be out there until you get it right. No more questions."

"They're clearing the camp," Patty said quietly. "They've done it before, but not this way."

"Why?" Henry asked.

"I don't know," Patty said. "Better to just go along with it."

"Quiet down!" Sam shouted. "Everyone not walking the perimeter will be on wood duty."

There was a collective moan from those who weren't on fence duty.

"You know how it works," Sam continued. "You haul wood up to the road, stack it neatly, and we'll pick it up with the truck later. We're going to need several cords. It's cold out. You've probably noticed." He gave his version of a smile, which looked more like a scowl.

"See those trees on the right side of the cabin?" Henry whispered.

Rebecca nodded.

"That might be a good place to watch the barn tonight."

"As long as Sam's pit bull doesn't sniff us out," Rebecca whispered.

CHAPTER THIRTY-SIX

They were broken up into small groups, then led to different fence sections by twos and told to wait for the sound of a whistle. Henry and Rebecca sat down next to an old stump.

"This is the most pointless task I've ever heard of," Rebecca said. "So much for sticking near the barn."

Henry agreed. "Why do you think they want the central ring cleared?"

"Maybe Robin and his looies hold satanic rituals there."

"We'll at least get a good look at the back of the barn. The perimeter fence isn't far from it."

"And our potential hiding spot near the cabin," Rebecca added.

"So, maybe this isn't a total waste of time."

"Here's another thing I was thinking about," Rebecca said. "Since the looies are the only ones allowed inside the barn, we need to try to gain their confidence."

"You mean suck up to them."

"That's exactly what I mean."

A whistle blew.

Rebecca got up. "I'll take the first loop."

"Keep an eye open for Derek's burrow. We might need it."

"Maybe they already found it and that's why they are making us walk the perimeter."

"Doubtful. Derek's the invisible man. He doesn't leave a trace."

Henry was tired. If it weren't so cold and uncomfortable leaning against the stump, he would have fallen asleep. Most people who trudged or stumbled past him along the fence didn't even look in his direction. But he had a good chance to look at them. Some of them had knives or hatchets belted around their waists; most of them wore down vests; all of them were wearing boots and gloves. He guessed most of them were in their twenties like Lani, who waved at him as she walked by.

A half hour later a looie he hadn't met showed up and gave him two small paper bags of food.

"One for you, one for your partner," she said. "Save the sacks. We recycle here."

"Nice day for a walk," Henry said.

She gave him a skeptical look.

"I mean, it's not raining, and walking is better than picking up firewood."

The woman stared at him.

She wouldn't tell you if you were on fire.

You're probably right, Henry thought. *She might light me on fire.*

She marched off toward the next sitter, fifty yards away, out of Henry's view.

Inside the sacks were half an apple, a small hunk of overcooked meat, and a handful of peanuts. He wasn't hungry. He put one sack in his bugout pack and the other on top of the stump for Rebecca.

The more he watched people trudging by, the more convinced

he was that the looies had no idea that Derek was inside. He was also beginning to think that maybe Gino and Chester were not in the barn. Someone on the outside would have to know. People watched the looies as carefully as the looies watched them.

They're in the barn.

Have you been inside? Henry thought hopefully.

No, I only go where you go, but it feels right. You're on the right track. You're exactly where you're supposed to be. You need to keep the faith, Bucko.

Henry didn't believe her, but he smiled. *Keep the faith, Bucko* was one of Caroline's favorite sayings. He wondered if Derek was watching the barn.

His question was answered five minutes later when Derek walked by along the fence. At least he thought it was Derek. He nearly shouted out, but the man shook his head, tossed a crumpled piece of paper in his direction, and continued on. If it was Derek, he had shaved his beard and was wearing sunglasses and a sock cap to cover his hair.

Hiding in plain sight.

Walking in plain sight, Henry thought.

Henry was going to retrieve the piece of paper but stopped when he heard something crashing through the trees behind him. Sam and his pit bull appeared. Sam watched someone walk by, then glowered down at Henry.

"You been around yet?"

Henry shook his head and stood up. He didn't want to be at eye level with the pit bull.

"It shouldn't be too long," Henry said, brushing himself off. "I've been here awhile."

"Takes about an hour and a half to go around. The ground is pretty rough in places."

A man walked by.

Sam swore.

The man froze, thinking Sam was swearing at him.

"Keep moving!" Sam shouted.

The man hurried on. Sam stamped toward the fence, stopped, and bent down and picked up the crumpled piece of paper. Henry thought he might have a heart attack.

"Slobs! Do they think this place is a pigsty? Did you see who threw this out?"

"No," Henry said. "It was here when I got here."

"Then you should have picked it up."

"Sorry. I wasn't thinking."

"Damn right you weren't thinking. Robin would throw you out for something like this. I wish I could catch whoever tossed it. I'd kick their ass."

He stomped back over to the stump, the paper held tightly in his huge fist.

"I'll take it," Henry said, holding his hand out. "I'll throw it on the fire when I get back."

"See that you do."

Sam dropped the ball of paper into his hand. Henry thought his knees might give out. "And when it's your turn to walk, make sure you pick up any trash you see."

"I will." He put the wadded paper into his pocket.

Sam walked into the forest with the pit bull trotting behind him.

A few seconds later Rebecca showed up. "You look like you saw a ghost."

"I saw an ogre by the name of Sam and his trusty dog," Henry said shakily.

"Yeah, I've seen some of the looies wandering around. You better get walking. They don't like us stopping for long."

"Walk with me," Henry said.

"Forget it. It's a hard walk. I need to sit down for a while."

"Just a little way. We've got to talk."

Reluctantly, Rebecca joined him.

"What's going on?"

"Derek was walking the fence. He shaved his beard. I barely recognized him. He tossed me a note when he walked by."

"What did it say?"

"I haven't had a chance to read it." He glanced behind him. The next guy in line was only twenty-five feet away. "Let's hurry ahead."

They picked up their pace. Henry waited until they were at least fifty yards ahead.

"Sam picked up the note before I could get to it."

Rebecca stopped.

"Keep walking. He gave it to me to throw away without reading it."

"No wonder you're pale."

Henry pulled the paper out of his pocket and unfolded it.

GINO AND CHESTER ARE IN THE BARN. THEY TOOK THEM OUTSIDE WHEN EVERYONE LEFT. I GUESS FOR EXERCISE.

Henry handed Rebecca the note.

"They're alive!" Rebecca threw her arms around him.

Henry returned the hug.

Rebecca let him go, then smiled at him. "I guess I better turn back. We're probably violating some rule by walking together."

"Probably so," Henry said, feeling a little awkward.

Focus, lover boy. It was just a hug.

"I left you some food," he said. "Burn the note when you get back to the stump. See you around."

"Funny guy," Rebecca said.

"Happy guy," Henry said. "I nearly lost faith."

"We can't have that," Rebecca said. She started to walk back to the stump.

Henry continued forward, reinvigorated by the news.

Walking along the fence was easy until he reached the first hill. He had to crawl on his hands and knees in places to get past the downed trees and branches.

Henry wondered why Rebecca didn't warn him about it.

Probably because she didn't have as much trouble getting through it as you're having.

Probably not, Henry thought. *There's enough downed wood here to heat the Rabbit Hole for years. The wood gathering is a complete ruse.*

Henry finally reached the top of the hill and relatively level ground, out of breath, sweating in the cold, hoping there weren't any more rough spots.

That's when Gort showed up outside the fence.

CHAPTER THIRTY-SEVEN

At first, Henry thought he was seeing things, but it was Gort, or a horrible version of him.

He was covered from head to toe in mud, leaves, sticks, and pine needles. He put his front paws on the fence and whined. The chewed rope was dangling from his collar. He looked like the victim of a hanging gone bad.

Gort whined again. Louder than the first time. Henry was afraid he would start barking.

"Quiet," he whispered.

Now what was he going to do? He couldn't let Gort follow him. Eventually he was going to reach the gate. What would he say to the guards about the dog following him outside the perimeter? He heard branches cracking. The guy behind him was breaking his way through the tangle. Henry had to get moving.

"I don't suppose you'd just go away?" he asked.

Gort whined.

"That's what I thought."

With Gort trotting next to him, Henry continued walking, hoping to come up with a plausible explanation by the time he reached the gate.

A half hour later he saw the road. It was about a hundred yards ahead up another hill covered with branches and downed trees.

Gort kept up, acting like they were having a fun romp through the woods.

When Henry reached the top of the hill, he looked as bad as Gort did. He heard a car up on the road and figured it was Robin's truck picking up wood. It wasn't. It was a 1959 red Cadillac with a smashed rear passenger door.

Henry put both hands on the fence and stared up at the car. Gort got on his hind legs and put his cold, muddy paws on his clinched fingers. The Cadillac stopped ten yards from the gate. The driver's door and front passenger door opened simultaneously. It was a long way off, and uphill, but it was clear enough for him to recognize Edgar and Albert stepping out onto the dirt road. Edgar was carrying a pistol. Albert was cradling his sniper rifle. They looked like geriatric gunslingers, wearing bulletproof vests. Henry remembered stuffing the vests into the duffels at the jewelry store.

"What is this place?" Edgar said.

Gort jumped down on all fours and sprinted up to the road.

"What's it to you?" a guard asked, pointing his compound bow at them through the gate.

Edgar didn't answer. He watched Gort run up the embankment to the road.

Albert put his rifle to his shoulder. "Don't compound your stupidity," he said calmly.

There were two other guards at the gate. They too had compound bows with nocked arrows.

"What are you talking about?" the guard said.

Albert smiled with his rifle still on his shoulder. "You just showed up to a gunfight with bows and arrows. That's not very intelligent."

Edgar squatted down, grabbed Gort's rope, and scratched him on the head, "Where you been, boy?" He looked toward the gate and grinned. "I was looking for my dog, and here he is. We were out hunting, and he chewed through his lead." He walked Gort over to the Cadillac and put him into the back seat and slammed the door, then closed the front doors so Gort couldn't get out.

"Never seen a gate up here before," Edgar said. "But I haven't been up here in a while. What kind of community do you have?"

"A closed community," the guard said.

"I can see that. Everything going okay for you?"

"We're fine."

"Must be cold."

"We're fine," the man repeated. "Where'd you get the car?"

"Had it before the juice went out."

"Lucky."

"It was that."

"How about the guns?"

"Had them too."

"Do you have more?"

"A lot more and plenty of ammo."

"Are you interested in trading?"

"I doubt you have anything we want."

Except for Gino, Chester, Rebecca, and you. Oh yeah, and Derek.

"We might have something you want," the guard said. "Why don't you wait here, and I'll get our head guy. I'm sure he'll want to talk to you."

The man following behind Henry caught up to him.

"Wow! Look at that car. What's going on?"

Henry told him to be quiet.

"How about letting us just drive in to see him?" Edgar said.

"No can do," the guard said. "We don't let armed strangers in unless the boss says so."

Edgar shrugged. "No sweat off my back. I'm just happy I found my dog before someone else did and ate him. We're outta here. You have a good day."

Henry watched them get back in the car. It looked like there was another passenger in the back seat, but it was too far away to see clearly. He couldn't believe they were leaving. He wanted to shout out or run up to the gate so they knew he was inside, but he stayed where he was with his mouth closed and watched them back the Cadillac up, do a three-point turn, and head down the road.

"You better start walking," the guy next to him said.

Henry heard another person coming up the hill behind him. A woman he hadn't seen before. He started up the embankment before she caught up to him. When he got to the gate, the guard said, "The guy in front of you is probably a hundred yards ahead. You're supposed to keep the circle tight."

Henry hurried along the road, still wondering why Edgar and Albert had driven away. When he was out of sight of the gate, he started jogging, slowing down when he saw the back of the next person in line. He passed the trail they had used the night before to get down to camp. The wood barn loomed like a giant tombstone below him. The doors were closed. Nobody was standing outside.

The road looped around to the back side of the barn, which was a mirror image of the front side, with a large sliding door and a small entry door next to it. Both were closed. He glanced up at the hay-loft opening. It was open. A woman dressed in camo was sitting on a plastic chair with a shotgun balanced on her camo-clad lap. He continued on without slowing.

He had to find Derek and tell him about the Cadillac. It took him another forty-five minutes to reach the stump. Rebecca wasn't there. Derek was. He got up and joined him.

"Keep walking," he said. "Rebecca is a couple people ahead of you."

"The Cadillac was at the gate," Henry said.

Derek nodded.

"You knew?" Henry asked.

"No, but I knew they would come up here eventually. I left them a rough map in the mailbox. Tell me what happened."

When Henry finished, Derek said, "I bet they were surprised to see Gort."

"I was too. Why did they leave?"

"It's best to back off if you don't know what's ahead. We didn't know about the fence before we got up here. It surprised them as much as it did us. You don't storm a fortified position with three people. That's a good way to get killed, or add three more hostages to Robin's collection. Even if the guard didn't know they were from the WC, he might have tried to take them down for their weapons. They're light on guns and ammo here. How did Albert look?"

Henry was so surprised to see them outside the gate, he hadn't even thought about Albert's health problems. "He actually looked good."

"Just an act, of course, the old goat. It's amazing how a pointed sniper rifle can make you look like you're in the peak of health. Wherever they went, they didn't go far. They've probably pulled off the road somewhere to figure out their next step. I think Robin will call the perimeter walk off soon now that the barn is closed back up. I walked by the place where I slipped under the fence. It's well concealed. They didn't find it and no one else has either. It's just ahead. I'm going to crawl out and see if I can find the Cadillac. I think you and Rebecca should come with me."

Henry shook his head. "As much as I would like to get out of here, I think we should stay. If we don't show up back at the inner circle, they'll get suspicious."

Derek didn't argue. They walked a little farther up and Derek stopped.

"This is it."

Henry looked at the ground around the fence and saw nothing unusual. Derek grinned and rolled a log away from the base of the fence, revealing a three-foot opening.

"When I get through, roll the log back in place. And make sure the guy behind you doesn't see you do it."

He squeezed through the opening on his back to the other side. Henry quickly rolled the log into place. It looked like no one had ever been there.

CHAPTER THIRTY-EIGHT

The round robin was called off half an hour later. Henry found Rebecca at their shelter. He quietly explained what had happened.

"Things are looking up," Rebecca said, smiling. "What's our next move?"

"I'm sure Derek will be back after he finds Edgar and the others."

They changed into their spare set of clothes, then joined the exhausted-looking Patents, who were sitting alone at one of the campfires.

"I told you that fence walk was a crock," Terry said. "One of the looies told me it was because an animal was outside the fence. There are hundreds of animals outside the fence."

"A stray dog, from what I heard," Patty said. "The owner showed up at the gate in an old Cadillac to pick it up."

"What do we do now?" Rebecca asked.

Terry shrugged. "Who knows? They'll think of something. I'm getting hungry again. Must be all that exercise I got this morning."

"I think it's close to noon," Patty said. "They should be coming out with something to eat soon."

As Henry put another piece of wood on the fire, they heard the sound of an engine. A few seconds later an old pickup drove past on the road above camp. The bed was filled with wood. It swung around to the back of the barn and disappeared from sight.

A few minutes later the cabin door opened, and Robin and Sam stepped out. Sam didn't have his pit bull with him. They went into the barn and came back out about twenty minutes later. Robin looked out across the camp for a few seconds, then came striding toward them with Sam at his heels. When he reached the campfire, Robin squatted down and warmed his hands over the coals.

"How was your first night?" he asked, shifting coals with a small stick.

"Okay," Henry said. "Cold."

"The shelter was trashed," Rebecca said. "We took everything out to let it air."

"The previous occupants were slobs," Robin said. "And lazy. That's why we threw them out. How was the perimeter walk?"

"Stupid," Terry said.

Robin shot Terry a sharp look, and Sam squared his stance and clinched his fists like he was going to beat Terry to death with them.

"I'll excuse that," Robin said. "But I have to tell you, Terry, you're pushing it, and one day soon your luck's going to run dry."

Terry met Robin's stare and looked like he was going to say something else.

"I saw that car up by the gate," Henry said, trying to save Terry's life.

Robin turned and grinned. "You did?"

"Yeah. I was walking up the embankment to the gate when it pulled up. I guess they lost their dog or something."

"Or something," Robin said, still grinning. "Did you see anything else interesting?"

Henry shook his head. "Not really."

"Tell you what, Caleb," Robin said. "Why don't you and Rebecca come into the cabin and I'll make you some hot cocoa. It's cold out here."

Robin turned to Sam. "Go back into the barn and check on things. I'll be in the cabin having cocoa with Rebecca and Caleb. Keep your radio on. I'll give you a call when I need you."

CHAPTER THIRTY-NINE

Henry and Rebecca followed Robin through the cabin door. It was warm inside. Robin wiped the dirt off his boots, and they followed suit. He took his vest off, revealing the pistol tucked into his waistband, and hung the vest on a hook.

"Go ahead and hang your coats up. I keep it hot in here."

They hung up their coats and followed him into a small living room. It was cluttered but clean, with two old sofas, three comfortable sitting chairs, a recliner, and a mismatch of different-sized coffee tables with unfinished jigsaw puzzles on them. That was a surprise. Robin did not seem like a puzzle person.

On the far wall was a massive bookcase brimming over with books. Most of the books looked like they were about animals. There were four doors leading off the room, three of them closed. The open door led to a kitchen with a woodstove. On top of the woodstove was a teakettle spurting steam from the spout.

"The water's hot," Robin said. "Let's go into the kitchen."

They followed him in. The kitchen had a sink and a countertop stacked with clean dishes. Above the counter was a long shelf with canned food and jars of flour, rice, sugar, beans, and other nonperishables. Across from the counter was an old wood-burning oven. On the other side of the room was a large, battered rectangular table with six chairs. Beyond the table was an overstuffed chair and ottoman next to a large window with a good view of the barn.

In front of the window was another comfortable-looking sofa.

Henry stared at the sofa in shock.

Robin walked over to the steaming kettle and grabbed the handle with a towel. "This is where I hang out most of the time when I'm in the cabin. I like the light from the window and the view."

Henry was not looking out the window at the view.

"Take a seat. The sofa's comfortable. I usually sit in the chair with my feet up when I get a chance to chill, which isn't very often, as you might imagine."

"I bet," Rebecca said.

"Is that a real tiger skin?" Henry asked, dry-mouthed.

CHAPTER FORTY

"Kind of hard to fake a tiger skin," Robin said, scooping cocoa powder into three mugs. "Don't worry. I didn't shoot it." He poured hot water into the mugs.

"Where did you get it?" Henry asked.

"Found it. Go ahead and sit down. It won't bite."

Henry did not want to sit on the skin, but not sitting on it might give him away. He and Rebecca sat down. She didn't appear to be disturbed by sitting on the pelt of an endangered species.

Robin brought over two mugs and set them on the table in front of them, which also had a half-finished jigsaw puzzle on it. Robin sat down across from them in the overstuffed chair and put his feet on the ottoman.

"Feel the fur," Robin said. "It's amazing."

Henry felt the fur. It was amazing. And revolting. He felt his world, such as it was, spinning out of control. Was this Niki's or Nuri's? If it was, how did Robin get his hands on it?

Robin took a sip of his cocoa and sighed. "Go ahead and drink. We found twenty pounds of it a couple weeks ago."

They sipped their cocoa. It was scalding hot. It warmed Henry all the way down to his stomach, which was churning because of the skin.

Robin drank his cocoa, savoring every sip with a satisfied grin like the Cheshire cat from *Alice in Wonderland*. After a couple minutes he put his mug down on the table next to the chair.

"Let's get down to it," he said, his grin broadening.

"Get down to what?" Rebecca asked suspiciously.

"Nothing in particular," Robin said pleasantly. "I'm just trying to get to know our two new recruits better. Most of the people who have shown up at the Rabbit Hole have been invited. For instance, that car today. It was unusual for someone to come here without an invitation. The road got very little traffic before the power went off. Less now because there are few cars running. It's a dead end. The road to nowhere. Tell me more about the car you saw today."

"Just a car," Henry said. "A couple of old guys in it looking for their dog."

"Armed," Robin said.

"A pistol and a rifle."

"And the guy with the rifle was pointing it at the guards."

Henry nodded. "But the guards were pointing their arrows at him. It didn't seem weird for them to be pointing weapons at each other. Everyone was just being cautious."

"What kind of car was it?"

"I don't know much about cars. Someone said it was a Cadillac. It was red. It had four doors."

"Did you notice anything unusual about the doors?"

Henry shook his head. "They were just car doors. I was a long way off."

"What were you doing?"

"What do you mean?"

"Did you stop when you saw the car?"

Henry acted like he had to think about this for a minute. "I guess I did."

"Why?"

"To catch my breath. It was tough going along that stretch of fence."

"Where did the dog come from?"

"It came out of the woods and ran up the embankment. It was definitely their dog. It looked happy to see them."

"What kind of dog was it?"

"I don't know. Some kind of mutt."

Robin's grin went even broader, which seemed impossible. "Just like you don't know much about cars. Do you know what kismet is?"

Henry shrugged. But he did know what kismet was. He had read about it in one of Derek's books one night. "Some kind of dog?"

"Very funny," Robin said. "Kismet is fate, destiny. The dog was a cattle dog, sometimes called a blue heeler. A lot of people have them downtown. They're loyal, smart, adaptable, protective, and they don't need a lot of food."

"I just arrived downtown, so I wouldn't know."

"I think the dog's name is Gort. Does that ring any bells for you?"

Henry shook his head, wondering if he could get out of the cabin before Robin shot him in the back.

Where would you go if you were lucky enough to get outside? You'd never make it to Derek's burrow, and you'd never find out about the tiger skin.

"Maybe this will help you, *Henry*," Robin said. "Klaatu barada nikto."

Busted.

Henry said nothing. He was too stunned. How had Robin figured it out? When had he figured it out? Where did Robin get the tiger skin? Was it Niki's or Nuri's?

Robin took a satisfied slurp of his cocoa and set the mug back down.

"You are Henry Carter," he said. "The son of Tom Carter, former zoo director, and Marie Carter, formerly Marie Ludd, head of the Wonderland Compound."

There seemed little point in denying it. "How did you know?" Henry asked quietly.

"Kismet." Robin pointed at the jigsaw puzzle. "Random pieces of fate. The power going off when I took the Wild Bunch to the zoo. You and your uncle showing up at Gunderson's when I was across the street. Hearing Gort's name and seeing the red Cadillac outside Gunderson's. Gary telling me about Edgar and Albert fixing the tractor at the zoo and Chester and Gino dropping supplies off from time to time. Random pieces, but all part of the same puzzle, and there are more." He pulled his sleeve up and looked at his watch, as if he were checking the time, but he wasn't. He was showing Henry another piece of the puzzle. It was a stainless steel Rolex Submariner in pristine condition.

That's not all he has.

Henry knew that he had more. A lot more.

Robin got up from the chair. "Come with me."

"Where?" Rebecca said.

Robin laughed. "Just into the other room. Don't worry. You're both puzzle pieces. You're safe . . . for now."

As they left the kitchen, Henry slipped a puzzle piece off the table and put it in his pocket. Every jigsaw puzzle they had at the farm had missing pieces. It irritated Henry to no end. He hoped it would irritate Robin.

CHAPTER FORTY-ONE

Robin unlocked one of the two doors leading off the living room.

"After you," he said, waving Henry and Rebecca into a dark, windowless room. He followed behind them with a lantern.

The room was small, maybe ten by ten feet. Robin hung the lantern from a hook in the low ceiling.

"This is our strategic planning room," Robin said proudly. "Go ahead and look around."

The walls were covered in sketches, hand-drawn maps with black-and-white photographs of the wind turbine, Stan and neighbors working on the wall, the three Ludd houses, the barn, the outbuildings, the yurt, the Cadillac, the flatbed, and the semi coming and going through the gate. There were blurry, but recognizable, photographs of Edgar, Albert, and several other uncles and aunts around the barn and out and about doing chores. There were two close-ups of Gino and Chester with battered faces that looked like mug shots. There was a photo of Henry riding his bike up the driveway to do his rounds, but it had been taken from behind and you couldn't see his face. There was a relatively clear photo of his mother standing on the deck. Henry stared at it, trying to figure out where it had been taken and how long ago. It was raining. She was wearing a heavy coat with the hood up. It had to have been taken from the lower field, not far from the deck where the fifth wheels were parked. Was the photographer inside a fifth wheel?

"Your mom," Robin said. "We're kind of proud of that one."

"It's not my mom," Henry said.

"According to Gary Dulabaum, it is your mom."

Rebecca stared at the photos of Chester and Gino.

"Why have you been watching the WC?" Henry asked.

"That's obvious, isn't it?"

"How long have you been watching it?"

"A couple months. More intensely the last few weeks as the wall was being completed. I wanted it finished before I made my move."

Free labor. It will protect the Wild Bunch as much as it will protect you. And I bet they didn't have the engineering skills to put it up.

"We thought we'd stay here," Robin continued. "Especially after we got the fence up. But after one uncomfortable night here, you've probably figured out that it isn't ideal."

"Why didn't you move into the zoo?" Henry asked.

"We probably should have," Robin admitted. "But by the time I thought of it, we'd already taken the fence down. Too much hassle to put it back up. We looked some other compounds over, but of course, none of them had a steady supply of electricity. I'm showing you all this because I want you to see that I have all the pieces. Let's go into the other room to talk this thing out."

Robin told them to sit down on the sofa, then took the two-way from his belt.

"Get Janet," he said. "I have a job for her."

"Roger."

Henry thought desperately about what he could do to get out of this. Robin was holding all the pieces. He and Rebecca getting into the Rabbit Hole had made a bad situation worse, not better.

Robin walked over to the bookcase and picked up a camera. It looked like the same kind of camera Ruth had used to snap pictures of the corpses in the lower field.

"Smile," he said.

They didn't.

Robin snapped several photos of them. There was a knock on the door.

"Yeah," Robin said.

Janet, the girl who had shown them into camp, walked in. "Sam said you have something for me to do," she said.

Robin gave her the camera. "Develop these."

Janet looked at the camera and said, "There's a lot more film left."

"Just do it!" Robin said.

"Sure thing, Robin," she said, and walked through a door without a glance at Henry and Rebecca. She closed the door behind her. *Darkroom.*

Robin sat in the chair across from Henry and Rebecca and gave them another broad grin. He pulled Henry's pocket journal out of his vest. Sam came into the cabin with his pit bull and stood next to Robin, who was slapping the notebook on his knee.

"One of the wood gatherers found your watch and the notebook under a rock near the edge of the road. Luckily, one of my lieutenants saw him pick your stash up before he tried to pocket it." He nodded to Sam. "You know what to do."

Sam pulled his pistol out.

The smile left Robin's face. "The fun and games are over, Henry. I'm going to ask you several questions. If I think you're lying, Sam will shoot your girlfriend."

"She's not my girlfriend," Henry said.

"I don't really care," Robin said. "I don't know how she got mixed up with this, but I'll have Sam shoot her anyway. Or maybe I'll have him sic his dog on her. Have you ever seen a pit bull rip into a human? No? Well, it's not pretty. Rebecca is what we call collateral damage." He looked at Rebecca. "Wrong place, wrong time."

"Don't tell him anything, Henry," Rebecca said.

"Go ahead and ask," Henry said quietly.

Robin smiled. "This notebook is pretty interesting. You're kind of a strange kid. Do you really have a ghost in your head?"

"Sometimes."

"Caroline? That must be weird."

Not as weird as you are, you freakin' wacko.

Rebecca gave Henry a surprised look as Robin continued.

"You see, my questions aren't so bad. I don't want to hurt anyone, not you, not Rebecca, not your uncles, not any of the Ludds. I just want your farm. I don't want the valley. Your neighbors will be perfectly safe where they are, but the Ludds will have to move away. It's not personal. I need the farm. It's as simple as that. Like I told you, I have all the pieces. Your mom would see that if she was sitting where you are. It was just a matter of time, like putting together a puzzle. How many guns do you have on the farm?"

"I don't know. A lot."

"How many more Ludds are going to come after us?"

Henry shrugged. "I don't know. There are a lot of Ludds."

"How did you know that we took your uncles?"

Henry was ready for this one. "Gary Dulabaum told me."

"I think that's a lie, which is unfortunate for Rebecca."

"I guess he didn't know it, but that's what he thought. I found the empty vial of ketamine in the administration building and pieced it together."

"Where did you get the map?"

"From Rebecca, just like she told you."

Robin scowled, but he recovered quickly, and the grin returned.

"What's your relationship with Rebecca?"

Henry glanced at Rebecca. She was staring straight ahead, almost as if she were in a trance.

"She's my half sister," Henry said.

CHAPTER FORTY-TWO

"We agreed that we weren't going to tell him!" Rebecca snapped angrily, finally joining the conversation.

Henry was surprised and greatly relieved. It was the reaction he'd hoped for but didn't expect.

"He would have found out anyway," he said.

"But we agreed," Rebecca said petulantly. "We should have talked about it."

"When?" Henry said defensively.

"Enough!" Robin said. "Explain!"

"Rebecca is my mom's daughter from another marriage," Henry said. It was the only way to protect her from Sam and his dog. He didn't think Robin would hurt a Ludd. If he could convince Robin, Rebecca would no longer be collateral damage. "She's—"

"Shut up!" Robin said, glaring at Rebecca. "You explain."

"It's true," Rebecca said resignedly. "I moved away from the farm a couple of years ago to live with my grandfather downtown. I hated the farm and the Ludds. They're crazy."

"Where's your father?"

"I don't know. He left when I was a baby. He might be dead for all I know."

"Your mother let you leave the farm and live with your grandfather?" Robin asked skeptically.

"How could she stop me, short of tying me up? At least she knew where I was."

"What about after the power went off?"

"She wanted me to go back to the farm, but my grandfather didn't want to leave his shop. In fact, she was trying to convince us to leave when Uncle Edgar and Henry were at the jewelry store. They swung by and picked her up on their way back to the farm."

"She hasn't checked on you since then?"

Rebecca shook her head. "She doesn't leave the farm."

Henry was amazed at Rebecca's ability to lie on the fly. He hadn't taken the story much past the lie that Rebecca was his half sister.

"So, Henry happened to stop by and told you that Gino and Chester had been taken to the Rabbit Hole, and you happened to have a map, which you happened to have found on the ground at Bull Run?"

"Kismet," Rebecca said.

She's good.

Henry couldn't have agreed more.

"What did you hope to accomplish by getting in here?"

"What else?" Rebecca said. "We wanted to find out if you had abducted Chester and Gino."

"So, there wasn't a riot in downtown last night?"

"There was," Henry said. "The cow herd was slaughtered, and people went crazy. It took us forever to walk around it and get up here."

"Why didn't you just go to the WC and tell them where you thought they had been taken?"

"I wish we had," Henry said. "And I wanted to, but Rebecca wanted to come up here first." He gave her a disgusted look, which she shrugged off.

"What about your uncles showing up at the gate? How'd they know to come up here?"

"Gary must have told them," Henry said. "They knew the zoo was one of our stops."

Robin regarded them for a long time, then said, "It's time for a family reunion."

CHAPTER FORTY-THREE

They followed Sam and his dog across the clearing, with Robin trailing them. Henry felt like he was being walked to his death.

More likely Rebecca's death.

You're right, Henry thought bitterly. *Gino and Chester will have no idea who she is. She'll be shot, or torn apart by a pit bull.*

I wouldn't be so sure. Robin wants to believe that Rebecca is your half sister as badly as you want him to. Another piece for his twisted jigsaw.

Sam opened the door and waved them into the dim, cavernous barn. It smelled of woodsmoke, kerosene, fried food, and the latrine in back of the clearing. The semi truck had been backed in and took up half the space, and barely cleared the ceiling. The trailer was closed. In front of it was thirty or forty feet of living space, with a couple of chairs and an old sofa covered with a second tiger skin.

Three camo-clad looies were sitting at a table playing cards. Henry and Rebecca hadn't seen them before. They put their cards down.

"This is Heather, Bill, and Carol," Robin said. "This is Henry Carter, also known as Caleb Brown. This is Rebecca O'Toole, who claims to be Henry's half sister."

"I've seen her at Bull Run," Heather said. "Do you believe her?"

Robin shook his head. "Where is everyone?"

"Up in the loft," Bill said. "You want me to get them?"

"No," Robin said. "How are Gino and Chester doing?"

"Still incoherent, like they were this morning when we took them outside," Carol said. "They've been sleeping since we brought them back."

Robin nodded. "It's the drugs."

Henry didn't think so. The effects of ketamine wore off quickly, which was one of the reasons it was used to tranquilize animals at the zoo. He heard footsteps above and looked up. The fifteen-foot ceiling was supported by massive wooden beams. He saw the outline of a couple of trapdoors, no doubt used to drop hay from the loft when the barn was used for animals. Now that his eyes had adjusted to the dim light inside, he could see that stalls ran the length of the barn on the right side where the looies were hanging out. The stall doors and walls had been removed and repurposed into sleeping areas, with cots and dressers and a place to hang up clothes. The stall next to where they were standing had been converted into a makeshift kitchen with a sink, shelves, and a woodstove. In front of it were steep stairs leading up to the loft.

The stalls on the left side were boarded up with newer-looking wood all the way to the ceiling. One of them was locked.

Robin reached into his pocket, pulled out a ring of keys, then pointed at the sofa. "You two sit down."

Henry and Rebecca stepped over to the sofa and sat down on the second tiger skin. *Niki's or Nuri's?* Henry asked himself. Robin picked up a lantern and walked over to the locked stall.

"They're not zombies," Henry whispered. "They're faking."

"I've got this," Rebecca whispered back, watching Robin unlock the door.

Henry had no idea what she was going to do.

Hard to say. She's smart. She's fighting for her life, as well as her grand-father's life. If she goes, so does he.

CHAPTER FORTY-FOUR

Robin opened the locked stall and walked inside. Henry couldn't see past the door, only the dim glow of the light on the wooden walls. Robin was inside longer than he expected. Were Chester and Gino sleeping, or feigning sleep? Was he questioning them about their niece Rebecca O'Toole? When he walked out with them, would he already know the truth? Everyone was looking at the open door, waiting.

Chester came out first, followed by Gino. Their eyes were glassed over. Expressionless. Zombies. The walking dead. Rebecca sprang off the sofa before anyone could stop her and rushed over to them, threw her arms around their necks and drew them near, sobbing, then whispered something to them Henry couldn't hear.

Robin stepped forward and yanked her away. Sam stepped over to help him. Henry jumped up from the sofa and tried to defend her. Sam threw him and Rebecca to the ground. Chester and Gino snapped out of their stupor and attacked Sam. The other looies joined the fray. Robin pulled his pistol and fired it into the ceiling. The pit bull ran under the truck and hid. There was a muffled scream above and a thud.

Robin cursed.

Everyone stared at the ceiling.

Think this is what Rebecca had in mind?

No, Henry thought.

He and Rebecca got to their feet.

"Go upstairs and see who got hit!" Robin shouted.

Sam and the others pounded up the staircase.

Robin pointed his pistol at Chester and Gino. "I ought to shoot both of you."

"Why?" Chester asked.

"Attacking my lieutenant, wounding another one upstairs."

"You pulled the trigger."

"What did you expect when you attacked our niece?" Chester said.

"So, this is your niece," Robin said skeptically.

"Yeah," Gino said. "Becky O'Toole."

"You know I don't like to be called Becky," Rebecca said.

"Old habits die hard," Chester said.

"You didn't mind it when you were a kid," Gino said. "What the hell are you doing here? Did they snatch you?"

"We came up here looking for you," Henry said.

"What were you thinking?" Chester asked. "You should have hightailed it to the farm and told—"

"Shut up!" Robin shouted. "Rebecca is not your niece. Do you think I'm stupid?"

No one answered.

Robin is a lot of things, but stupid isn't one of them.

"You two seem to have made a remarkable recovery," Robin continued.

They didn't answer. Robin pointed his pistol at Rebecca.

"Not smart to shoot one of your hostages," Gino said.

Robin cocked the trigger. "I have plenty of hostages. More than you know."

"We know you're trying to take over the Wonderland Compound," Chester said.

"Whatever negotiation you're planning isn't going to go over well if you shoot Becky," Gino added.

"How do you know I'm trying to take over the WC?"

"It's not like the stalls are soundproof," Chester said. "Your people talk a lot when you're not around."

Robin looked up toward the hayloft, where his guards were now examining whoever had been injured. Henry knew it would be bad for whoever was discovered being too chatty in the barn.

"I'll tell you something else we heard," Gino said. "That a red Cadillac showed up at your gate today. That's bad news for you."

Robin grinned. "It will be worse news for you if they try anything."

"You're dreaming if you think they're going to give up the farm without a fight," Chester said.

"We have you and Henry. Marie Ludd won't sacrifice you for the farm."

"I wouldn't bet on it," Gino said. "It's not just the farm she'll be worried about. It's the entire valley and the people who live there. Marie's good at making hard decisions. It's the reason we've been so successful. You think she's going to toss all of the Ludds and our neighbors out on the street because you have us?"

"I don't want the valley," Robin said. "I just want the farm."

Chester shook his head. "There's no difference between the farm and the valley now. It's one community. You're talking about a couple hundred well-armed people. All I've seen here are bows and arrows and the pistols and shotgun you took from me and

Gino. You kill us, it's war. The Ludds know where you are. They'll slaughter you. You've heard the rumors."

Robin's confidence appeared to falter a little.

"You'd have to leave here," Gino said. "Not that this is much of a place, from what I've seen. You'd have to split up. Probably have to move out of the state, maybe even outta the country."

"We have a ton of coin," Chester added. "How many people do you think the Ludds could hire to track you down?"

"People would track you down for free if the WC invited them to live there," Rebecca chimed in.

"I don't believe the rumors," Robin said. "You forget that I've had people watching the WC for months and reporting back to me. They've seen only a handful of people carrying weapons. Most of the Ludds carry rakes and shovels and push wheelbarrows around. That goes for your neighbors as well." He looked at Henry. "If your mom doesn't trade, I'll kill all of you one at a time and dump you outside her gate until she changes her mind."

Sam came clumping down the stairs.

"Bad news," he said. "You hit Julie in the leg. Femoral artery. She's bleeding out. We can't stop it. Wrong place at the wrong time."

Collateral damage.

Robin didn't look that upset about Julie, nor did Sam.

"Is the girl a Ludd?" Sam asked.

Robin shook his head. "The Ludds are liars. We were just discussing hostages. Chester and Gino don't think that Marie will give up the farm for them or Henry. They say that there are a couple hundred well-armed people there who will slaughter us if we kill them."

"They can try," Sam said.

Henry remembered his mother saying the exact same thing when he told her someone might try to take the farm.

"Looks like you're missing some of the pieces to your puzzle," Henry said, fingering the piece in his pocket.

"You think so?" Robin asked, smirking.

The other looies came down the stairs. They walked over to Robin and Sam. A couple of them had obviously been crying.

"Julie's dead," one of them said.

Robin bowed his head. "I'm sorry to hear that. She was with me from the beginning." He looked up. "Bring her down, put her in the pickup. We'll bury her outside the fence. No point in upsetting the others. If someone asks about the gunshot, we'll tell them it was an accidental discharge." He looked at Sam. "Lock them up and stay inside until I get back."

CHAPTER FORTY-FIVE

The stall was ten by ten, with two single mattresses on the floor and two against the walls, with a flickering candle between them for light. There was a five-gallon bucket in the corner for a toilet, which accounted for the smell Henry had found so noxious when he first stepped into the barn. Gino and Chester sat down on one of the mattresses. Henry and Rebecca sat on the mattress across from them.

"What happened at the zoo?" Henry asked quietly.

"Unloaded the truck and got darted," Chester answered.

"Took a while for the drugs to take effect," Gino added, starting their back-and-forth dialog.

"We would have shot them, but we didn't see anyone."

"Must have been in the administration building."

"Got wobbly."

"Next thing we know, we're locked in this stink hole."

"Played possum, but we listened at the door the whole time."

"Took us outside yesterday. We would have made a break for it, but we didn't know where we were."

"Wouldn't have gotten very far."

"Heard about Edgar's Caddy and Gort, figured you were with them. Didn't know you were inside."

"Guess they're going to try to exchange us, and now you, for the farm."

"You shouldn't have come up here. I'm not sure your mom would have done the exchange for me and Chester, but I think she'd do it for you."

"In a heartbeat."

Henry shuddered, remembering what Robin had said: "If your mom doesn't trade, I'll kill all of you one at a time and dump you outside her gate until she changes her mind."

The guy's a psychopath. He just shot Julie, one of his originals, and barely blinked. Your uncles will be the first to die.

Henry told them what had happened since they had been abducted at the zoo. When he finished, Chester looked at Rebecca. "As far as I'm concerned, you and your grandfather are in if you want to come to the WC."

"If we make it out of here alive," Gino said.

Henry was surprised that they didn't appear to be upset. They had been tranquilized and kidnapped and they were acting like it was no big deal.

Maybe you were wrong about the drugs wearing off.

Henry didn't think so. "Are there any other prisoners here?" he asked.

"Not that we've seen," Chester said.

"Or heard about," Gino added. "Robin's people are talkative."

"As soon as Robin leaves the barn."

Gino nodded. "As soon as he or Sam comes in, they clam up. When they're gone, it's a talkfest."

"Did they feed you?" Rebecca asked.

"A few scraps of meat," Chester said.

"Our meat," Gino said. "Overcooked."

"What do we do?" Henry asked.

"We've been looking for an opening," Gino said. "So far, we haven't seen one."

"They'll make a mistake eventually."

"Until then, we wait," Chester said. "There's nothing else we can do."

They lapsed into silence.

Rebecca and Henry were exhausted after their rough night in back of the shelter and the fence walk.

"If you're cold, you can use our blankets," Gino offered.

They both shook their heads.

"It's going to take a while for them to get back," Chester said. "Ground's frozen."

Unless they just dump Julie in the woods.

"We were up most of the night listening. Hoping to hear something useful."

"Didn't."

"Fell asleep just before they brought you in."

"Barely."

"Might as well try to get some shut-eye. Need to be alert for whatever comes our way."

Chester and Gino wrapped the blankets around their shoulders, stretched their legs out in front of them, and were asleep within minutes.

"I'm frightened," Rebecca said.

"I am too," Henry said.

But there was something else he felt. Something had happened to him when he left the farm. It was as if he had woken from a long sleep and stepped out of a dream back into reality. He wished it hadn't happened, but he was glad it did. In some ways he felt more relaxed than he had at the farm. Freer, maybe, emboldened.

As horrible as reality is, at least it's real.

Henry took Rebecca's cold hand. "Sorry I got you into this."

She squeezed his hand. "My dad used to say, 'Life is messy, and wonderful, but mostly messy.'" Rebecca looked at him. "Do you really hear a ghost in your head? Is that why you talk to yourself sometimes?"

Better think quick here. You don't want to say the wrong thing.

"Yes. Her name is Caroline, and she died when the switch happened. You would like her, she's tough and smart."

Rebecca smiled. "She sounds all right to me. On the bright side," she continued, "we ruined two of Robin's jigsaws."

"Two? I only took a piece of the one in the kitchen."

"I saw you take it and was inspired. I took a piece from the big puzzle in the living room."

Great minds think alike.

An hour later they heard the barn door open and slam closed. People began shouting.

CHAPTER FORTY-SIX

Gino and Chester jumped up from the mattress, threw their blankets off, and hurried over to the door to listen. Henry and Rebecca joined them.

"What's going on?" Rebecca asked.

"Shh!" Chester and Gino hissed simultaneously.

Henry heard the voices but couldn't distinguish what was being said. After a while the voices quieted down. Chester turned to them.

"Robin's back in the barn. I couldn't hear everything, but from what I gather, Edgar and the others have crashed the gate and are in the Rabbit Hole. They put a couple of shots into the pickup as it headed down the road, and Robin's guards put a couple of arrows into the Caddy."

"Edgar's not going to be happy about that," Henry said.

"I bet he's not happy about smashing the Caddy through the fence either. The only reason Robin and the looies got away was Edgar had to stop to untangle his car from the chain link."

Gino joined the conversation. "I guess Robin has decided to hole up in here and fight them off."

"Or negotiate," Chester added.

Henry doubted that was going to work, having witnessed Albert and Derek's negotiation techniques at the jewelry store.

The stall door swung open. Robin motioned them out with

his pistol. He held a two-way in his other hand. Two looies stood behind him, armed with bows.

Sam's voice came over the radio. "We're ready up here."

Robin keyed the mic. "We'll be up in a minute. Switch channels. Stand by." He looked at the looies. "You two stay down here. Cover the front and back doors. I doubt they're going to bust in with the hostages in here, but stay alert."

"What's going on?" Chester asked.

Robin smiled. "Showtime. Single file up to the loft."

Henry went up the steps first, followed by Rebecca, Chester, Gino, and Robin. Sam and his dog were waiting at the top of the stairs. The loft door at the back of the barn was closed. The door at the front was wide open. Between the two doors was another living area with a potbellied stove surrounded by cots, sofas, and chairs. Several looies were scattered around, holding their bows. All of them were standing well away from the open door.

"Tie them to the posts," Robin said.

The looies grabbed Rebecca, Gino, and Chester, tying them to posts with their hands behind their backs.

"What about me?" Henry asked.

"You're first up," Robin said.

"First up for what?"

"Your relatives showing up here have changed my plans," Robin said. "But don't worry. The results will be the same. I still have all the pieces."

Henry had noticed a change in Robin since he had locked them in the stall. He was nervous and jumpy, like a coiled spring. This in turn made Henry nervous. He tried to shake it off and keep his wits about him, looking for an opening. If he didn't find an opening, this was going to get worse.

Much worse. Robin has extra pieces. He won't hesitate to eliminate them if he has to.

Robin looked at Sam. "Right channel?"

"Yeah, I've been listening to their chatter. I haven't looked, but I think they're spread out. Watch yourself." Sam handed the radio to Henry and headed back downstairs.

"What's this for?"

"I'll let you know." Robin grabbed Henry by the back of his collar and pushed him toward the light.

CHAPTER FORTY-SEVEN

It was late in the day, but the light shining through the loft was bright. Henry shaded his eyes, happy his hands weren't tied behind his back. Ten feet from the opening, Robin stopped him.

"This is how it's going to work." Robin pushed the barrel of his pistol against Henry's temple and cocked the hammer. "You're going to work the radio. If you say the wrong thing, I'll blow your brains out. If your uncles make a wrong move, I'll blow your brains out. Got it?"

Henry nodded.

Still holding his collar and the gun to Henry's head, Robin pushed him to the brink of the opening, using him as a human shield. The Cadillac was parked below with the top up, torn in a few places. The front bumper and grille were smashed, and the sides and hood were scratched. They must have driven it along the side of the barn to reach the inner circle. Henry looked beyond the car to the clearing. The fires were smoking, but no one was there. He had a good view of the shelters and tents. The flaps were all open and they seemed to have been abandoned. The forest surrounding the clearing was quiet except for a slight breeze ruffling the branches. There was no sign of Derek, Edgar, or Albert.

"Tell them where we are," Robin said over his shoulder.

Henry was certain Derek, Edgar, and Albert knew exactly where they were, but he raised the radio and keyed the mic. "We're in the loft overlooking the clearing."

"*We see you,*" Derek said.

Henry had no idea where he was hiding.

"*Where are the others?*"

"In the loft behind me, tied up."

"*Is Sam with them?*"

"He's downstairs."

"Who's talking?" Robin asked.

"Derek."

"Who the hell is he?"

"You might know him as T-Rex."

"The guy across the street from the jewelry store?"

"Albert Gunderson's nephew."

Robin swore.

Apparently, Robin doesn't know about all the jigsaw pieces you have.

Robin let go of his collar but kept the gun to his head. "Give me the radio."

Henry handed it to him.

Robin keyed the mic. "Okay, this is what I want you to do . . ." he began, but he was interrupted by someone getting out of the back seat of the Cadillac.

It was Henry's mother.

She looked up at him from behind the car. "You okay?"

"I'm fine." Henry was so shocked to see her, he was barely able to get the words out.

"What about Chester and Gino?"

"They're okay."

She was wearing a baseball cap, a down vest, jeans, and hiking boots. She was clutching a two-way radio in her right hand.

"You must be Robin," she said. "Take the gun away from my son's head."

Robin clipped the radio to his belt and grabbed Henry's shirt collar. He did not move the pistol.

"Hello, Marie," Robin said.

Henry couldn't see Robin, but he could feel his warm breath on his neck.

He probably has that stupid grin on his face.

"I'm sure Albert is trying to get me in his crosshairs," Robin said. "But attempting to shoot me would be a mistake. It's a tight shot. He might hit Henry. If he misses, I'll kill Henry. When Sam hears the shot, my people will kill Gino, Chester, and the girl. No hostage rescue, if that's what you have in mind. They'll all be dead."

Edgar came on the radio. *"So will you and your people,"* he said. *"I'll burn the barn down with you inside."*

Edgar had to be close to have heard the conversation. Henry wondered if he was standing around the corner of the barn.

"Which one was that?" Robin asked.

"Edgar," Henry said, feeling strangely calm, wondering if this was what you felt before you died.

"Listen to me," Robin said, ignoring Edgar's threat. "I want the four of you to get into your car and drive back to the WC. By noon tomorrow I want you and all the other Ludds out of there. Leave everything else intact, including the wind turbine, vehicles, weapons, ammunition, gems, and gold. You will leave the farm with nothing more than what you can carry on your backs. I fully expect you to cheat, but if you cheat within reason, I'll let it go. I realize that you'll have to take things with you to establish yourselves somewhere else. My intention is not to harm you or the hostages, but to take over your farm."

"What if we don't cheat within reason?" Marie asked.

"Then I'll keep the hostages until you've made it right."

"What about the other people in the valley?"

"I'm not interested in them. I only want the farm and the wind turbine. I would have never enclosed the valley like you did. That was a waste of time and effort. I would have just enclosed your farm. Your neighbors are free to do whatever they want."

"I don't trust you."

"I'm sure you don't, but we have more in common than you think."

"Like what?"

"We're both trying to protect our people the best way we can."

"By kidnapping?"

"It's better than taking over your farm by force."

"In your dreams," Edgar said.

"Why don't you step out into the open where I can see you?"

Edgar came out from the side of the barn, carrying a pistol, and stood next to Marie. He looked up at Henry and smiled. "You okay?"

"I am," Henry said, almost returning the smile.

"Where are the others?" Robin asked.

"You were right about the crosshairs," Edgar said. "You're a trigger pull from death."

Robin gripped Henry's collar tighter and shifted.

"Just give it up," Marie said.

"I know what happened to Tom," Robin said.

CHAPTER FORTY-EIGHT

"He has a tiger skin in his cabin!" Henry shouted, hoping they didn't shoot Robin before he had a chance to explain and hoping he didn't get shot before he learned the truth.

"We found Tom in the Arboretum," Robin said. "He'd been mauled. There were two dead tigers and a keeper lying next to him. At the time I didn't know what had happened, but it looked like he had shot the tigers trying to save the keeper, or maybe he was trying to save himself. The rifle sitting next to him was empty."

The Arboretum was above the zoo. They hadn't driven through it on their way downtown that day. Henry wondered if his father's bones were still up there, or if Bathsheba and other animals had gnawed them to dust. He stared down at Edgar and his mom. They looked as horrified as he felt.

"Our old pickup still worked," Robin continued. "Sam, one of my lieutenants, is an ex-hunter and taxidermist. It seemed a shame to leave the pelts up there to rot, so he skinned the tigers, and we brought the pelts up here and tanned them. Every time I see the skins, I think of those poor captive animals."

Which hasn't stopped him from eating captive elk venison.

"Niki's in the cabin," Robin said. "Nuri's in the barn. I've kept them alive in a way." He released Henry's collar and unclipped the radio. "Bring him out."

Henry thought about jumping through the opening so Albert

or Derek would have a clear shot. He might break something, or he might die, but getting rid of Robin was the only way to end this. He leaned out the opening, but Robin grabbed his collar and yanked him back before he could jump.

"Careful," Robin said. "You might have hit him."

Henry struggled to get away. "What are you talking about? Hit who? You're crazy. I don't care if you shoot me or . . ."

The door below them opened. Sam pushed a wheelchair through.

His mother gasped. "Tom!"

Edgar started around the Cadillac.

"Everyone, freeze!" Robin shouted.

Henry looked down on his father. His hair had grown out in a tangled mess. He was very thin. He had a thick beard. He wouldn't have recognized him if his mother hadn't called his name. Sam was crouched behind the wheelchair for cover, with a gun to his father's head.

The last piece.

"Still want to burn the barn down?" Robin asked gleefully. "I saved your husband, Marie. He would have died if it hadn't been for me. And he still might if you don't do what I say, along with your son and your brothers. This negotiation is over."

A leap of faith. Take him down, Bucko.

Henry leapt through the opening, pulling Robin with him.

A shot rang out, then another. Henry crashed through the soft top on his back. There was the crunch of something hitting metal. His mother ripped the rear door open. Henry lay sprawled on the back seat. He couldn't breathe. Gort was looking down on him from the front seat, barking. Henry wanted to tell both of them that he was okay, but it was impossible without air. Another shot rang out, muffled, farther away. The breath finally came with a deep chest heave.

"Is anything broken?" his mother asked.

Henry shook his head, although he wasn't certain.

"Dad?" he croaked.

"I'll check. Stay here."

She rushed away.

Henry had no intention of staying in the car. He grabbed the front seat and sat up slowly, trying to wrap his mind around what had just happened. Gort licked his hand. He was sore, but nothing felt broken.

"Take him down, Bucko?"

It was a thing of beauty!

Caroline laughed.

CHAPTER FORTY-NINE

Henry pulled himself out of the back seat and stood unsteadily, bracing himself on the side of the car. Robin lay on the ground on his back five feet away, staring at the darkening sky through sightless eyes. Henry was reminded of the crash the day of the switch. The Cadillac's trunk was crushed. Robin must have bounced off it.

He couldn't see his father because his mother was in front of the wheelchair holding him, weeping.

"He's fine, considering."

The familiar voice came from above. Edgar was standing in the loft, pistol in hand.

"You'll get your turn if your mom doesn't squeeze him to death. You okay?"

Henry nodded, stunned by what had just happened.

"You ruined my soft top."

Henry smiled. "Sorry. What happened?"

"The barn's clear. Albert shot the giant behind the wheelchair. Derek took out another guy up here. The others ran away. Look." Edgar pointed.

The camo-clad looies were running down the road, with Sam's dog leading the way. Sam was lying dead in the open doorway behind the wheelchair.

Henry ran over to his dad.

CHAPTER FIFTY

October 5

It's my birthday. I'm in the treehouse.
I have a day off, more or less.

Gort is lying at my feet, snoring.
Rebecca and her grandfather, the Patents,
Gary Dulabaum, and Sprint are in the Olofs'
house, where they all live now. (Gary has
changed his mind about having roommates.)
I split my time between the treehouse, the
Olofs', and Derek's yurt. Derek is downtown on the *Osprey*, listening to rumors
and spreading a few of his own about the
terrible Ludds.

Six houses have power now, including
the Olofs' and the treehouse, not that I
use much power up here. Edgar thinks we'll
have thirty houses powered up by spring.

The harvest was good this summer,
but below expectations, so food is still
scarce. Chester and Gino come back to the
compound with less and less food every
day. We've been canning and preserving

for months like panicked squirrels pre-
paring for winter.

There is some good news, or at least
hopeful news. We aren't the only wind
turbine pumping out power. A few more
have been erected outside the WC. They
were disassembled in eastern Oregon and
hauled over Mount Hood. Edgar and Steve
helped get the turbines up and running.

There are more cars and trucks on the
road. Mechanics have figured a way to
get vehicles running, but the special-
ized parts are hard to come by and very
expensive. And then there is fuel, which
is as scarce as food, but Edgar, Albert,
and Terry Patent, who was a chemistry
professor before he retired, are working
on a solution.

The military showed up in March and
declared marshal law and curfews, which
everyone ignored because it was impossible to enforce. A few local police are
back on the job too, but they aren't
being paid. Most people believe the offi-
cers are working because they are given
cars and fuel for their patrols, which
makes scrounging easier for them. I guess
that's a form of payment. They stop by

here several times a week to make sure we're okay. Stan says they're not patrolling, but "trolling" because Mom always gives them a little something before they leave.

After the wall was complete, Stan didn't know what to do with himself and Mom didn't know what to do with him. She tried to talk him into taking charge of perimeter security, but he would have none of that. "I'm an engineer, not a security guard," he told her. So, she sent him to eastern Oregon. She wanted him to pay particular attention to the dams on the Columbia River and find out what had to be done to get them working. Before the switch, most of the power for western Oregon came from the hydroelectric dams. He drives Robin's pickup, which we took when we left the Rabbit Hole. Gino and Chester found a camper for it. Stan comes back to the farm most weekends. He claims he's making progress, but it could be years before the dams are churning out power again.

Rebecca and her grandfather have fit in so well, it's as if they've always been here. It took a little convincing to get her grandfather to leave the shop, but he soon forgot that he had ever had a shop. During the day he wanders around the valley with his binoculars and notebook, bird-watching. At night he peers into his microscope, watching microorganisms.

Rebecca spends her days with Mom and my aunts, organizing, planning, and canning. She's more useful than I am. She hasn't left the WC since she arrived.

The Patents haven't left either. Terry spends most of his time in the barn with Edgar and Albert. Patty spends her time fixing up the Olofs' house and has almost brought it back to its former splendor after Gary captured and set free the raccoons.

Gary is still taking care of the zoo animals, but they are no longer at the zoo. They have been moved or set free. Many of them are in the compound. When I got here this morning, the mandrill baboons were peeking through the treehouse window at me. I think they were looking for Gary because he supplements what they can't find in the woods with monkey biscuits, which he bakes in the Olofs' oven.

Sprint has taken over my message duties, joyfully peddling up and down the valley filling people in on what's happening in the WC.

When we got back from the Rabbit Hole, Mom stepped down from running the WC, handing over most of her responsibilities to my aunts and uncles so she could take care of Dad.

He was malnourished and his right leg and arm were useless. He doesn't have a clear memory of what happened in the Arboretum the day after the switch. He remembers Niki coming out of the woods from nowhere and attacking Mike Keele, the animal keeper foreman. He remembers shooting her and rushing up to Mike to see if he was still alive. After that, he remembers nothing.

"It's a blank," he told us. "Nuri must have grabbed me from behind. I had deep claw rakes on my back and legs. Somehow, I must have kept ahold of the rifle and shot him, or maybe it was an accidental discharge when he hit me. I don't know. The first thing I remember is waking up in a dark stall lying on a mattress, feverish, in excruciating pain. People came in from time to time, but they were more like faceless shadows than humans. In my delirium I couldn't understand what they were saying or why they were torturing me. After weeks of this I realized they were cleaning and treating my wounds. My fever abated and I started to have periods of lucidity. I could talk to them, although they rarely answered any of my questions. When I managed to survive, they didn't know what to do with me."

Some of the Wild Bunch wanted to dump him on the street or in the woods and let nature take its course. Others wanted to keep him so he would learn what it was like to be a captive animal. Robin didn't care what they did with him until he learned that the WC had power, vehicles, coin, and guns. They got him a wheelchair and fed him the same food he and the loo-ies were eating.

"The stall I was kept in was relatively soundproof. I couldn't really hear much of what was being said in the barn. I got information in bits and pieces. I heard about the power outage and the Wonderland Compound. I can't tell you how relieved I was that you had all survived. I knew I was in Forest Park. I knew Robin was wait-ing until the wall was finished to make

his move. I heard the truck come into the
barn, but I didn't know where they had
gotten it, or that Gino and Chester were
on board. I didn't know about Henry and
Rebecca. I couldn't walk, I could only
hobble. Escape was impossible, but that
didn't stop me from thinking about it
every minute I was there . . ."

Rebecca called to Henry. He had promised that he would walk down to the farm with her. He opened the window and saw her standing below, looking up at him.

"I'll be down in a few minutes," he said. "I have to pack a few things. I'm staying in the yurt while Derek's away. If you're in a hurry, you can go ahead. I'll see you at the farm."

"I'll wait," Rebecca said, smiling.

"I'll lower Gort down to keep you company."

Gort had gotten up, stretched, and was now sitting on the dumbwaiter, impatiently waiting to join Rebecca beneath the old oak tree.

Henry returned to the typewriter.

I wanted to get this down today before I
forgot . . . I've thought a lot about Robin
since the day I took the free fall with him.
I thought I might feel guilty about what
happened to him, but I don't. I didn't aim

```
for the soft top. It was a leap of faith,
or maybe a leap of fate. I could have
just as easily landed on the trunk...
```

Kismet.

"I thought you couldn't come up here," he said.

I don't like what you've done with the place.

Henry hadn't heard from Caroline since he had returned to the farm. He was glad she was back.

CHAPTER FIFTY-ONE

The light came on in the yurt. It was still dark outside. Henry sat up, blinking, wondering what the emergency was. His father was standing next to the bed, holding himself up with his walker.

"Sorry to wake you," he said.

"No problem. What time is it?"

"Four."

"Early." Henry swung out of bed. "Did you walk all the way down here with the walker?"

His father smiled. "I did."

"Wow. Your leg is really improving."

"Good days and bad. Today's a good day. I was thinking about taking the day off from Mom and Doc's torturous physical therapy."

Henry didn't blame him. He had helped with the therapy several times over the past several months, and *torture* was the perfect word for what his father had to endure. This still didn't explain why he was in the yurt so early in the morning.

"What are you going to do?"

"I know you were up late last night celebrating your birthday, and you're probably tired, but I was wondering if you want to go with me."

"Go where?"

"Chester and Gino are heading to the coast to pick up tuna. I'm going with them. I thought you might like to join us."

What better way to celebrate the first anniversary of the switch?

Henry grinned.

"I'd like that," he said.

ACKNOWLEDGMENTS

Books are written in solitude, but they are never written alone. I want to thank my three editors at Scholastic. Anamika Bhantnagar, Matthew Ringler, and Orlando Dos Reis for helping me over the finish line. I'd also like to thank Janell Harris, Chris Stengel, and the rest of the team at Scholastic. A special thanks to the wonderful librarians Joan Arth and Jared Myers who were the last people to read the story before it was born.

ABOUT THE AUTHOR

Roland Smith first worked with animals at the Oregon Zoo, and he has been involved in animal rescues and conservation work around the world for more than twenty years. He is the author of numerous books for young readers, including *Jack's Run, Zach's Lie, Peak*, the Cryptid Hunters series, and the Storm Runners series. He is also the coauthor of numerous picture books with his wife, Marie. Roland lives with Marie on a little farm south of Portland, Oregon, and in a little house in Bentonville, Arkansas. You can find him online at rolandsmith.com.